my secret positano

WITH LOVE FROM ITALY

TESS RINI

ISBN: 978-1-7376372-3-3 (e-book)

ISBN: 978-1-7376372-4-0 (paperback)

Tessrini.com

Publisher: One Punch Productions, LLC

Cover design and interior formatting by *Hannah Linder Designs*

To my grandparents, Francesco and Theresa
Thanks for being my first love story

one

"Brava, Brava, Kate." The driver twisted his head in order to look at her as she sat in the back seat, grinning and adding a wink. Kate sat terrified. Fear gripped her throat as the car rapidly swept around another hairpin turn, sliding inches away from a guardrail that hugged the cliff.

"Lorenzo, please watch the road," Kate pleaded yet again from her dry throat. Beads of perspiration formed on her forehead.

He chuckled before turning his attention back to the road.

Apparently, frightening young American women was Lorenzo's idea of afternoon entertainment. He had met her at the Naples airport shortly after noon, queueing up with all the other drivers enthusiastically offering to take visitors to their destinations. She had chosen the friendly looking man with his newsboy cap and laughing dark eyes. She explained to him she was scared of the winding road to Positano, famous for its hairpin turns and steep cliffs. Now she was certain she should have asked a few more questions.

The car zigged and zagged around more turns before finally slowly descending into the town of Positano on the Amalfi Coast of Italy. As they ventured up the extremely narrow one-way street, he pulled as far right as he could. Lorenzo jumped out quickly. Hauling her suitcase out of the trunk, he touched his cap, and was back zipping up the hill before Kate could catch her breath.

"Ciao, Lorenzo," she called weakly after him.

Beep beep went his horn in salute as he drove off, deftly skirting two motorbikes that were zooming past him on the narrow street. Glancing across the road, Kate spotted the sign for her hotel, positioned next to bright pink wisteria, which trailed down the side of its white walls. She couldn't wait to check in and settle her stomach. Motion sickness was something she had never overcome from childhood. Even now as she was closing in on twenty-eight years old, she often got sick on planes, but long car drives and boats were the worst offenders. The drive from Naples to Positano, particularly the last few miles, was like the pinnacle of the Motion Sickness Olympics—especially with Lorenzo at the wheel.

"I think I earned a gold medal," Kate mumbled, grabbing her suitcase handle and purse. She stepped off the small curb on to the cobblestone street toward her hotel.

Beep!

The sound of a tiny horn was right on her, and Kate jumped back to avoid colliding with a motorbike. In doing so, she lost her footing, tripping over the curb behind her. As if it was happening in slow motion, she felt herself falling. And not just any fall. No, she had to be the overachiever when it came to being a klutz. Kate landed sprawled over her suitcase, her legs tangled, her skirt riding up. Her ankle already throbbed. She took a deep stunned breath.

"The Gold Medal for Falling goes to Kate..." she joked again in an attempt to distract her from facing what she already knew was going to be bad.

"*Mi scusi? Posso aiutare?*"

Kate looked up toward the rich baritone voice. Its owner loomed over her, partly blocking out the sun. She squinted at the tall Mediterranean man with dark designer sunglasses over his eyes. She couldn't quite see his face, but he appeared to be near her age. He was wearing a simple polo shirt and jeans that looked new and pressed.

The man held out a hand toward her.

"*Grazie.*" She shifted uncomfortably. "*Inglese?*"

"*Si*, yes. Let me assist you," he answered in perfect English.

She felt his cool hand against her clammy one. She grimaced —the tangled way she was lying on the cobblestone street was more involved than simply grabbing his hand. She glanced down with horror and yanked her floral skirt down over her thighs.

A small sound came from the man, as if he was trying to hold back a laugh. "*Signorina*, if you would allow me to help, I think this could be easier." Two strong hands gently came around her waist, and he plucked her from the ground, untangling her from her suitcase and setting her on her feet.

"Oh my God!" she shrieked. Kate immediately leaned into the man, holding her right foot up, tears forming in her eyes.

"*Mi dispiace.* I am so sorry," he translated, as if he forgot she was American.

"It's my ankle," she shuddered, desperate to not crumple back over. His strong hands continued to hold her tight, bringing her closer to him.

"If I could just lean on you for just a second, I'm sure I will be okay soon." Kate trembled.

Taking off his sunglasses, he stared anxiously down at her five foot five frame. His gaze slid over her, past the nondescript blouse and skirt she had worn to travel in, and down her legs to the ankle that was swelling and beginning to redden against her pale skin. "I don't think so," he advised gently. "I think we should find a doctor."

Without a word, the man stowed his sunglasses in his pocket and bent to pick Kate up as if she weighed nothing.

Why did I eat those three cookies on the plane? She thought wildly. The idea that those cookies put her over her bodyweight limit made her chuckle. He glanced at her quizzically, as if wondering if she was now hysterical. He carried her across the cobblestone street toward a store next to her hotel. As they came through the door, he shouted to a young man who looked to be about twenty. The younger man hustled out, returning shortly with Kate's suitcase and purse. Meanwhile, the man gently placed her on a high stool near the counter.

"If I could just go to my hotel. . ." She trailed off as the man put up a finger, his cellphone already to his ear, speaking sharply into it.

Heat spread across her cheeks. Why hadn't she taken more Italian online? She heard *dottore* and *incidente*—doctor and accident.

Kate ran a hand through her hair. God only knows what she looked like. Glancing around, her eyes widened at the array of ceramics in vibrant blues, yellows, reds and greens that were scattered all over the shop. She admired the bowls, platters, and plates that sat on glass shelves, arranged by pattern. Part of her wanted suddenly to shop, but her sagging shoulders betrayed her. Her thoughts were broken by the man who was now speaking sharply to her.

"Where are you staying, *Signorina*?"

"I have reservations at the Hotel Santa Maria."

He spoke into the phone and then snapped it off. Taking in her fatigue and pallor, he asked her what her name was, this time in a more soothing tone.

"Kate Malone. My family and friends call me Katie," she added, and she felt her face grow even hotter. "I mean, after you've carried me and all, I feel like we're pretty well-acquainted." She almost slapped her forehead with a hand. She always made bad jokes when she was nervous.

The man smiled gently at her. "I am Marco, and this is Alfonso." He gestured to the younger man.

"Um, well, nice to meet you both. I'm sorry to cause you so much trouble..." she mumbled, shifting on her stool, avoiding his eyes.

"I will take you to your hotel and the doctor will meet us there."

Before she could utter a sound, Kate found herself being carried once again by Marco's tanned arms. She leaned against his protective broad shoulders, suddenly too overwhelmed to argue. He carried her out the front door, and the sultry heat once again hit her. They went next door to the white stucco building, Marco climbing the stairs easily. This gave her the first opportunity to study him closely. She took in his smooth olive skin, with a little razor stubble near his jaw line. His nose was straight and prominent, and his chin was strong. His black hair was thick and a little wavy, but neatly styled.

Kate didn't realize they were already at the reception desk until Marco spoke. Introducing her to a man named Giovanni, Marco made short work of checking her in, quickly inquiring that the hotel had everything they needed—her reservation was correct and credit card was already on file.

"Welcome, *Signorina Malone, Signore Rinaldi!*" The older man greeted them warmly. His stature was small next to Marco, his gray hair thinning at the top. Giovanni handed Marco a key card as if this was the most natural check-in procedure of a guest.

"*Stanza Cinque*—Room Five," Giovanni called after them.

Marco carried her up the small flight of stairs and down the hallway. Kate looked down at the beautiful floors, tiled in blue and white, as he quickly tapped the key card and entered. The room was small but relaxing with its walls painted in a quiet blue. An enormous bed dwarfed the room, and its white coverlet and pillows looking inviting.

Gently placing her on the bed, Marco remained bent over, his concerned gaze intent on her. He arranged pillows behind her as she leaned against the headboard, grateful for the coolness of the room. She winced a little as her ankle hit the coverlet. Marco looked at her sharply, but straightened, silently watching her.

Alfonso appeared at the open door lugging her suitcase and purse inside, and he gave her an appreciative glance. Marco spoke quietly to him. Alfonso nodded and ran off. He returned quickly with a plastic bag filled with bottles of water and smiling, shut the door.

"I'm sure I'll be just fine now," Kate insisted in a wobbly voice. Her friends and family teased her about being "the quiet one," and she was finding this entire scenario very uncomfortable. This amazing looking man now sat down in a chair opposite her, making her more unsettled by the minute.

He handed her a water bottle before speaking. "I will stay and help translate for the doctor. He is my personal physician. He does not speak English that well. If you were my sister, I would want someone to come to her assistance."

She took a tentative sip of water before asking, "Do you have a sister?"

"No." He grinned at her.

Kate smiled weakly, and squaring her shoulders, she finally looked at her ankle. The good news was that it didn't look worse. The bad news was her stomach was now catching up with her, following Lorenzo's drive. She glanced around frantically, and Marco, eying the sudden green hue of her face, moved with lightning speed. He quickly handed her the plastic bag the water bottles had been in.

And that was when Kate threw up in front of a handsome Italian stranger.

two

M arco winced as he averted his eyes when Kate got sick. Why in the world was he spending so much time tending to this American woman? There was something about her that already intrigued him, and he had no idea what it was. As one of Italy's most eligible bachelors, Marco was used to women falling at his feet. This one had literally done so but appeared to be oblivious to any of his charms. If anything, she had acted like she didn't want to be anywhere near him.

He went to the balcony doors, opening them to let in fresh air, standing with his back to her to give her some privacy. After a few minutes, he went to the small modern white bathroom, bringing out a wet cloth, handing it to her silently.

"Feel better?" he inquired nonchalantly.

Kate was now holding the bag, her face growing red again. At least the red was an improvement over the green pallor she had a few minutes ago.

"Yes, thank you," she whispered, tying the bag and not raising her eyes, looking clearly mortified. He grabbed a nearby trash can and put it by the bed. She gave him a grateful look before leaning over, placing the bag in the trash, still not making eye contact.

Handing her the water bottle again that she had thrust on the nightstand before getting sick, he gestured for her to drink.

As she was sipping and pointedly not looking at him, Marco took a moment to study her. Her shiny, thick brown hair hung in waves to her shoulders. Her dark eyebrows framed her brown eyes. When he looked closely, he could see golden specs in those wide eyes. She was a little on the shorter side and curvy, from what he could observe of her short-sleeved blouse and skirt. He found her creamy skin fresh and tempting. But it was her lips that drew him in—full and naturally pink. He had watched her face transform when she had smiled at Alfonso, showing off her straight white teeth. A dimple near her serious mouth now transfixed him, and he suddenly wanted her to look at him the way she had at the younger man.

"So, what brings you to our beautiful Positano?" he prodded gently, hoping to coax more out of this woman, who was eyeing him nervously.

"I'm here to spend time seeing the Amalfi Coast and write a novel," she answered softly, now looking toward the balcony, as if she were eager to see more of the town that was below them.

He tried again. "All alone?"

"Yes."

"What do you write?"

Kate studied him for a moment. She lifted her chin defiantly. "Romance."

"Wonderful! You are in a *very* romantic town."

She looked at him quizzically. "You're not going to laugh at me?"

He drew his brows together. "Why would I do that?"

"Oh, I don't know. Just another single American woman traveling through Italy, hoping to write a romantic novel."

"Are you published?"

"Well, it depends on what you call published." She was still not looking at him, smoothing her skirt. "I write and design websites. But now I want to pursue something I've always wanted to do," she answered shyly.

He nodded. "I think that's great that you are chasing your dreams."

Kate's head snapped up, clearly assessing his answer. She appeared to decide he was worth knowing more.

"Well, you see..."

Knock knock

He almost cursed out loud as the knock on the door broke the spell. She was just opening up, and now the doctor had probably arrived.

Marco opened the door, greeting his long-time personal physician. Dr. Amato spoke English perfectly well—it had been a small white lie he had told Kate to ensure he could stay with her. Speaking in Italian, he explained the fall, and the doctor put down his bag and came over to greet Kate and examine her.

Taking off her white tennis shoe, the doctor gently rotated her foot and ankle every which way. Finally, after several minutes, his brow furrowed, Dr. Amato proclaimed it to be a sprain. Ice and rest were the best course, he told them in halting, but good English. To be sure, she should come by his clinic tomorrow just for a quick X-ray, he explained. He would send up some crutches in the meantime for the *signorina* to get around. He told her to elevate it as much as possible, for the quicker the swelling went down, the faster she would heal.

Marco asked him a few follow-up questions. The doctor gave him a quizzical look, his eyes glinting. "*Si, domani.*" Packing up his bag, he handed Kate his card and repeated, "Tomorrow." He nodded warmly.

Marco closed the door after him and turned around, smiling at her. "Well, that's good news. How about an *aperitivo*?"

KATE LOOKED AT MARCO, her mouth slightly open. Was this guy for real? He was one of the best-looking men she had ever seen in her life, and he was clearly attentive and kind. What was he doing sticking around tending to a random American woman? Even worse, he had been here to witness her spectacularly throwing up and now she was probably looking like the motorbike had actually run over her. Her clothes were wrinkled, her makeup long gone. God only knows what her hair looked like—it was probably frizzing in the sea air.

"Um, I thought you said the doctor didn't speak English."

"I said he didn't speak English *that well*," clarified Marco. At her narrowed eyes, he grinned. "A small fib, Katie." He put up his hands in surrender. "I wanted to stay to help, and I could see you were ready to dismiss me. I will take you out for an *aperitivo* as an apology."

Kate had read about the Italian *aperitivo* and had been excited to experience them. She had learned Italians believed in opening one's appetite with a drink and a snack. *Aperitivos* ranged from small to elaborate, depending on the restaurant. Despite her desire to try one, now was not the time. She looked at him, her eyes widening in dismay. "Marco, honestly, thank you for everything, but I think it has been quite a day. All I really want to do is take a shower, put my pajamas on, and rest—even if I have to hop on one foot."

Kate knew she sounded like a grandmother, ready to don her flannel nightgown and head to bed, but she was apprehensive about staying any longer in this handsome man's presence.

"I could have something brought up..."

"I can't thank you enough for everything." She pointedly looked at the door, putting out a hand, not sure how to signal it was time for him to go.

Taking her small hand in his, he took time to study her light pink nails. Turning her hand over, he rubbed her palm thoughtfully. Electricity flashed through Kate. *If this is how he can make me feel by just touching my hand, how would it be if he kissed me?* She felt her cheeks blush at her own ridiculous thoughts. Marco's eyebrows raised, but he said nothing.

"Tomorrow then," he promised, walking to the door and glancing back at her one more time. Katie gave a small wave and felt ridiculous. He grinned at her, and she found herself returning one just as large. He went through the door, clicking it closed softly.

Katie let out the big breath she hadn't realized she had been holding. This stranger unnerved her but excited her at the same time. She wasn't used to attention such as this—not as a child or an adult.

Growing up, Kate always had her nose in a book, her imagination soaring with each story she read. Her sister Meara was different, constantly on the move. A force of nature, with a bold personality, she now held a high-powered job in the high-tech industry.

In contrast, Kate lived in a small apartment in San Francisco with Teresa, her best friend since the first grade. She worked on websites, and her social life consisted of going out with her friends who liked her because she was a good listener. Therefore, she was the one to call when their boyfriends broke their heart, they needed a sitter for their young children, or a catastrophe hit. A loyal and unassuming friend, Kate was "simply the best," her friends proclaimed.

Kate knew her friends took advantage of her, but she enjoyed being needed and accepted her life. It was only lately that restlessness had stirred her, and she wanted more—she just didn't know what.

When she and Allie, a friend from college, had planned this Italian getaway, Kate, ever the researcher, scoured the Internet and social media, painstakingly planning it. When she saw a post showing Allie's boyfriend, Justin, on one knee with an open ring box, Kate knew instantly the trip was off. Sure enough, Allie immediately went into wedding planning mode and proclaimed she didn't have the money to travel now. "You can be a bridesmaid," she had gushed.

Kate looked for another friend to accompany her. Teresa had just become a nurse and had little vacation time at her new job. With the trip just a couple of weeks away, no one else could move that fast. Rather impulsively for her, Kate decided maybe this was the opportunity she needed to finally begin her writing venture. She had planned to spend most of her time on the Amalfi Coast, picking the picturesque town of Positano as home base. She wanted to take day trips to Sorrento, Amalfi, and other local towns. She was determined to make the most of this trip.

Telling Meara about it had been a mistake. "You're wasting your money." Meara's tone was dismissive while video chatting with Kate as she packed. "Why don't you just rent a small apartment or something in Monterey and go write there? You don't have to go all the way to Italy and spend all that money. And you'll be all alone..."

"I've always wanted to go to Italy," Kate interrupted, continuing to pack, trying not to look at her tablet so she wouldn't have to see her sister's beautiful face twisted in disapproval. Meara could only be described as stunning, with gorgeous dark red hair and emerald green eyes. When she walked down the street, men literally stopped in their tracks. It always fascinated Kate to watch. Meara dated a series of high-profile men also in the tech industry but said she hadn't found "the one."

Meara rarely came home, which left Kate looking after her father. Their mother passed away several years earlier after a brief battle with cancer. Kate wondered sometimes if her own life would be different if her mom had lived. She had let Meara influence her sometimes to take the safe route. Their father, struck down by grief, had been a shell of himself for so long, he didn't even notice. He spent most of his time at the Irish pub he owned, which seemed to bring him the most joy. Most of the customers were regulars and, though they were growing older, they came by for a pint and a chat.

A knock at the door startled her. She swung her legs off the bed, wondering how she was going to hop to the door, when it opened. Alfonso tentatively looked in. Seeing her, he gave her a big grin as he carried a pair of crutches. He put them alongside the bed and helped her stand.

Biting her lip, Kate stood on her good leg while Alfonso steadied her and handed her the crutches.

Tentatively, she took a step.

"*Brava!*" He smiled. He handed her the keycard to her room and explained Marco had taken it in order for the crutches to be delivered. "*Ciao*," he waved, and almost bumped into Giovanni, who stood at the door holding a tray and an ice bag.

"*Signore Rinaldi* told me you needed an early dinner," he proclaimed. Entering the room, Giovanni took it to the balcony and placed it on the small table.

Sweeping his hand to show the extraordinary view, he said proudly. "Dine with Positano."

She hobbled out the door to the balcony and gasped. She could see the multi-colored houses scattering the hills and the sea beyond. It was breathtaking and worth every extra penny she had used to spring for the sea view room.

"Oh, Giovanni, it's beautiful," breathed Kate.

"*Magnifico!*" He nodded. "And now you will sit and eat."

She gave the older man a grateful glance. "*Grazie.*"

Giovanni showed himself out, and Kate quickly hobbled to the bathroom to brush her teeth. Sighing when she saw her bedraggled self in the mirror, she took the time to wash her face and brush her hair. Feeling better, she went back to the balcony and sat down, sliding her leg gently on to the companion chair, plopping the ice bag on top of it. She was suddenly starving. She took the cover off the tray to see a selection of cheeses, Italian meats, rustic bread, a glass of crisp white wine and a small dish of pasta, dressed simply in a lemon butter sauce.

Breathing in the smells of garlic and deliciousness, Kate finally began to relax. She looked at the vertical town below, watching as its residents and visitors climbed the hills, coming from spending the day on the beach or out shopping, their arms full of bags and packages. Something caught her attention on her right, and she saw Marco walking up the street with several boxes, Alfonso scurrying behind him.

Marco must be the manager of the ceramics shop, she realized. Suddenly, he looked up as if he felt her eyes on him. She felt herself blush. She raised her wineglass to him in a silent toast.

He smiled, acknowledging her with a nod. Alfonso bumped into him at his sudden stop, making Kate laugh out loud for the first time that day. Marco grinned, turning around to say something to the younger man. Alfonso ran ahead, presumably to open the door. Marco shot her one last look and entered the door, out of sight. *Out of my life*, she thought, feeling a bit too sad about the loss of someone she had just met. She sipped her delicious wine and pursed her lips at the sudden crispness. Her heart now felt a little heavy.

three

The previous day's mishaps were now a fading memory, and Kate woke up feeling more like herself. She had slept well, her ankle propped up on a few pillows. She had blinked her eyes open as dawn streamed through her balcony windows; she had forgotten to close the blue velvet curtains tied to either side of the balcony doors. She was glad she had left them open, now watching the beautiful colors of the sunrise spread across the bright blue sky.

Last night after she had consumed all the dinner, Giovanni had returned with another ice bag and a pistachio-rimmed cannoli. He had urged her to eat it and sat with her, telling her about how he had grown up on the edge of town. His parents had opened a bed and breakfast when they had inherited a small building in the center of the town. After working there as a young man, eventually it was handed down to him and his sister. He explained they had recently remodeled it with the help of an investor. They could now compete with some of the more modern hotels. They were very grateful to the investor, and now they were booked solid through the season, he told her proudly.

Kate felt fortunate to have chosen this hotel. Interrupting her thoughts, she decided she had better rouse herself and attempt a shower. Giovanni had thoughtfully brought her a shower chair, and she managed with the hand-held attachment. She had to be a little more creative while dressing herself. Glancing down at her ankle, which the doctor had bandaged, she could see purple bruising spreading down toward her foot, but it didn't appear to have swollen anymore since the previous evening. Just as she was sitting on her bed, brushing her still-damp hair, there was a knock on the door.

Thinking it was Giovanni who had said he would bring her breakfast, Kate grabbed the crutches and hobbled over to the door. She sucked in her breath when she opened the door to find Marco standing there.

Dressed in a crisp, short-sleeve button-down shirt with khaki pants, he appeared refined. Kate glanced down at her lavender skirt and matching top. She felt a little frumpy, but she had grabbed what was on top of her suitcase, taking the easiest course to getting dressed.

"*Buongiorno*, Katie," he greeted her softly.

"*Buongiorno*," echoed Kate. After last night's toast with the wine, she was feeling shy again today. She turned back to sit down again on the bed.

"How about some breakfast?" Marco eyed a pair of walking sandals on the floor that she had gotten out earlier. "Let me help you with these."

Before she could answer, he was sliding the shoes gently over her feet and fastening them. It was a little trickier maneuvering it over the bandage that encompassed her ankle and part of her foot, but he slid it inch by inch, as if he was apprehensive about causing her any pain.

His dark handsome head was bent over the task and Kate breathed in his spicy cologne. God, he smelled good.

Marco straightened up, grabbed the crutches again, and held them in one hand. Without saying a word, his strong hands—so different from Alfonso's tentative help the night before—came around her as he helped her stand, adjusting the crutches under her arms.

"Let us go. Breakfast awaits." He held the door open for her, careful as she hobbled by. "I could carry you again, but something tells me you'd rather walk," Marco teased.

She felt herself blush, telling him he was right. "Thank you. You know I'm fine by myself, right? I was going to have some breakfast and then make my way to Dr. Amato's clinic."

"Of course, you can do it yourself," he said soothingly. "But why do it yourself when I'm here to help?" He had now adopted a wheedling tone which caused her to smile and shake her head.

Slowly they walked to an elevator Kate hadn't noticed yesterday. Marco had simply carried her up the stairs. Descending on the small elevator, he put a steadying arm around her, and once again, she drank in his closeness and breathtaking smell. She was almost disappointed when the elderly elevator doors parted. She limped through them slowly as he held the door.

Kate almost cried out in happiness when she saw the beautiful, large breakfast room before her. Tiled just as the floor had been in bright colors, the interior room led out to a terrace, which had several white metal tables and chairs. Large tables lined the walls inside, boasting platters and baskets of Italian breads, desserts, cheeses, and meats. Kate noticed the cereal boxes in the corner, seemingly a concession to finicky Americans.

Giovanni scurried up to greet them, showing them to a corner table on the terrace overlooking the town. He disappeared shortly, returning to bring them cappuccinos in blue-and-white cups with saucers. A heart was formed in the milk.

Kate beamed at Marco, unable to keep her happiness to

herself. She took a deep sip of the cappuccino and almost moaned.

He watched her intently, and then a grin appeared. "You have a little foam on your lip." His finger caressed it away.

Kate's cup clattered down onto the saucer. She shakily reached for a napkin and patted her lips. Her heart did a funny little bounce as she looked over at his dancing black eyes, gently mocking her, almost defying her to say something.

Giovanni returned, holding plates filled with the offerings from the large tables, as well as eggs and tomatoes. It was apparent they did not need to help themselves and that he wanted to serve them. He came back with a basket of pastries and even more food until the tiny table could hold no more.

As they slowly ate, Marco was an entertaining companion. He provided details about Positano, how much it had grown and the famous movies filmed there years ago. He told her about some of the neighboring towns as well, cleverly inserting details she hadn't read about in her research.

Kate hung onto his every word, soaking it in, as she was dying to be out exploring. She frowned in her cup, disappointed that her trip was getting off to such a slow start.

"Now, what have I said to make that dimple return?" he inquired, sitting back with his cup, his eyes mischievous.

"Dimple?"

"Yes, dimple. It appears at the most illogical times. Not when you smile, but when you frown or are thinking about something intently."

"No one has ever told me that." Kate smiled reluctantly. "You are an interesting man, Marco. I give you that."

"Interesting is just the start," he declared smugly. "Come on, let's go."

~

KATE'S VISIT to the doctor was quick and painless. The X-ray confirmed there were no bones broken, and now that the swelling had gone down, Dr. Amato insisted she wear a soft walking cast just for a few days. Thankfully, the crutches were no longer needed. However, Dr. Amato cautioned she should take care and not overdo it on Positano's famed hills.

Rubbing her already sore arms, Kate had to agree the cast was better, though it was a fashion eyesore. She stuffed her sandal in her purse and walked slowly beside Marco up the incline to the ceramics shop. She knew he purposely was slowing down his long stride, but she still struggled to keep up with him. As they neared the shop, he asked her if she would like to go back to her room to rest. Though her hotel room was beautiful, the thought of being cooped up on this beautiful day was heartbreaking. Kate looked at the vibrant blue sky and the vacationers packing the streets and couldn't bear to sequester herself. Though she had longed for time alone to write, she wasn't feeling the least creative, watching the world go by her door and unable to take part. She hadn't seen much of Positano yet to even be inspired, and now she almost felt a sense of loneliness.

"Do you need some help in the shop?"

Marco gave her a surprised look.

She met his gaze. "I'd love to help do anything. Whatever I can assist with using one good leg!" As soon as she said it, she felt embarrassed. She was practically begging the man. He probably thought she was coming on to him.

Marco rubbed his chin hesitantly.

"You are the manager, right? I'm not asking you to hire me or anything. I just wanted to volunteer. I can help Alfonso," she clarified nervously.

To her astonishment, Marco chuckled, guiding her into the shop. "You are not like most women, Katie. I'm just not sure what to do with you."

She glanced up at him. Was that good or bad? Shrugging, she

looked around happily at the shop's interior. It was so bright and full of beautiful ceramics. Marco called for Alfonso, speaking to him in Italian. Alfonso glanced hesitantly at her, his big head of curly hair looking even more disheveled today. He listened patiently and kept nodding at Marco's instruction. Alfonso approached her with a grin. "You come with me?"

Kate nodded, leaving Marco, who was already heading to a back office she hadn't noticed yesterday.

Alfonso led her behind the counter and helped her onto the tall stool and then placed another one for her to put her leg up on. He brought her a large box of orders and asked her to sort them, giving her detailed instructions on how he wanted it done. He told her visitors often ordered larger quantities to be sent directly to their homes.

After he walked away, Kate studied the orders, her eyes growing larger. Some orders were in the thousands of euros. The shop did an impressive business, even if this was just a small slice of it.

As she systematically worked, Kate looked around, admiring the shelves of ceramics—there was even a patio set in the corner. Whatever could be made into different Italian patterns was packed solidly into the shop. She watched Alfonso greet customers, his cheery personality putting them at ease, as he showed them the different patterns and their origins. The rooster was traditional, he explained in his practiced English, while the lemons signified the region.

A couple hours soon went by, and with the orders now sorted, Kate clipped them together in piles and waited. Alfonso was busy with customers and Marco was nowhere to be seen.

Carefully, she stepped down from the stool and walked over to an arrangement on a nearby table. Instinctively, she rearranged the table, adding different pieces that complimented the settings that were there. She glanced around the shop and found a vase with flowers. Adding it, she retrieved a few other items of decor. Limping slightly, she gathered those and rearranged the vignette once more.

Stepping back to admire her work, she hit something rock hard. Long arms grabbed her from behind and steadied her.

Marco.

"Katie, what are you doing?" he asked curtly.

"I'm sorry. I know I was supposed to sort the orders, but I finished, and I just thought this needed a little something. If you want me to put it back the way it was, I will." She glanced nervously at him, already picking up a couple of pieces.

His hand stretched out, stopping her. "No, *per favore*. I apologize if I was abrupt. It was because I saw you standing on your bad leg. This is beautiful what you have done. Feel free to attack the entire shop!"

"Really? Because I would love to—as long as it is okay."

He shrugged. "Do whatever you want. But first I think we will go in search of lunch."

Saying something to Alfonso over his shoulder, Kate felt a thrill as Marco casually put an arm around her and led her outside. The bright sun blinded her for a moment, and she felt the sudden warmth on her skin.

Marco waited patiently for traffic to subside on the one-way street going up the hill. He then led her to an open-air restaurant, which was covered to keep the sun at bay, but had no windows or doors. At the sight of Marco, a waiter hurried over, ushering them to a table in the back.

Kate glanced around, taking in the Italian ceramic pots filled with vibrant pink, red and yellow flowers and greenery flowing over them. Despite the casualness of the restaurant, the table was set with fine linens and more Italian ceramic plates.

"This is beautiful." She sighed.

He looked at her again and shook his head. "You find so much enjoyment in such small things."

"I don't know about that but look around. The people, the colors, the flowers—it's all so amazing."

Kate glanced quickly down at the menu, but under her lashes, she noticed Marco didn't even look at it. She realized he probably came there every day.

When the waiter appeared, he greeted Marco by name. Marco reached over, patting him on the shoulder. They ordered wood-fired pizzas that Marco promised would be extraordinary. He ordered a beer for himself and suggested a lemon spritz for her to try.

"I've never had one." Kate enthusiastically nodded, which sent him grinning again, his eyes squinting through his long black lashes, his laugh lines prominent. A woman would kill to have those lashes.

She glanced again at all the floral surrounding them and then suddenly looked away, overwhelmed by a memory. Memories of her mom came to her at the strangest times. Her mother had adored flowers, working long hours in her garden, watering little pots scattered on their porch, even when she was ill.

"Katie?" Marco inquired softly, noticing her withdrawal.

She looked at him now, blinking away the tears that had come to her eyes. "Oh, I'm sorry. I got lost for a minute. Have you ever had a memory suddenly wash over you?"

At his frown, she continued, trying to get over the awkward moment. "I mean, suddenly you think of something out of the blue at the strangest time?"

A sad, fleeting look crossed his face. "You mean *someone*?"

She nodded. "I was thinking about my mom and how much she loved flowers. She would be so amazed at all the flowers here. I've never seen anything like it."

He put his hand over hers where it was resting on the table. She felt the warmth of his hand and the odd shockwave go up her arm. "Tell me more."

Stalling, Kate took a sip of the lemon spritz which the waiter had set before her. Her face lit up. "Okay wow. That's really good."

He grinned, but the grip on her hand tightened.

"She was my cheerleader," Kate began, stirring her drink. "Just my everything. She died of cancer when I was twenty-two. She was my best friend, my confidant—she believed in me."

"I can see why."

Kate made a tiny face and rolled her eyes. "You just met me!"

"It's still true," he insisted, an edge to his voice. "Trust me on this. I have met people who I have little faith in. I know the difference."

"You seem to understand grief. Have you lost someone?"

"Ahhh, very perceptive, Katie." He gazed back at her before looking off into the distance.

"My uncle recently passed away. He was the owner of the ceramics shop. My father...well, that's a story for another time. But my uncle became a father to me. It's been difficult for my family."

"Oh, so you manage the shop for him. You grew up in the business?"

"Katie..." he began hesitantly.

Suddenly, the pizzas arrived, and the waiter was rearranging the table in order to fit the large plates.

Kate's eyes widened. "I'll never be able to eat all this!" She gently picked up a piece of her Margherita pizza, its thin crust slightly charred. Marco did the same with his sausage-and-tomato pizza. Looking over at her, he grinned and touched the end of his piece to hers.

"Salute!"

Giggling, Kate took a bite of hers and nearly moaned again. The Margherita pizza with just tomato sauce, homemade mozzarella and bright green basil was simple, but its fresh ingredients made it fantastic. Maybe she *could* eat this whole thing.

Marco and Kate kept eating, their conversation on hold.

Without any discussion, they automatically set pieces of their own pizza on each other's plate for one another to try.

Kate was well into her second piece when she realized Marco was not going to continue discussing his loss. Being an introvert and not overly sharing her own life, she understood. Finishing her piece, she looked up to see him watching her.

"Oh geez, I have tomato sauce on my face, don't I?" She anxiously scrubbed her mouth.

"No, you're fine." He smiled. "You're such a breath of fresh air. You don't ask me questions or try to pry into my life."

"Maybe I lack curiosity," murmured Kate.

He shook his head, still smiling. "I don't think so. I can tell by the way your head is on a swivel that you are curious and eager to explore everything."

Kate looked at him for a minute. It seemed like he wanted to say more but was watching her guardedly.

Making it easy on him, she launched into a series of questions about the town, remembering some facts she had read about its history and the church at the bottom of the hill. In her quiet way, Kate was a good conversationist, and between bites of pizza, the two continued to talk easily to one another. The pizzas were carried away, and a small plate of Italian cookies and two cups of espresso were placed on the table. Marco continued to tell her about Positano, neighboring Capri, Sorrento, and all the exploring she must do.

Finally, signaling the waiter, Marco was presented with a bill. He threw down what seemed to be an incredible number of euros. He accepted a pizza box for Alfonso that Kate hadn't even heard him order. As they got up, he looked at her, his eyes sincere. "Thank you. I haven't enjoyed a lunch like this in a very long time."

"I should thank you. You've gone above and beyond. You rescued me, fed me, took me to the doctor, gave me something to occupy my time—it's too much!" She wanted to let him know how much she appreciated him.

His eyes glinted with something she couldn't quite read. Was it amusement or something else? "*Prego*. You're welcome, Katie. I have been honored to spend some time with you and to tell you a little bit about the town I love. And we're just getting started," he promised.

four

K ate's following few days in Positano took on a pattern. She rose early, did a little writing on her balcony while watching the town stir to life. She had dutifully outlined a story before arriving, but now she struggled to fill a page. She determinedly kept writing until it was time to go down to the breakfast room, where she always found Marco waiting for her.

Sitting at their usual table in the corner, he would look up from his tablet and smile at her. He wore small rectangle glasses she found incredibly sexy on him. As always, he was the perfect gentleman, standing up and sliding her chair out, while signaling to Giovanni or one of the staff to bring her a cappuccino. He then would inquire about her night and talk about everything from the weather to what the day would bring. He seldom brought up anything personal, Kate noted, and when she tried to ask a few questions, he would steer her in an impersonal direction.

Following breakfast, they would walk to the shop where Alfonso was always waiting with his big grin. Kate would ring up sales, dust ceramics and re-do displays while Marco disappeared into the office. Lunch across the street was followed by more work. One night, the three of them had gone out to the small seafood restaurant two doors down. The next night, Marco apologized that he had a business dinner that couldn't be avoided. She wandered down slowly to a wine bar near the hotel, having a solitary bite to eat.

Kate's ankle was feeling better. She wasn't going to run any marathons, but she normally wouldn't, anyway! Despite the slight soreness, she was considering taking the awkward boot off for a test walk outside. That morning she had walked a little around her hotel room with no mishap. The bruising was still a nasty shade of yellow and purple against her fair skin, but it could be a few more days before that disappeared.

"Wanting to break loose, aren't you?" Marco interrupted her thoughts as she ate her Italian roll with prosciutto and cheese—which had become her favorite breakfast.

"How did you know?" She raised her eyebrows and gave a small laugh. "You and Alfonso have been so wonderful. I can't imagine what I would have done. Unfortunately, I am only here for a short time, and I want to go exploring, even if I have to do it slower than usual."

He stared at her; his black eyes warm. "We have enjoyed it and Alfonso has now grown used to having you, but you are right. We should go exploring!"

She shook her head. "I didn't mean for you to take me. I know you're busy managing the ceramics shop. I'll be fine on my own."

An odd look went across Marco's face swiftly before being replaced by a persuasive one. "You would banish me to the windowless office when I have all of Positano to show you?" he teased, raising his eyebrows. "I should not see the light of day, while Kate is out enjoying the sea and flowers and all of our lovely town?"

"Of course not!" she said, rolling her eyes at his drama. "I know you're busy, though."

"Let's say my work is at a bit of a standstill right now," he murmured. "I would be honored to show you Positano, Katie."

Honored.

There was that word again. Marco was so different from the men she met at home. "Then let's do it!" she consented excitedly, and as always, her enthusiasm made him chuckle.

After breakfast, they went back to her room so that she could grab a purse and sunglasses. Pushing aside her usual independent spirit, she asked his opinion about wearing the boot. He advised her to keep it on one more day. He cautioned Positano's hills alone could tax anyone's legs. Better to be safe.

Kate agreed reluctantly. Wearing her favorite red and white wide-striped sundress and a flat sandal on one foot, black boot on another, she ventured out with Marco into the sunny day. He smiled at her as they left the room, his eyes looking at her appreciatively. He made her feel like she was the most beautiful woman in the world. It was a strange feeling for her since she had never felt that way. Her heart beat faster just looking at him.

They headed down the hill, stopping into each store as they went. She noticed all the shop owners greet Marco enthusiastically, many coming right up to him, speaking in rapid Italian and hugging him as if they hadn't seen him for quite a while. Maybe he didn't get out very often. It was almost as if he didn't live and work there.

Marco stood patiently as she examined everything the shops offered, from linens, clothes, and candles—all imprinted with lemons. Lemons were on everything. Bottles of limoncello and lemon olive oil were widely available.

They walked into one shop and a bright dress with lemons all over it was prominently displayed. Kate laughed when Marco held it up in front of him. She had seen a lot of older women wearing those dresses, along with floppy hats and big purses.

"That screams tourist." She shook her head, still smiling. "I think I'll try to be a little less conspicuous—but it looks good on you!"

They continued their light-hearted debate, exiting the shop, with Marco saying something to the shop owner, who waved and called a quick *ciao*. As they ventured down the hill, the small roadway became a pedestrian-only street. The crowds became thicker, and the cobblestones were a little tricky to navigate. Marco grabbed Kate's hand, a natural move as he ventured to protect her from the jostling crowds and the uneven steps. Still, his warm, strong hand holding hers sent a tingle down her spine.

Kate took in the beauty of the bright-colored flowers, which overflowed from Italian pottery as they moved farther down the street. She was enamored to see bright pink wisteria trailing down overhead from a trellis. Marco patiently waited as she stopped to take photos, trying to take it all in and remember it at the same time.

Halfway down the hill, they walked into a shop with a giant lemon candle displayed outside. Marco called out to the two women managing the shop. This time, it was more than a simple exchange, as the three seemed to have a lot to discuss.

"*Mi scusi*," Marco finally acknowledged her. "Francesca and Allegra, this is my friend, Kate," he introduced her, emphasizing the word *friend.*

Kate tried not to frown. Why did it bother her? They *were* friends, after all. Exchanging pleasantries about her stay with the women, she got the feeling they wanted to continue their conversation. Feeling like an interloper, she wandered away, giving them space.

Picking up candles and smelling them, she listened to their discussion in Italian. It sounded as if the conversation was becoming serious, but she couldn't tell. Italian sometimes sounded more passionate, whether it was meant to or not.

Kate studied both women as they talked. Francesca was the taller of the two, with long blonde hair pulled back and styled perfectly. Her slim figure was wearing a dress that was simple in its cut, but very chic. Allegra was smaller and petite, her short brown hair stopping just below her ears. She, too, wore a dress, but hers was shorter, and she was sporting impossibly high heels, making her almost Francesca's height.

Glancing back at Marco, Kate saw he was now at the counter looking at a ledger Francesca was holding open. He seemed absorbed in the task. Shrugging, Kate exited the shop and began strolling down the hill, walking farther than she realized. She was relieved when she saw a nearby bench to sit and rest her ankle. She was enjoying watching the people go up and down the hill, laden with bags and packages. Many were in beach wear, strolling down the hill with coolers and picnic baskets, heading to spend the day on the sand.

Kate took out her phone and typed her impressions. She used her notes app constantly to capture ideas for her writing. Sights, sounds, and smells surrounded her, and she wanted to make sure she remembered everything. She put a hand to her neck. The sun was beating down and Kate was considering whether she should move when a hand gently touched her shoulder.

"Katie, I am so sorry." Marco looked down at her apologetically. "Francesca had some things to discuss with me, but I didn't mean for it to interrupt our day."

She gazed up at him. How did she tell this man that it was normal for her to feel almost invisible at home? His thirty minutes of engagement were so inconsequential compared to what she was used to. She remembered her last date, who hadn't looked up from his phone for most of their dinner together.

"No worries." She smiled at him as she stood. Instinctively, she grabbed his hand to help her stand as if it was the most normal thing in the world. "It gave me a chance to rest my ankle, and now I'm ready to roll again." He smiled back, looking relieved that she wasn't upset about his absence.

They continued walking down the hill, bypassing some of the

touristy T-shirt shops. They stopped by the street vendors and artists selling paintings and jewelry. Marco pointed out some landmarks in the paintings, explaining where they were on the Amalfi Coast. Kate looked up at him, pretending she was interested, but in reality, it gave her a chance to stare at his attractive face. His eyes were hidden behind his dark sunglasses, but she focused on his mouth. Suddenly, he was also staring down at her and lowered his head slightly. His lips were descending...

"Twenty-five euros!" shouted the artist.

"*No, grazie,*" Marco responded politely, the moment broken. They continued walking then and he told Kate there were better paintings ahead if she was interested in taking one home. They came upon another stand, where Kate stopped to admire the jewelry. She tried on a bracelet, its delicate beads the vibrant blue that seemed to be all around them, from the sea to pottery. Marco was busy looking over some sunglasses. As he joined her, Kate rolled the bracelet off.

His fingers stopped her. "A small remembrance of Positano."

"Marco!" Kate smiled at him, thanking him. True, she knew it was an inexpensive present, but was still touched that he had quietly slipped the artist a few euros.

They soon came upon a small flight of stairs, and Marco grinned at Kate's gasp. The stairs led to a cream-colored church, beautiful in its simplicity, standing amongst the nearby flowering plants and blue skies. Marco explained it was the Church of Santa Maria Assunta, truly the heart of Positano.

"Can we go in?"

"I think we need to wait," he responded dryly.

The church's bells were ringing merrily, and Kate looked at him quizzically, as they joined a crowd that had formed in the small piazza. Suddenly, a bride and groom appeared, giddily running down the stairs to the crowd's cheers. Kate and Marco clapped as well, watching as the bridesmaids followed, all in colorful dresses. The bride and groom looked at each other, oblivious to those present, kissing and smiling at one another. The groom lifted the bride up, her veil still touching the ground.

Marco wasn't watching the couple, but staring at Kate, his expression unreadable. "I think it's all clear. We can go in now."

They entered the now silent church, instantly feeling its coolness from the morning heat. A white runner and kneelers at the foot of the gold altar and a massive spray of colorful flowers were the lingering signs of the wedding.

Still holding Kate's hand, Marco guided her up a side aisle. They paused at the altars lining the walls; Kate was overwhelmed at their beauty, stopping to study the intricate art pieces.

Marco gestured to a pew, and they entered it from the side. Kate kneeled quickly, feeling gratitude for her journey. Sitting down after a minute, she looked at him from under her lashes, noting his serious face. They were silent, taking in the church's beauty and the stillness of its interior.

Marco sat looking straight ahead, his face a solid mask. "It's been a very long time since I've been in here."

"How long?"

He turned to look at her, his black eyes steady. "Since my wedding."

five

M arco took in Kate's shocked expression and then looked away, wondering if he had just spoiled their day. He still felt guilty about leaving her while he talked with Francesca and Allegra. He had felt a moment of alarm when he couldn't find her, wondering if she had been upset and left. As the owner of the shop which sold all his family's products, he wanted to check in with them and let them know a little about what was going on.

Kate had been a wonderful distraction this week, especially given the mess he had inherited involving his family's massive corporation. As the largest producer and exporter of limoncello and other lemon products, the corporation was extensive. In addition to the lemon products, they also produced and sold olive oil, and in recent years, his uncle had invested in other local companies. His uncle's death had started an avalanche of issues and problems. Though it had been expected that Marco would eventually take on the role of CEO when he turned thirty-five, the shareholders—mostly his uncle's old friends—were taken aback. Now rising to the position sooner at thirty-three, some shareholders thought Marco was too young. They were talking about the possibility of selling their shares and cashing out at this point in their lives.

There was an enormous number of legal tangles as well, and Marco was working as fast as he could to ensure no one sold. His mother and two brothers also owned a number of shares, as well as his cousin Lucca. Though his mother and brothers were involved in the business, Lucca had left Italy and had shown little interest in the company. Now Lucca was somewhere in Africa, where he had been on safari with his jet-set crowd. Despite having several people looking for him, Lucca remained largely out of sight. Marco was hopeful Lucca would emerge soon—he needed to continue to have the family hold its majority interest to stave off any hostile takeovers.

The look on Kate's face brought him back to the present.

"You're married," she said dully, instinctively moving away from him.

Marco glanced around, but the church was still empty, except for a worker who was methodically rolling up the white linen runner.

"No, Katie, I'm not," he answered quietly. "I never was. Unfortunately, my fiancé didn't decide that she did *not* want to marry me until I was standing right there." He pointed to the front of the altar. "It was a horrible day for me and my family." He put a hand through his hair, remembering how his brothers had jetted him away, touring Greece on his yacht, drinking way too much for several days until work had beckoned him back.

"Gianna"—he said her name bitterly—"didn't even have the decency to tell me herself. She sent her father to whisper to me the wedding was canceled. Apparently, she was just using me."

"For what?"

Marco looked at Kate, wanting to explain, but he had already said too much. While he wanted to share what was going on in his life, he had pledged long ago that he would not let his power

and influence become the replacement for love in another relationship. Gianna had become swept away, wanting the gift of his
name and influence to open doors for her and buy expensive
clothes and jewels. His brothers had both warned him, but he
had been so taken by her and her wide-eyed assurance that none
of that meant anything to her.

Meanwhile, she had fallen in love with a junior executive in
his company, a man Marco had deeply trusted. Marco's frequent
travel and busy schedule had left Gianna and James many
opportunities to spend time together. In fact, Marco would never
know what it finally was that had led Gianna to taking off that
day. He had soon learned from everyone in Positano she had
gone to New York and joined James, who was supposedly doing
well for himself on Wall Street. Francesca, who thrived on
sleuthing on social media, had shown him one or two posts, but
when he bit her head off, she dropped the subject. Though he
had apologized later, she wisely never brought up the topic
again.

That was what was so strange about today, Marco mused. He
hadn't meant to even bring it up with Katie. He found these last
few days with her such a breath of fresh air, and he had enjoyed
his time with her. Her enthusiasm for the smallest thing was so
intoxicating. Just the way she had reacted to the inexpensive
bracelet that she was now twisting around on her wrist had him
shaking his head.

Kate was so unassuming, almost hiding in the clothes she
wore. While today's dress was sweet, it went below her knees
and seemed like something an older woman would choose. In
fact, all her clothes seemed like that. He frowned. He wondered
how she would react if he bought her more expensive clothes—
the kinds of things she deserved to wear with her beautiful curvy
figure.

Katie had gently prodded him about his personal life, but had
not pressed him, and he appreciated it. He felt there was more to

her own life that she had not shared as well. When he had asked a few probing questions of his own, she had answered cautiously, choosing her words carefully. After Gianna's betrayal, Marco's instinct made him sense there was more to her story, but he also wondered if it was his own paranoia. With Kate, it was easier to give her the benefit of the doubt. That was why when she had kneeled in the church, so humble and authentic, he had blurted it out. Now he looked at the wariness in her brown eyes, and he felt a mixture of relief and regret. He realized now he hadn't answered her question about why Gianna had left.

"I believe she was using me for several reasons. We haven't spoken since. She married an American and moved there. It seems a long time ago and much too lengthy for us to get into now. I'm not even sure why I brought it up." He brought his hand up to her face, touching her cheek gently with his knuckles. "I hope I haven't ruined our day."

"Of course not! Are you kidding me? This is the best day ever," Kate reassured him, teasingly elbowing him, clearly trying to break the spell. "Let's roll," she urged with her American slang he found so amusing.

They exited the cool church and felt the sun's blast almost immediately. Putting on his sunglasses, he asked her if her ankle could handle a few more stairs. At her nod, he smiled, wanting to take her to one of his favorite restaurants. He was a little apprehensive as, of course, he knew all the staff there. He had determined that Kate's knowledge of Italian was very limited, and hopefully, she wouldn't catch on that he was not a simple shop manager. He was also an investor in this restaurant. Most of the people they encountered had attended his uncle's funeral and had heard rumblings about what was occurring in his family's corporation. They were eager to know it was on solid footing, as it could affect their own livelihood, but mostly because the Rinaldi family was well-loved among the residents of Positano.

Marco led Kate to the restaurant overlooking the sea,

greeting the manager by name. Kate excused herself to go to the restroom, and he sat down at the table, taking time to enjoy the view and sip the cold white wine the waiter had immediately brought him, knowing his taste. He wanted to ask some questions of his own, and lunch might just be the time to do so.

six

K ate was relieved to have a few minutes to herself. Things were so unbelievably tense in the church. She had held her breath the entire time, waiting for Marco to explain his almost wedding to her.

Kate thought she deserved another medal, this one for acting. Her false bravado was difficult to pull off when he had asked if he had ruined the day. Of course, he had not ruined it, but her heart felt heavy now. The day lacked the innocence it had before the church, when she could almost pretend they were a couple.

Kate didn't consider herself insecure, but she did not experience men like Marco. They simply didn't look at her. They looked at someone like her sister—striking with the right clothes, who knew what witty thing to say. Kate sometimes still struggled with shyness when she met people. She had looked forward to this trip for that reason—pushing herself out of her comfort zone since she would be on her own.

With new resolve, she now decided that Marco's past would make it easier to relax. She could enjoy being his friend, knowing he was not interested. He had looked so disgusted telling her about the experience. Clearly he was still deeply affected.

She wished he had told her Gianna's last name. No, she instantly knew that would be bad, as she wouldn't be able to resist searching online for Gianna's photo. Kate already instinctively knew what she looked like, imagining a gorgeous Italian woman. She was undoubtedly like the women in the lemon candle shop who took sophistication to the next level.

Kate quickly used her lip gloss and dropped it back in her purse. Making a silly face at herself in the mirror, she squared her shoulders and left the comfort of the restroom. She glanced around the open-air restaurant. Of course, there was Marco in the best seat in the house, right out in front, next to the railing with a beautiful view. He was busy looking out over the sea and for once, he wasn't aware she was approaching.

"*Mi scusi*, Katie," he said, standing after she sat down.

She opened her mouth to say something about being lost in his thoughts but closed it again. She wanted to move on from the tension of the church.

"I hope you don't mind. I ordered before the kitchen got too busy," he remarked.

Looking around, Kate noticed the tables that were empty when they first arrived were now all occupied. "I'm sure anything will be delicious." She nodded happily.

The waiter arrived then, as if on cue, his tray full of dishes.

"Did you order one of everything?" She giggled as the waiter kept setting small plates before them. She was happy to see the caprese salad with ripe tomatoes, fresh mozzarella, and vivid green basil. There was an arugula salad with shrimp, a Caesar salad with anchovies and shaved parmesan, and a wide variety of bruschetta.

"I was hungry." He shrugged.

The two began sharing the plates, commenting on the cuisine, and purposely keeping things light. Conversation was so easy with him. Usually, she was more self-conscious when she ate with a date, thinking maybe she should be one of those women who only picked at her food. Marco didn't seem to think about it, or maybe she was already in the friend zone so it didn't matter. Kate sighed audibly without realizing it.

"Sighing, Katie?" he exclaimed with a mock frown. "Aren't you having fun?"

"Oh no," she rushed to reassure him with a white lie. "Sorry, it was an 'I'm getting full, and I better stop sigh.'"

Marco then let out a big sigh. She looked at him grinning, eyebrows raised.

"That is the 'I'm going to order dessert sigh,'" he explained, signaling the waiter.

They laughed, but despite Marco's big talking, he finally settled for a small plate of biscottis and a cappuccino.

He suddenly looked at her with a glint in his eye. "We're uneven, and I think it's time we settle the score. I shared something deeply personal to me in the church, and so now it is your turn. Tell me a secret," he whispered dramatically. "Or if not a secret, just something about your life. What do you Americans say? I am all ears!"

She smiled nervously, self-consciously rubbing her arm, where she had a long scar.

"Let's start with something easy. How did you get that scar?"

"Well, it wasn't from falling off a curb." She grinned. "It happened when I was little. I was playing with my friend, Jacob, when I was around eight years old. He was chasing me for some reason. I ran up to our treehouse and then grabbed the rope swing. I was going to land on the other side of the yard."

"I had done this maneuver several times," she continued earnestly at his raised eyebrows. "This time I didn't stick the landing, and I lost my grip and fell, breaking my arm badly." She rubbed it again, remembering the pain it had caused. "Several operations and casts later, I have this scar as a reminder." She rolled her eyes ruefully.

"A badge of honor." He nodded with appreciation. "We'll share our scars some other time."

Something about that sentence sent a little thrill down her spine, except realistically, his scar was probably on his knee or ankle, she surmised.

Marco continued to stare at her persistently. "Next?"

"Oh well, let's see. So I told you what I do and that my mom died a few years ago…"

"Cancer sucks." He nodded, and she murmured her agreement.

"Is your father still alive? What is he like?"

Kate thought for a moment. It wasn't a tough question, but she chose her words carefully. "You'd love him. Well, everyone does. He runs an Irish pub in San Francisco. It's kind of like that television show where everyone knows everyone," she explained, citing the name.

He nodded, waiting for her to go on.

"Dad has owned it my whole life. He cut back when mom was sick, and his staff stepped up and ran it for him. But when she died, it comforted him to be back behind the bar. He loves me, but sometimes we don't really know what to say to each other."

Sensing her discomfort, Marco gazed at her. "I completely understand," he soothed. "Sometimes our quiet supporters are a little too quiet, eh?" he added, not explaining himself.

"I don't want you to get the wrong idea. He was very encouraging about me taking this trip. It's just that he often tells me I'm not reaching for my star. He always talks about my star." Kate rolled her eyes. "What does that even mean? And how exactly do I find it?"

"It may be easier than you think. Remind me and we will see if we can find it tonight." He grinned at her.

~

THE REST of the day unfolded perfectly. After lunch, they strolled down the stairs to a walkway that bordered the beach. They walked past rows and rows of beach chairs on the sand, covered with tiny blue umbrellas, lined up in an orderly fashion, waiting for visitors to rent them.

Kate stopped to take it all in and, as always, Marco laughed at her excitement. She whipped out her phone for the hundredth time to take photos of the beach, the hills above them, and the church with its colorful dome in an intricate pattern of yellow, green, and blue tiles shining above them. She took photos from every angle, even sneaking a few of Marco, who had walked over to look at an artist's paintings. If nothing else, she would have a few photographic memories, she told herself a little sadly.

Kate walked over and joined Marco, who was busy contemplating the paintings. "Which one do you like?"

"They're all beautiful," she answered, meaning it. Glancing at him, she realized he was already taking out his wallet. She stopped him with her hand.

"Please don't buy me anything else. You have treated me to countless lunches and dinners. You bought me my bracelet already."

Marco just frowned at her.

She addressed the painter in her poor Italian.

Both he and Marco grinned. Kate smiled, too, shrugging. She hoped she hadn't just insulted the artist.

The man gestured to his price list, and she nodded. Kate and Marco examined the selection, their heads close together. They focused on a smaller watercolor that captured the hills perfectly, outlining the pastel-colored houses and flowers. "This one," they both proclaimed at the same time and smiled at each other.

Kate handed the painter euros, accepted the wrapped painting, and thanked him. At least she could get *grazie* right. He tipped his hat to her, and she beamed at him in return. She turned to see Marco looking at her with narrowed eyes. He reached out his hand to take the painting from her as she put her wallet back in her purse.

"What? What is that look for?" she teased.

"I wanted to buy it for you," he pouted.

"Oh, Marco." She grinned at him, putting her arm through his. "You are so generous, but you have spent so much money on me. I can buy my own souvenirs. You're an amazing man," she added, anxious he know she appreciated him.

As soon as it came out, Kate was horrified. She looked down, feeling her face begin to flush. It was what she felt, but she couldn't believe she had just blurted it out. Fortunately, he said nothing, almost sensing her discomfort. If he said something about her right now, it would be so forced. Instead, Marco stopped at the stairs going back up the hill. Shifting the painting to his other hand, he got out his phone.

"Selfie-spot," he told her with a laugh. "All the tourists take one here."

Kate smiled and leaned in. They took a series of shots, some silly, some more serious. It was funny to see the reserved Marco say "selfie," let alone take one.

"I'll share them with you later," he promised, shoving his phone in his pocket.

They slowly climbed the hill, stopping often. It was only later that she realized he had no interest in most of the shops but was letting her browse at her will. He gestured to sit on a tile-covered bench in the shade, telling her to rest her ankle. Marco disappeared into the crowd, and Kate leaned her head back, not realizing how the heat and the crowd had tired her out.

He soon returned, holding two cups. "Freshly squeezed lemon granita."

Kate sat up excitedly. "Oh my God, I love lemon! How did you know?"

Marco's lips twitched, but he said nothing as they ate. She loved its icy, flaky texture. It was somewhere between a sorbet and a snow cone. She paused, realizing that he was watching her savoring the ice, pursing her lips at the sudden tartness. Embarrassed, she looked away before quietly sneaking a few more bites.

They sat on the bench for a while, watching people, jokingly commenting on the number of women in lemon dresses walking by. After a time, Marco grabbed their cups, tossing them into a nearby trash can. Holding his hand out, he helped her stand.

"One last errand." He led Kate into a nearby shop, which was tucked behind a bigger store, its space small. An elderly man sat at a workbench, focused on a pair of sandals, tools surrounding him.

"Katie, this is Armando, the finest sandal artist on the Amalfi Coast."

Kate accepted Armando's greeting and kiss on each cheek as he nodded proudly at Marco's praise. He seemed to be asking Marco questions in Italian, but Marco finally raised his hand. "We will talk later, my friend. Now it's more important that we get Katie fitted for a pair of Positano's famous sandals."

Armando showed her the shelves of fine leather sandal forms with an accompanying example of the finished product. He pointed out the various designs and colors. Next, he showed her an array of jewels. He told her the jewels were created by Neapolitan masters, who welded each single bezel and very small stones by hand. She could choose any sandal and jewels to add to them.

Marco explained Armando had been making sandals his whole life, sitting at his father's elbow. Now Armando's two sons worked with him most days. There were many shops that offered similar items, but Armando was a true artist, and would fit the sandal perfectly to her feet.

Armando beamed, ushering Kate to sit down. He brought several styles over to her, and she tried them on her left foot, eyeing them from all angles. Marco watched silently. Every so often, she would glance at him and sometimes see him subtly shake his head no. She sat back, eyeing the wall, and spotted the perfect pair.

"Those," she said, excitedly pointing at a light brown pair of sandals. The sandals were simple, but exquisite, with two straps that went across her foot and another strap that crisscrossed at the ankle. Given her clumsiness, Kate joked to Marco, she needed a pair that would strap on to her feet. He laughingly agreed.

From the jewels, she picked out a few of the lighter blue ones to remind her of the color of the sea as it brushed the sand. Armando suggested the placement of the small stones on the foot straps, and Kate nodded. From there, he measured her feet to a mold, helping her delicately take off her soft cast.

When he was finished, he stood, chatting easily with Marco in Italian. Kate strapped her cast reluctantly back on and stood gingerly. Her ankle had stiffened up, and it took a few minutes for her to apply pressure gently. Marco frowned a little as she hobbled next to him.

He eyed her narrowly. "We overdid it."

"Oh, Marco, don't act like an Italian mother. I'm fine."

"Still, we will take it easy tonight."

"We will?" She looked at him warily.

His eyes glinted. "We will. That is if you will agree to have dinner with me."

She gave a small laugh. "I'll have to check my schedule. By the way, what do I owe for the sandals?"

"Oh, you pay when you pick them up," he explained smoothly, holding the shop door open for her. They both turned and waved at Armando. "*Ciao.*"

Marco walked Kate up to her room, handing her the painting and helping her open the door. They stood just inside the doorway.

"I'll see you tonight about eight." He looked so intently at her that once again, Kate thought he might kiss her, but the moment was lost when a smiling Giovanni bustled over, holding an ice pack. "This will help your ankle after your day out."

Kate thanked him, touched by his thoughtfulness. She didn't know Marco asked him to bring it up when they had first walked in. The men left together, with Marco giving her one last thoughtful look before gently closing the door.

seven

After they left, Kate changed out of her now sticky dress and put on shorts and a tank top. She went out on the balcony for a few minutes, but the sun was overbearing. She came inside and was grateful to lie down, the ice pack on her ankle and foot.

Waking up startled, she glanced at her phone, realizing she had slept almost two hours. It was time to get ready. It was then she saw a text from Marco. They had exchanged phone numbers after lunch, realizing they hadn't done so.

Marco texted he would pick her up out front. Since he was always the gentleman coming to the door, the new plan made Kate curious. She eagerly swung her legs over the bed, testing her ankle. The rest and ice had done wonders. She was going bootless tonight, no matter what.

Kate took time showering and getting ready. She tamed her frizzy hair into submission, it falling in soft waves to her shoulders. She looked over her clothes, biting a fingernail. When she had packed, she had not expected to go out this much. Thankfully, Teresa had urged her to throw in a few more dresses. Kate examined one of those, a bright pink wrap dress. It was a little lower cut than she usually wore, hence why the tags were still on it. Teresa insisted it would be beautiful with Kate's dark hair and eyes, but she had never had the nerve to wear it.

She finished her makeup, adding a little more than she normally wore, and slipped on the cool dress. Taking a selfie in the mirror, she eyed it apprehensively. She texted the image to Teresa with a question mark. She hadn't texted her dad or Teresa since the short texts she had sent when she had arrived. She hadn't even looked at social media. It felt truly like an escape to stay off the grid for a bit.

You are stunning!

Kate grinned.

Need complete honestly—pinky swear!

As if they were still six years old, the women still held the pinky swear as the utmost code of honestly.

100%

Kate's grin grew wider. Before she could think about it, she texted a photo of Marco that she had snapped when he wasn't looking. She would have rather shown Teresa the selfie, but he had not shared them yet.

WOWZA! Who or what is that? Teresa added hearts and a surprised emoji.

We're just friends.

You won't be for long in that dress!

Kate giggled—her friend always gave her confidence. Glancing at her watch, she saw it was almost time to meet Marco. After saying a quick goodbye, she slipped on sandals, eyeing them warily. Though they weren't too fashionable, they were fairly flat, so she felt comfortable walking in them. Though now, after trying on Armando's buttery soft leather sandals, Kate could feel her own pinch her feet.

She collected her purse and phone and slipped on the bracelet Marco had bought her—the only jewelry she wore except the small diamond hoop earrings that had been her mom's. Kate left her room, walking gingerly down the hallway. It felt like freedom to have the clunky boot off, but it also was a little unnerving.

She eyed the elevator but decided to take the stairs slowly. The ancient elevator made her anxious. It had been okay with Marco—everything was okay with him. Kate felt a sense of safety and trust she had rarely felt, but she didn't want to analyze that now.

She went down to the street and wasn't sure what to do. Glancing at her watch, she saw it was eight o'clock on the dot. She had noticed she and Marco were similar in their habit of being on time.

Beep Beep!

Kate glanced up to see Marco in a red Alfa Romeo convertible, pulling over to the right side of the road.

"Get in quickly, if you can," he yelled with a grin. "But watch for motorbikes!"

Kate made a face at him, but glanced down the road carefully, walking across and jumping in.

Marco checked his side mirror, pulled out, and sped up the hill.

"I'm sorry I couldn't get out to open the door for you." He grinned as he gave her a quick sideways glance, his black hair ruffled with the wind. "There was no place to park."

"Marco, this car is gorgeous. Is it yours?"

"Borrowed from a friend," murmured Marco, his eyes straight ahead on the hairpin turn coming up.

"Nice friend."

Kate's hair blew in her face as they climbed higher and higher, turn after turn. The warm scented breeze felt wonderful, and she brushed the strands back impatiently. Abruptly, Marco pulled over to a small parking area next to a restaurant on the cliff, its lights glittering already in the dusk. He got out, reaching into the back seat for a box, before coming around to Kate's side to help her out. He looked admiringly at her pink dress, his gaze traveling down to her feet.

"You look beautiful, Katie. I see you lost something, though."

"I cast it aside." She giggled, making a face at her own pun. When would she stop making bad jokes when she was nervous?

Marco chuckled, handing her the box he was holding formally. "I had a feeling you might. That is why I asked Armando if he had time to get these done."

He opened the lid, and she stared down at her new pair of sandals. The light blue stones glittered against the leather. "Put me on," they twinkled at her.

Kate looked up at Marco, her eyes widening. "These are the most beautiful sandals I've ever owned!" She immediately sat back down in the car, taking her own sandals off and slipping the new ones on. They glided on and fit perfectly. Marco grabbed her hands to pull her back up and she stared at her feet, admiring them from every angle.

"How much do I owe you?"

He shrugged. "Let's not talk about money on such a beautiful night."

"But, Marco..."

He shook his head. "They are not expensive, I promise. Please allow me a few opportunities to treat you."

She opened her mouth and then closed it again. Marco was staring at her, his head tilted, his grin growing bigger at her consternation. She decided not to argue. It was already a magical evening, and she was going to enjoy every minute. She thanked him quietly, and he acknowledged her gratitude with a nod, still smiling.

Glancing toward the nearby restaurant, she gasped. "This is breathtaking." The open-air restaurant was on the cliff, over-looking all of Positano and the sea. Its blue-and-white tiled floor sparkled, and tables were scattered throughout, covered by fine white linen with candles reflecting off the wine glasses set neatly before them. Nearby pots of brightly covered flowers were set alongside the perimeter. Kate let Marco usher her inside, his hand lightly on her back. The host greeted him with a big hug and turned to Kate and gave her an enthusiastic kiss on each cheek. He led them to a table next to the wrought iron rail overlooking the town, speaking to Marco the whole time. Marco answered quietly, nodding his head.

The scene below captivated her. Dusk was turning the colors of Positano bright pink and orange. She barely noticed as Marco ordered a bottle of prosecco.

"I'm sorry! I just have to," she apologized, pulling out her phone.

She took a few photos and then quietly slipped her phone back into her purse. Teresa had texted her several times, but she resisted answering. She didn't want to be rude to Marco. It was more important to be here, gazing at him and enjoying their evening. Kate took in the beauty of the hills and sea, pointing things out, inquiring about landmarks.

He quietly answered her questions, but his eyes were on her and not on the scene before them. Kate finally turned back to meet his intense stare. Nervously, she smiled.

Marco smiled back, just as wide. They sat gazing at each other for a minute, oblivious to anything. It was the waiter who interrupted, setting up an ice bucket and showing Marco the label before popping the cork.

After their glasses were filled and the bottle was nestled back into the bucket, Marco raised his glass, softly toasting, "To a perfect night. *Cin Cin.*"

"*Salute!*" The only Italian toast she had learned, she told him.

That made him chuckle as they sipped their prosecco.

"This tastes delicious. I like it better than champagne." Secretly, she wondered if prosecco was as expensive as some champagne was. The restaurant looked expensive, too. She had seen the receipts from the shop. While it was doing well, it must cost a lot to live in Positano. There was also something about the way Marco dressed—elegant and refined was how she would describe it. Tonight, he wore black pants and a crisp white shirt, and though they were nondescript, they looked expensive. The long sleeves were rolled up, showing his strong brown arms. A gold intricate watch was on one wrist. She realized he must do well, but she didn't want him to spend all his money on her. He had mentioned his widowed mother, and she guessed he probably took care of her like many Italian men. Kate knew from her father's business how money could ebb and flow. It wasn't always a guarantee that it would continue to come in.

Marco was looking at her steadily, his eyes glinting in the candlelight. "It is made in Italy. I prefer it, but I only drink it when I have something to celebrate."

"Oh, cause I got my cast off? That's really nice of you!" she exclaimed, not seeing the glint in his eye.

"I'm glad you agreed to come out tonight, Katie. I promise it will be one of the most delicious dinners you have ever had."

Kate's stomach rumbled at the thought. She found herself relaxing. She was all in, if it meant enjoying this night—something she would remember the rest of her life.

The waiter brought them an antipasto dish and a basket of crusty bread. As they sampled the Italian meats and cheeses, Kate laughingly told Marco she had never met a piece of cheese she didn't like.

That led to a discussion of their favorite foods and dishes. Marco insisted they play his trading secrets game. Kate thought for a minute before admitting she loved ice cream or gelato in any form. And pizza—she loved pizza. Marco nodded approvingly. He said he grew up frequently eating fish from the region, but confessed an American cheeseburger was his weakness. Couldn't get enough of them, he confided.

Kate talked about her grandmother's cooking. She grew up standing at her nonna's elbow, watching her make Sunday *sugo*

—a Bolognese sauce. Her favorite foods were all the Italian meals her grandmother and mother had made. Kate told him just thinking about them brought her comfort, and he agreed. He felt the same way about his mother's food, he told her.

Happy to share that memory, they continued talking about their childhood. He told her about his younger brothers, Stefano and Niccolo—or Nico, as they called him. They were all close in age and constantly got into trouble, laughed Marco, describing their childhood antics. They had grown up on a lemon grove outside Sorrento, he explained, where they were expected to work the farm and do chores. Marco appeared to be very close to his brothers, talking about how they continued to tease each other and support one another. It sounded idyllic, and Kate sighed.

MARCO REALIZED Kate grew quieter as he talked about his family. He had hoped that if he shared a little more with her, she would open up as well. She started to at lunch but had seemed to withdraw just as quickly.

He couldn't take her eyes off her tonight. Her shiny brown hair was gloriously tousled from the car. It looked delightful on her, he thought, so tired of perfectly coiffed women who would have complained the car ruined their hair. The candlelight was now reflecting off her soft brown eyes, making them even warmer. When she smiled at him before, she had licked her pink lips showing her lovely white teeth.

And then there was that dress. *Dio.* He took another sip of prosecco, enjoying the view. The dress hugged her curves in all the right places and showed off her body—something she seemed to want to hide most of the time.

He wasn't sure about the sudden change in her mood. Hoping to draw her out, he asked questions about her job. She brightened, telling him about how she had built her freelance business, learning to write for websites and the coding to redesign them. She seemed comfortable in this arena, talking at length about how important it was to work with search engines so websites were successful.

"You must be very good at your job."

Kate gave him a shy look at his praise.

Now that she seemed relaxed, he tried a direct approach. "Tell me about your sister."

Looking at the view, she took a long sip of her water. "How do you know I have a sister?"

"You mentioned to Alfonso that you were looking for a gift for her, and he told me in passing." Marco looked at her questioningly. "I didn't think it was a big secret."

She gave him a nervous smile. "It just caught me by surprise."

As luck would have it, the waiter came to clear their plates and brought their pasta course. Marco hadn't ordered anything —the chef was simply preparing dishes for them.

After setting the enticing plates of fresh lemony linguini with crab before them, Marco ordered a bottle of pinot grigio, which was promptly brought and opened. It was only after Marco had tasted it and the wine was nestled in the bucket that he raised his eyebrows, obviously prompting her.

"My sister's name is Meara, and she's just eleven months older than me. Irish twins." She shrugged. "We were closer when we were kids, but then…" Kate stopped and bit her lip. "Then we weren't…for several reasons." She looked down again at her food, not eager to continue talking.

"Wait." Marco's eyes widened in surprise, as if he was putting it all together. "Your sister is Meara Malone?"

～

KATE HAD EXPECTED THIS LOOK. She twirled her linguini around her fork, no longer interested in eating it.

And here it comes. She braced herself, waiting for the accolades, the comments about how Meara was the tech world's wonder child. Her brains and beauty and quick success up the corporate ladder were well-publicized. Just last month, she had been on the cover of a popular business magazine, climbing the stairs to a corporate jet, her tall, trim legs shown off by a sleek black suit. Her beautiful, dark red hair was glinting in the sun. Kate didn't even read the article, she just stared at the photo for a long time. It was baffling how Meara seemed to have gotten every Irish gene, favoring her father in looks. Meanwhile, Kate looked more like her mother's Italian ancestry—the short, stubby side, she often complained.

Whether it was Meara's startling beauty or her rise to fame in the tight-knit Silicon Valley world where she had risen as one of the youngest CEOs of a major firm—she was constantly in the headlines. It hadn't even escaped Positano. Kate sighed. She wasn't envious of her sister—she didn't want her cutthroat life. She just didn't like being compared to her, which had happened too frequently, given they were born so close together.

Maybe it was because her father had come to America as a child of immigrants and had struggled and saved to build a life for himself that he appeared to admire Meara's wealth a little too much. He kept copies of her magazine covers behind the bar at the pub, always quick to own being Meara Malone's father. Kate, helping at the pub, could barely keep her eyes from rolling when the subject came up repeatedly.

She now looked at Marco. He wasn't asking questions, and he wasn't marveling at Meara's accomplishments like most people did when they found out. He just simply looked at her, his face unreadable. Now he picked up his fork and knife and they began to eat. They stayed silent for a while, Kate's mind was whirling. She hadn't wanted to have this conversation with him. She wanted to keep Marco to herself and not let the world intrude. For once, she had something—even if it would just be a memory of her own—that was just hers.

The waiter came to clear their plates, and Kate used the time to choose her next words. "I wish we were closer. It's complicated."

"What happened?" Marco inquired softly, twirling the stem of his wine glass, watching her carefully, as if one movement would startle her.

Maybe it was the quiet way he asked, but she suddenly trusted him implicitly. She had never talked about it to anyone except Teresa, who had grown up well-versed in the Malone Family Dynamics.

"Meara and I were so close in age, some people thought we were twins even though we look so different," she began. "She was always striking. People would stop our mother on the street to comment." The memories came rushing back to Kate. She remembered standing there awkwardly while their mother was careful to point out her other daughter to Meara's admirers.

"She was always smarter, more confident, better at sports— and of course, beautiful. I felt like I couldn't catch up."

She looked off into the distance, her face remote. "You know, it never really bothered me. I was really close to my mom. We did everything together. I had good friends and a wonderful childhood."

"But then someone special came along," prodded Marco.

"How did you know?"

"There always is," he stated firmly, his eyes intense.

"Yes. Jacob and I had grown up together." She touched her scar absently. "When we got to high school, we were always together, and he would cheer me on whether I was playing volleyball or even at my piano recital." She smiled slightly at the memory of his standing ovation. "I thought we were just friends, but then he asked me to the prom, and it seemed like things changed between us. People saw us as a couple, and I thought so, too."

"Then we went to different universities, but they were only a couple hours away," she said. "I didn't want to date anyone else —I lived for weekends when I would usually go visit him. Meara went to the same university."

"One weekend I got there, and he was nowhere to be found. I sat outside his fraternity until one of his friends walked by and said Jacob had left with some redhead who had come by."

"I just knew," she told Marco quietly. "I waited all night in my car outside. He never came home. I left at dawn, embarrassed. I didn't want him to know I had been there. Then I saw a photo of Jacob and Meara at a party together that someone posted. I got a text from him the next day apologizing but admitting he had been in love with my sister for years. He said he still thought of me as a good friend. A good friend," she repeated bitterly.

"Did your sister love him?"

"You know, that's the ironic thing. When I confronted her, she swore to me she felt nothing for him—that he had been like a little brother. She said she had just stopped by looking for me, assuming I was down for the weekend, and he asked her to a party. I know it's stupid, but it still hurt. I loved him so much. He was *my* friend, *my* boyfriend..." Kate trailed off.

"Then our mother got sick right around my graduation. I came home immediately. Meara did not. She had started her career by then. She came in the end, but it was when mom was almost gone. Meara left soon after the funeral."

"We talk every so often. She tries to give me advice when we do—mostly financial advice. Someday I hope we can come together on a different level, but for now, I just like to keep her there and me here." Kate gave a humorless laugh, picking up the salt and the pepper and spreading them widely.

The waiter appeared just then, frowning at the salt and

pepper rearrangement. He placed plates of sea bass and scampi before them. Kate breathed in the adjacent fragrant fennel salad that smelled of licorice.

She took a bigger gulp of wine than she intended. Liquid courage, she thought wryly. It was a little disquieting how silent Marco was, but then he reached over and grabbed her hand that was on the table, gently stroking it. The nerves tingled all the way up her arm. Her heart swelled that he wasn't placating her with platitudes about her beauty or personality. He just listened. It was a rare quality.

"I haven't been in touch with her since I've been here. I just wanted this time to myself."

Marco finally nodded slowly. "I'm glad you told me this. It explains a lot."

When she looked at him questioningly, he withdrew his hand and smiled at her. Picking up their utensils, they ate slowly. Marco made small talk, telling her about fishing as a young boy and some of the seafood that was prevalent on the Amalfi Coast. They both shared similar tastes in fish, with Kate admitting that she could never stomach an oyster.

Marco's eyes widened with amusement. "I've seen what happens when your stomach isn't right!"

"Hey, you're not supposed to remind a lady of that," she flushed. Kate couldn't hold back the giggle, though. "That was really not one of the finest moments of my trip."

He sat back, smiling at her. "How about now?"

She looked at him seriously. "Now is perfect."

WHEN THEY HAD FINISHED EATING, Marco got to his feet, holding his hand toward her.

"May I have this dance?"

Kate looked over at the small dance floor, where a few

couples were enjoying the sounds of an Italian ballad. She nodded and let him lead her to the dance floor, where she melted against him, her heart thudding.

Marco smiled down at her, his hand intertwined with hers, his arm holding her close. He suddenly loosened his grip and looked at her, concerned. "*Dio*, I forgot about your ankle. Are you okay?"

Kate reassured him she was fine, quickly changing the subject. "What did you mean at the table?" she asked quickly before she lost her nerve. "What does it explain about me?"

"I think I have an antennae now after Gianna. I could tell you were holding back—almost hiding something. The hairs on my neck go up. Always be honest with me, Katie." He stared hard down at her.

"Okay, I'll be honest," she blurted. "What are we doing here? I mean, you are spending all this time with me—I'm on vacation. I'll be leaving soon."

He looked at her steadily. "The honest answer is, I don't know. You are the first woman I have wanted to spend time with in a long time. I go out with various women, but I just haven't been interested in anyone. You're so different from the women I meet, Katie. Don't ask me to tell you how or why right now. Can we leave it there?"

His black eyes continued staring, searching her face for her reaction.

Though she felt her spine tingling, she nodded. Every nerve in her body screamed this was going to end badly. Despite that, she couldn't help it. Life was short, right? She made her decision and nodded, leaning against him as his arms tightened. She felt the magic in the air. She had thought it was her lovely Positano. Her heart hammered against her chest. She knew now it was more than that.

∾

WHEN THEY RETURNED to the table, Marco signaled for the bill. They needed to get out of the there. Holding Kate in his arms had been too tempting. He badly needed to kiss her, and he wasn't going to have their first kiss be in a crowded restaurant. He had fought the urge all day, wanting it to be special.

With the bill also came two short glasses of limoncello, an Italian liqueur. Nodding, the waiter made sure Marco knew they were from his company. Marco paid quickly, hoping that Kate's Italian was as poor as it had been on the waterfront. He knew it was selfish. He spent time tonight prodding her for details about her life, but he still wanted some parts of his to remain a secret for now.

He hadn't been completely honest with Kate when he told her he didn't know why or how she attracted him. He did know. It was her innocence, enthusiasm for the smallest thing, and appreciation for every small token or gesture. He knew that wasn't completely unique to every woman, but Gianna had soured him. He asked out most women because he needed a plus-one for an event. He took a date to charity events, corporate dinners, and other occasions where it was simpler to have someone by his side than to fend off single women present. His dates knew who he was, how much he was worth, and expected certain things. Kate took whatever he offered. Actually, not everything, he corrected, thinking back to her proud denial of the painting on the waterfront. It was important for Kate to feel as if she wasn't taking advantage of what she assumed was Italian hospitality.

He was glad she had told him about Meara and their relationship. He had sensed there was a large presence in her life, something that had made her unsure of herself. Though she seemed confident in some areas, he saw her often withdraw. He knew he would have to work harder to build her trust.

Kate was a beautiful woman because she didn't know it. She transfixed him the moment he saw her. He loved her curves and was longing to take his fingers and glide them through her thick, shiny hair. Her face came alive, and when she smiled, it was like the heavens were being handed to him. Her musical laugh made him want to work hard to make it happen again. He felt powerfully drawn to her. And that dimple. It played hide and seek with him at the strangest times.

Marco was careful not to say what she was obviously expecting when she told him who her sister was. He had seen the suspicion in her eyes, the wariness that he was going to wax on about Meara's accomplishments. From what he had read, Meara was a shark, a woman who would sell her own nonna to get where she wanted to be. His only shock had been how different his understanding of Meara was from what Kate appeared to be.

He also knew Kate expected some obligatory compliments. It had probably been done over and over as a child, as a second thought by someone gushing over Meara. Kate had obviously learned along the way that these statements were disingenuous.

When he told Kate what he thought of her, he wanted them to be at a point where she would accept it as sincerely as it was being given. Now she was staring at him, almost as if she was trying to read his mind.

He wanted to lighten the mood. "Have you ever had limoncello?"

"No, but you know how much I love lemons!" She took a tentative sip. Pursing her lips. "Oh, that is so good!"

Marco smiled and clinked his small glass with her.

"*Cin Cin!*" She took another sip. "My Italian is really coming along," she teased.

Marco asked her in Italian if she wanted to go for a drive. Kate narrowed her eyes at him, obviously trying to make out a word or two. He grinned at her. "We'll keep up with those Italian lessons!"

He held her chair, and they strolled to the car. After he

helped her in, Marco ran around to his side. He had purposely stopped drinking halfway through dinner, knowing he needed to drive. In fact, he hadn't even really drunk his limoncello because the biggest secret of the largest limoncello producer in Italy was that their CEO was not fond of it. He winced, thinking about what the shareholders would say about that.

"A quick drive?"

"Of course." She was already leaning her head back, taking in the cool sweet-smelling night air. "It smells so good here."

Marco drove a few miles up the hill to a spot that featured a view he had wanted to show her. Pulling over into the scenic area, he parked the car and turned to her, taking his seatbelt off. She looked back at him with the same intensity. Turning, she found the catch and snapped her seatbelt off as well.

Marco wasn't sure who moved first, but suddenly they were together, and he gently brushed his lips with hers. Her full lips were as soft as he knew they would be. She tasted like lemons, but with a sweetness he couldn't describe. His kiss became stronger, confidently devouring her. Finally, his lips left hers, only to travel across her cheekbone and settle on the dimple he had come to adore. He returned to her mouth, eager to taste her again. After several minutes, he reluctantly pulled away.

"Katie," he sighed. "If I don't stop now, I'm not sure I can."

She nodded, looking as stunned as he was. "Do we have to go back to the hotel yet?"

"No *cara*, let's just sit her for a few minutes and enjoy the view." He put his arm around her, and she leaned her head on his shoulder. They sat gazing at the view before them. Lights twinkled all over the hill, disappearing into the inky darkness of the sea.

"Beautiful," she breathed.

"*Si*," he agreed, wrapping his arm a little tighter around her with his eyes on her.

eight

Kate woke up the next day and stretched. Smiling, she nestled back into her comfortable bed. The soft sheets the hotel used caressed her body. She peeked at the light coming from the balcony. According to where the sun was in the sky, it was much later than her normal sunrise. Picking up her phone, she found a text from Marco.

Enjoy your day! I am looking forward to seeing you tomorrow.

She hugged her phone, remembering how last night they had stayed looking at the view, content to be quiet and just be together. It was only after she trembled in the cooling air, that he reluctantly took his arm away to fasten his seatbelt and start the car. Marco was able to park across the street from the hotel since there was little traffic. He had insisted on walking to her room, where he kissed her with the same controlled passion. He walked backward down the hall as she held the door open, his expression showing regret at ending the evening.

Marco had said he was going on a short business trip, but he would be back in time to take her out the next day for a surprise. She asked him who would manage the shop while he was gone, and he had casually dismissed it, telling her Alfonso would be fine.

Kate's phone buzzed suddenly. She was happy when she saw it was Teresa.

Dying here. You never got back to me! How was your night with Mr. Hunky? Did he like the dress?

Kate laughed out loud. She and Teresa had used that term to describe hot guys ever since they were teenagers. Part of Kate still felt like she was back in high school—certainly she hadn't felt like this for a long time.

She looked at her watch. It would be almost midnight at home. She propped herself up against the headboard, fluffing her pillows, she hit the call button.

"*Buongiorno* Teresa," she sang in her best Italian accent.

"Oh my. Your date is worth a phone call! Spill it, Malone. I have been dying all day. I waited up tonight until it was an okay time to text you. You're lucky I didn't wake you up earlier!"

Kate giggled. It felt good to hear her friend's voice and know she cared so much. She launched into the story, skipping some of the more private parts. Teresa would call it "the good stuff." She felt it necessary to protect Marco's privacy, though. Not that Teresa would ever get to meet him, but Kate felt protective of the thoughtful man, who was already meaning something to her.

At the end of the story, she heard Teresa's sigh. "It's like a movie. I couldn't be happier for you."

The best part was Kate knew she was telling the truth. Teresa *was* happy for her. She was a loyal friend who had watched Kate's struggles, always her champion.

"Teresa, what am I doing? I mean, it's a vacation romance. I'm going to have to come home, eventually."

In fact, Kate didn't actually have a return trip ticket, not wanting to pin herself down. She had left it open, knowing she could work remotely if she wanted to. Her goal was to get her book written, no matter what. Her savings wouldn't allow her to stay indefinitely, but she was hoping to stay several more weeks.

"Kaaateee," Teresa drew out her name in exasperation. "Just have fun. Don't take it all so seriously. Just roll with it."

"What if I lose my heart?"

"Then I'll help you find it again."

"I know you will," Kate acknowledged quietly.

They talked for a few more minutes, but Teresa's yawns were becoming more frequent, and they said goodbye with the promise that Kate would call if she needed anything.

"Give him a kiss for me," Teresa teased as she hung up.

Kate stared at the ceiling for a long time after that, contemplating this unplanned relationship of sorts. Her mind was a mess of swirling emotions.

Finally, she got dressed in a simple, sleeveless, light-pink top and white jeans. She intentionally chose white tennis shoes—better to ensure her feet were well taken care of today. She looked at her watch, surprised Giovanni wasn't up to check on her. He was like a doting father, and she appreciated his care. She hadn't felt attention like that in a long time.

Kate grabbed a quick cappuccino and waved Giovanni off from breakfast. Last night's dinner was superb as promised, and she wasn't hungry yet. Instead, she spent the morning re-walking the route she and Marco had taken the day before. She stopped in at the candle shop and chatted with Francesca and Allegra about trivial things. It felt good to spend some time with women around her age.

As Kate passed a shop farther down, she stopped in her tracks. In the window was a cobalt blue, one-piece swimsuit that caught her attention. She didn't like the thought of trying on bathing suits, especially after a gazillion slices of salami and cheese these past few days. Nevertheless, she walked into the cool shop, pointing to the swimsuit. She found herself in the dressing room, trying it on within minutes. She had brought her old suit from home, knowing at some point she might want to take a dip in the Tyrrhenian Sea. She wasn't sure what was driving her to shop. It could be the Mediterranean women she had seen and envied yesterday. They looked naturally exquisite, even on the beach. What if Marco decided that was their next adventure? Kate sized herself up in the mirror and decided the suit did a few things for her. It gathered effectively near her stomach and was high cut, making the most of what legs she had. The color was her favorite, too. Looking at the price tag, Kate groaned. At this rate, she was going to have to cut her stay short.

She dressed quickly and left the dressing room. As she walked to the counter, she saw a rounder of cover-ups and bought a blue-and-white one that looked like it would hit her mid-thigh. The idea of a cover-up made her feel a little more secure.

After making her purchases, Kate walked slowly down the hill, stopping every so often to take in the sights and smells. She found her stomach rumbling and went to a nearby cafe, finally deciding on a panino, a grilled sandwich oozing with warm Italian meats and cheese. She sat on a stool inside, next to a window, watching people go by.

Finally leaving her perch, she trudged up the hill, her package trailing from her hand. It was hot, and her ankle was a little sore today. Suddenly feeling a little lonely, she spotted the ceramics shop and had an idea. She had asked Teresa what she had wanted as a souvenir, and her selfless friend had not asked for anything. Kate had decided to bring Teresa something from the shop and today would be the perfect day with Marco's absence. If he was there, he would insist on giving it to her.

Opening the door with its little bell ringing merrily, announcing her arrival, Alfonso came out from the back. Instead of his normal cheery self, he looked frustrated.

"Alfonso, is everything okay?"

Alfonso greeted her with his normal kiss on each cheek.

"*Sì.*" He nodded absentmindedly, running his hands through his curls.

Kate explained she wanted a gift for her friend. She already knew what she wanted—a pretty oval blue platter rimmed with lemons. She admired it now, picking it up for Alfonso to wrap. The boy was an expert at bubble wrap.

Once finished, he handed her the package, finished with the store's signature paper. He looked horrified as Kate handed him her credit card.

"No, no." He held his hands up.

"Yes," Kate insisted, pressing the card at him. "Alfonso, this is a gift I am buying. Please don't say anything to Marco. It's something I want to do."

Alfonso shrugged, giving up and running her card. Handing her the receipt, he asked her if she had a few minutes to watch the front while he tended to something in the back. She agreed, happy to help her new friend. A few minutes turned into thirty minutes, and Kate began to get bored. It was the quietest part of the afternoon, with tourists probably resting in their hotels from the heat. She wandered back to ask Alfonso if he still needed her and found him at the computer. Even though his back was to her, she could see he was clearly frustrated, blasting the computer in Italian with words she wasn't sure she wanted to know the meaning of.

"Alfonso?"

"*Mi scusi,* Kate." He turned to her in exasperation. "It's this computer!" he shouted, looking like he wanted to knock it off the desk.

Seeing her eyebrows raised, he explained the website had crashed that morning. While it wasn't urgent, he felt responsible. He had called the number Marco had left for technical help, but no one had returned his call.

"Well, it's your lucky day!" She grinned, explaining what she did for a living. "It's probably just a simple error."

He didn't seem to understand what she was talking about, but he looked amused at her cheerfulness. Getting up, he let her take his seat at the desk in front of the laptop. Kate sat down, picking up her hands as if she was about to play a complex piece on the piano, wiggling her fingers. Alfonso laughed at her silliness.

At the bell's tinkle at the front door, she told him to go tend to customers, but Alfonso seemed reluctant to leave her alone. "Go!" She waved, smiling at him. He slowly backed away, as if he was unsure of what to do.

"I'm fine, Alfonso," she reassured him, taking his hesitation as guilt for possibly imposing on her.

Kate bent over the laptop and shook her head. There were dozens of windows open, slowing the processing. She closed them so she could focus on her work. After a few minutes, she found the offending piece of software that was popping up and blocking the site. Now, the website came up instantly.

She reloaded it a few times just to be sure. Satisfied, she was about to stand and go tell Alfonso when she took another look at it. Like most Italian businesses, it had an Italian side and an English side. Whoever had made the website had put little to no energy into it. The descriptions of items were vague and did not contain any good search criteria.

Kate started moving things around on the homepage, bringing some of the more popular items forward. She wrote better copy for some items, describing them in greater detail. She used descriptive words that she surmised one might search for when looking up Italian pottery. She automatically linked it and auto translated it so it would show on the Italian shadow side.

Alfonso came back now and then to check on her, looking over her shoulder. She showed him what she was doing, and he was pleased, high-fiving her awkwardly and gesturing for her to continue.

After some time, Kate felt stiff. She had been sitting there for longer than she had realized. She sat back in her chair, rubbing her neck, pleased at her work. She glanced around the nondescript office that had a small desk and a couple of chairs. The wall was littered with various invoices, calendars and some kind of production sheet. On the desk next to her, she saw a few folders with a logo that said "Oro." She cautiously moved the files over to another part of the desk, moving the laptop closer to her.

Scrolling down the homepage, she noticed the same name on the bottom of the website: Oro Industries. Hmmm, maybe a parent company?

Pulling her phone out to search for it, she heard Alfonso approaching and quickly put her phone down. She showed him her work and he praised her, telling her he saw the difference already in how attractive it was.

"I want to fix just a couple more things and then I'll call it a day."

Alfonso nodded, retreating again.

Kate finished the home page and scrolled down one more time to make sure all was in order. Thrilled with her work, she automatically closed the browser window and gasped when the computer's wallpaper now appeared. There it was, as big as the world to see—a photo of Marco and a beautiful woman. Their heads close together, they stood in front of the Eiffel Tower. Kate focused on Marco's face—he looked really happy.

"What do we have here? Snooping, Kate?" a voice asked silkily.

∾

KATE WAS LIVID. She had spent the entire afternoon helping Marco's shop. She was confident her improvements to the website and the search functions would be beneficial. She turned around to observe him standing behind her, handsome as ever, but slightly disheveled. He wore an elegant suit, his silk tie loose, his hair a little messy, as if he had been running his hands through it. He was now staring at her suspiciously.

"How can I be snooping when there's a giant photo right in front of me?" she asked coolly.

Standing up, Kate turned and faced him. Usually not confrontational, she felt the need to assert herself, putting her hands on her hips and staring him down.

"Where's Alfonso?" he demanded, his eyes like steel. "You shouldn't have been left alone back here."

Kate shrugged, picking up her purse and package. "Why? Was I going to steal something? By the way, I bought this in case you need the receipt." She waved the package at him, skirting the chair, and brushed past Marco, marching toward the door.

Alfonso emerged from the basement just then, clattering up the stairs with boxes. As Marco prepared to follow her, Alfonso stopped him, speaking in rapid Italian. Marco looked over Alfonso's head at Kate, his eyes narrowing.

She shot him one more shriveling look—the look she had perfected to stop her cousin's naughty toddler in his tracks. With that, she grabbed the door a little more vigorously than she meant to, the bell tinkling violently.

"*Arrivederci,*" Kate called over her shoulder, her face flushed. And she meant it.

nine

Kate paced her hotel room. She thought about calling Teresa, but a quick glance at her watch told her Teresa was still at her work at the hospital.

Kate had cooled off a little. She had taken a refreshing shower and put on the cushy hotel bathrobe. Toweling her hair now, she sat on the bed, her mind going back to the photo of who she assumed was Gianna.

If Kate was honest with herself, she had to admit that some of her anger wasn't even directed at Marco. It was jealousy, plain and simple. Seeing the photo of them together had jarred her heart. Knowing he had a past and then seeing it were two different things. And couldn't one ex be plain? Did every single one have to be gorgeous? Kate and Teresa had often remarked about that. It was so easy to search the former love lives of men they were interested in. Every single time they came up with a gorgeous ex—making Kate and Teresa groan and ready to throw their phones at the wall.

"And did she have to be his wallpaper?" she asked out loud to the silent room. Kate got up and wandered out to the edge of the balcony. She remained in the room where no one could see her but she could still enjoy the view. She felt embarrassed, even though nothing had really changed, except photographic evidence of Gianna. Marco's annoyance at her had hurt. This whole thing with him had been such a bad decision. Anyone could see it wasn't going to end well. She didn't want to run into him now. That would be so awkward!

Kate still had a few more days at the hotel. She would cancel and move on. She had splurged on this hotel, knowing it was at the center of the town. Her next stop was a small studio apartment somewhere on the hill. It was less expensive, given the number of steps that led up to it. She hadn't worried about it when she booked it, confident she would write and be nestled in for a time.

Kate dragged her suitcase to her bed impulsively and began to pack. Something about this decision felt empowering—like she was taking charge of her life. Then she had a sudden realization—going to her computer, she confirmed that her plan wasn't going to work. The apartment was booked until her arrival.

Chewing on her fingernail, she thought about finding another hotel. Dragging her suitcase up the hill was not appealing. She had wanted to explore some of the nearby towns— Sorrento and Amalfi, for sure. She would stay there but ask Giovanni about the bus and ferry schedules and spend her remaining time away from Positano.

With that decision, Kate felt better. She had a plan. She would travel around the region, her time with Marco a treasured memory.

A soft knock at the door brought her out of her stupor. She knew Giovanni was worried about her. He had glanced her way as she had rushed by him earlier, tears in her eyes. But what if it was Marco? Kate stood undecided, her eyes wildly searching the room, almost as if she was looking for a place to hide. She could stay silent and pretend she wasn't in the room or was in the shower. The person knocked again.

"Let me in, Katie," Marco's quiet voice commanded from the other side of the door.

Before she could stop to analyze her movements, she opened the door, determinedly keeping her face neutral.

Marco stood there, his tie and jacket now gone, his sleeves rolled up and under his arm he held a rectangle box. He looked at her so intensely, she admitted defeat and opened the door a little wider to let him in. Kate closed the door, her hand self-consciously going through her tousled drying curls. She grabbed the lapels of the waffled white robe closer to her, tying the knot tighter.

"What do you want, Marco?" she asked curtly.

He put the box on the counter and turned to her. "I'll start with an apology. I'm sorry. I should never have accused you of anything."

"Alright, thank you. I appreciate that. And now if you're done..." Kate went to open the door when she saw Marco's eyes go to her suitcase.

"You're leaving?" he asked roughly, clearly astounded. "We have one disagreement, and you're leaving?"

"No, I... uh, I don't know," she muttered, wildly trying to find an explanation.

Taking a breath, she tried again. "Both you and I know this— whatever this is—will go nowhere. And you should talk! You aren't ready to be with anyone yet. You're obviously still in love with Gianna."

"What are you talking about?" he bit out.

"She was your wallpaper, Marco. *Your wallpaper!*"

At his confused look, she sighed loudly and went to open her laptop. "*This* is my wallpaper."

Marco sat down on the bed, holding her laptop and staring at the photo of a young Kate, her arms wrapped around her mother from behind. It was Kate's eighteenth birthday, and she remembered it like it was yesterday. Tears formed in her eyes even thinking about it. Their faces radiated happiness. Her mom's delicate hands were holding Kate's. That small gesture showed how much the embrace meant to her.

He looked up at her with an unreadable expression.

Kate sat down next to him, taking the laptop away from him and closing it gently. She clutched the bathrobe's opening a little tighter, covering her pale legs. Maybe she should have offered to get dressed for this discussion—she was clearly at a disadvantage.

"Katie." He looked at her, a slight smile coming to his face. "Is this where I tell you that the laptop you were working on wasn't mine?"

"But whose..."

"It was one of my uncle's computers. He was thrilled when Gianna and I got engaged. For being an older man, he was better at technology than I am! When you said wallpaper, I had to think for a minute what that even was. He must have put that up at some point. I haven't even looked at that computer—I leave it in the office for Alfonso to use. Other than email, spreadsheets and the internet, I don't do much on my laptop. I actually avoid technology when I can. I don't even have social media." He shrugged.

Kate eyed him warily. It wasn't that she didn't believe him. There was something else gnawing at her, and she didn't want to admit it.

"Alfonso told me all the work you put in, fixing the website," he said, looking at her closely. "After you left, I saw it—it looks great. I have to admit, I don't know if I ever paid attention to it— the ceramics shop was really my uncle's baby."

Kate quietly thanked him. She couldn't help telling him about some improvements she made, including some of the more technical changes.

He put his hand up and teased. "Remember, I just got done

telling you I didn't even know what wallpaper was. I don't think I've graduated to coding."

Kate looked amused, still nervously twisting her bathrobe tie. Marco was eyeing her steadily, before getting up abruptly and walking to the window. "So, are you staying?"

Kate was too ashamed to tell him about the real issue bugging her. Seeing him with someone else had deeply affected her. She would sound so insecure if she told him the truth—yet, who wouldn't be? Instead of answering him, she stared at her feet, admiring the pedicure that was still hanging in there from before she left home.

"Katie?" he turned now, raising his eyebrows.

"What's in the box?" she inquired, suddenly eyeing it on the high counter behind the door where he had placed it.

Marco chuckled and picked it up, handing it to her.

She took the lid off the box carefully, parted the tissue paper, and started giggling. Pulling out the dress, she shook it out. Marco had bought her a lemon dress. She had to admit it was cuter than most of the shapeless ones they had seen on their outing. This was a sleeveless wrap dress, cut low in the front. It was vivid blue with the lemons more subdued and discreet.

Kate was forced to smile. "So, is this an Italian thing? You say you're sorry with a lemon dress?"

Marco shook his head, grinning at her. "Not that I'm aware of. I bought it in Sicily. I saw that you…er, like that style of dress. That one last night on you was lovely."

She thanked him, avoiding his eyes.

"Katie, how about we rewind the clock? I came back early because I was hoping we could have dinner together tonight."

Kate took a breath, running her hand gently over the dress. She could see the "DANGER, DANGER" sign almost flashing before her eyes. She felt like she had spent her whole life in someone's shadow. Here she was, stepping into Gianna's shadow, but she couldn't stop herself. All she had to do was take one look at him and she turned into a puddle. Despite her best intentions, she nodded.

"Then I suggest you get dressed in anything—anything at all. Because if you don't, I'll just have to go back to staring out this window!" he said roughly. "I'm trying to be a gentleman. Get dressed and we'll find somewhere special to dine."

She looked at him, her eyes widening, a pink flush coming to her cheeks. "I'll be just a few minutes," she promised, getting up and grabbing some clothes to head into the bathroom.

Sticking her head out before she closed the door, she asked, "Hey, can we go out for pizza?"

His laughter was her reward.

ten

Marco sipped his cappuccino, looking at his expansive view of Positano from his villa on the hill. He could hear his staff in other parts of the house and the groundskeepers outside working in the garden surrounding his infinity pool. He had already swum this morning, waking up at dawn, his mind a mixture of emotions. He reached for his phone and reminded Kate what time he would pick her up. Getting up, he headed to his spacious stone shower. Shedding his robe, he let the multi showerheads pulsate on his tight neck and back.

After their disagreement yesterday, they had ended up having a light-hearted evening. Kate had insisted on a restaurant with "no utensils." Marco indulged her by taking her to a pizza window where they had dined, sitting at nearby casual tables. Once again, they had automatically shared each other's pizza, toasting with their slice by touching the points together. Marco thought he could eat pizza every night just to hear Kate's delectable moan when she took a bite. Every time she did it, he had to steel every nerve in his body not to just haul her over and kiss her passionately. As it was, they had exchanged lingering kisses at the door to her room. He knew he needed to tread lightly, as their misunderstanding had done some damage. He could see the wariness in Kate's eyes.

When he walked in and saw Kate looking at the photo of him and Gianna, it had felt like a gut punch. Not only did he not want to share anything from that terrible time in his life with Kate, but just seeing that photo again made him cringe. He had been so naïve. He had believed Gianna's lies of love, proposing in classic fashion at the Eiffel Tower after a weekend in Paris. He remembered her squeal of delight at seeing the ring she had picked out days prior. She had played it well, teasingly telling him what she liked when they were "just looking." But she had made a beeline for one of the most expensive rings in the case. When she ran out of the church at their wedding, he assumed she had taken that diamond with her. He hoped she had thrown it into the sea.

He was telling the truth when he told Kate he seldom thought about Gianna. He had taken his helicopter back yesterday instead of spending the night in Sicily because he wanted to spend the evening with Kate. When he walked in tired after a fight with his brother, it had just triggered him to see her gazing at the photo.

Poor Alfonso—Marco felt guilty taking his anger out on him. Marco stayed to hear him out, though he wanted to chase after Kate. He didn't even care if she *was* snooping, though he knew deep in his heart that wasn't the case. Alfonso had explained at length, and they looked at the homepage. Marco had to admit he was impressed by her work. The site looked fresh and interesting and seemed easy to navigate. He had never spent time even looking at the site since the store was such an inconsequential part of their business. Alfonso assured him the difference, singing Kate's praises. Marco grinned—Alfonso was half in love with her himself.

He had also briefly panicked at Kate being alone in the office. He knew he had left files from their corporation, Oro Industries, haphazardly on the desk. Alfonso had apologized for that, too, but he had dismissed it. The younger man wasn't used to having Marco around, working in the office. Marco was only staying away from the corporation's headquarters in Milan on the advice of his Chief Financial Officer, Salvatore. Sal had told him shareholders were circling, wanting to address the upcoming earnings report. It seemed wise to tell them that Marco was brokering a new deal and was unreachable. Marco thought it was a good plan until he could secure the stock and find Lucca.

Marco had intended to just stay at his villa. It was only after going to visit Alfonso and meeting Kate that he had wanted to stay close. He grimaced as he looked in the mirror now, carefully shaving—she thought he managed a ceramics store.

On days like yesterday, he wished he did. He had traveled to Sicily to talk to Nico about the issues affecting the corporation. Nico had been preoccupied and uninterested. If it was up to Nico, he'd be out tending to one of their many farms. Marco knew his brother was happiest working in the dirt, whether it was the lemon grove or the olive trees—both intricate parts of their empire. Lately, Marco had to drag him more into the corporate side of things, and Nico wasn't happy. He had been angry at Marco yesterday, and Marco finally gave up, lashing back, telling Nico he needed to stay put. Marco knew he was being selfish, but he needed his family right now. He trusted Nico, and there were few people he could trust. Nico had finally slammed out, but not before adding that Stefano was equally unhappy. That was not news. Stefano, who oversaw their massive wholesale business, had already let Marco know his feelings quite clearly.

Marco knew deep in his heart that they were all still grieving for their uncle. Zio Angelo was the only father his two younger brothers could remember. Marco knew Nico's yearning to get back to nature was connected to his sadness—it was where he felt most at home from the early days of working on the farm with Zio Angelo.

There was also a part of them that continued to grieve for their father—not his death, but his departure from their lives. When Marco had looked at Kate's sweet photo with her mother, it had made him wonder what his life would have been like if he'd had such a moment with his father. Marco thought back bitterly to the last time he had seen him—at the hospital right before his death five years ago. Marco had felt nothing for the man who had deserted his family. He had come to his father's bedside and listened to apologies but couldn't find the forgiveness his father sought. Marco remembered as a child waiting for his father to return, his mother in tears. Even with all the love she gave them, plus the attention of his uncle, nothing could heal the abandonment he felt.

Marco now traveled the length of his bedroom and went to his massive walk-in closet. He decided on a pair of black shorts and a white polo, stopping to assess the view of Positano at his feet. He could see dozens of boats already out in the sea on this blue-sky day. Grabbing his watch, sunglasses, and wallet, he shoved his feet into deck shoes and headed out the door, eager to join Kate.

He hoped she would like his plans for the day. God knows he needed to keep her out and about. He was determined not to take their relationship to the physical level for a while. He needed time to gain her trust and respect. Last night he had nearly lunged for her in that bathrobe, her hair all tousled. She looked so damn sexy that he had nearly changed his mind then and there. Admittedly, he didn't know how she felt, but he could tell by their kisses she was very attracted to him.

Marco had planned the day thoroughly. He regretted he'd have to tell Kate a few white lies, but he felt it was for the best right now. He entered his multi-car garage, choosing to take the Alfa Romeo again. She had already ridden in it and wouldn't ask too many questions.

As he roared down the hill and out of his gate, Marco

thought again about Kate. The timing of this new person in his life couldn't be worse. He knew on some level that he should be honest with her. He wanted more time to just be Marco, Ceramics Shop Manager, to her. He saw how much more relaxed she was every day around him. Her confidence was growing, and he loved it. He couldn't wait to see her.

～

KATE WAS READY FOR MARCO, standing outside in her new lemon dress and white tennis shoes he had specifically mentioned she wear. He hadn't told her to come down, but since she found herself ready early, she might as well wait on the street. Clutching her bag with her new suit and coverup, she was feeling apprehensive. He had told her to bring one, so she had packed it as well as her old suit as insurance.

She was excited when she saw the Alfa Romeo coming up the hill, stopping when a tourist darted in front of it. She shook her head—drivers had to have nerves of steel. Motorbikes whizzed by, but Kate stood firmly behind the curb, having learned her lesson.

Marco waved and slid into a nearby parking lot—an alleyway next to the restaurant they had gone to for their first meal together. He spoke briefly to the manager of the restaurant, tossing him his keys, and walked across the street to her.

"*Buongiorno,* Katie!" he called. "I had intended on coming up. Are you always so prompt?"

"It's a habit." She smiled and was surprised when he leaned in and gave her a sweet lingering kiss.

Trying to recover, she gazed up at him. "I hate being late. Can it be my secret for the day?"

Marco gave her a wide grin. They had made a point of telling each other something personal every single day.

"Of course."

"Thank goodness! Got that checked off early. What's yours?"

A fleeting look crossed Marco's face. He rubbed his hand over his cheek in thought. "Let me think about that. I'll come up with one. I promise, I promise!" He chuckled at her raised eyebrows.

He held her hands and slowly appraised her. "It looks wonderful on you. I was hoping you would wear it," he admitted with twinkling eyes.

Kate opened her mouth and closed it again. It was better that he didn't know that she had come close to not wearing it. It was a little shorter than she usually wore, and she was a little self-conscious in it. The look on his face now made it worthwhile.

Asking if she had her swimsuit and sunglasses, Marco grabbed her hand, and they began walking down the curving street. Kate loved feeling the warmth of his hand, and she knew it was because it made her feel special. They waved to Alfonso, who was taking tables outside, setting up a few trinkets to draw customers in. It seemed Positano was just waking up, as they watched other shopkeepers beginning to open their doors.

As they passed a pastry shop, she glanced at all the tantalizing fare in the window. "You didn't have breakfast, did you?" he inquired.

"No, I did as instructed," she answered, raising her eyebrows.

He squeezed her hand. "*Grazie.*"

They descended the last part of the pedestrian street, making quick work of the stairs to the sea walkway. They strolled past the young boys setting up the beach chairs. Kate nervously eyed the chairs, wondering if that's how Marco intended them to spend their day. Truth be told, she wasn't much of a person who liked to sunbathe. Though she favored her mom's side of the family with her dark hair and eyes, she never tanned, only burned.

Kate couldn't see Marco just lounging for the day, either. He seemed like the type to want to keep moving. Her thoughts were soon interrupted by Marco leading her down to the marina. As they neared a large speedboat, a young man greeted them. Marco easily jumped into the boat and then helped her step up on the edge and hop in. Fortunately, he grabbed her as she slipped, almost taking another fall.

Marco laughed, holding on to her. "I think I'm destined to always pick you up!"

Kate laughed, too, knowing he was right. "If you only knew how many times a day you might have to pluck me up off the ground. It could be your new job."

"Tell me where to apply," came his quiet reply.

Kate felt the flush rise on her face. She refocused his attention. "Where are we going?"

"You'll see!" He grinned at her, letting go of her hand. "Katie, this is Luigi,"

Luigi stopped untying a rope to wave, touching the tip of his black cap.

Kate felt a little apprehensive. She looked at the sea and the much larger ships sailing around. She felt guilty—she knew Marco probably could only afford to rent a small boat, but she was worried about the motion sickness that so often plagued her. It hadn't affected her on ferries or the time she had taken a dinner cruise on a big ship at home.

Marco showed her to a seat in the back of the boat, and she watched as he went up to the helm. Carefully steering the boat out, he guided it slowly out of the marina. In no time, they were in open water, traveling fast, and Kate hung on the back for dear life. This was going to be a tricky day. Good thing she didn't have anything in her stomach. Bouncing along the waves, the cool water splashed her face. Her hair was flying every which way. She could only imagine the sight she was going to look when this was over.

She tried to stare at the horizon like she had read to do to help with motion sickness. She fixated on a piece of land in the distance, not wavering her gaze. Out of the corner of her eye she saw Marco looking over his shoulder, a concerned look on his face. Suddenly the boat slowed and coasted.

Kate heard shouts of welcome, and she glanced over to her right to see them nearing a mega-yacht. Marco was focused on pulling behind the massive ship, bearing the name *Margherita.*

Marco killed the engine and came back to her. "Are you alright?"

"I'm just fine," she said, trying to make her voice sound normal. Internally, she kept repeated her mantra to herself, "I won't throw up. I won't throw up." She rolled her eyes. How many times was she destined to get sick in front of this guy? She had already checked that box.

He studied her intently. "I should have asked if you suffer from motion sickness."

"Just a little," she lied.

He looked at her closely. "I am so sorry, Katie. We'll take care of that. Come on, let's board the ship."

He helped her navigate the platform to the ship, waving to Luigi and grabbing her hand. "I'll introduce you to the crew, and then we'll find some breakfast," he said casually, as if he boarded a yacht every day.

Marco led Kate up the stairs to an upper deck. The crew was lined up, including the captain, who warmly greeted her. There seemed to be so many crew members who were ready to introduce themselves, along with their role. Kate met deck hands, the purser, steward, chef, housekeepers, and more. She dutifully shook each of their hands, smiling and thanking them.

They then went to a nearby table that had a sunshade pulled over the top and featured deep-cushioned chairs. Marco ushered Kate into a comfy chair and sat across from her, watching her closely. She hadn't heard a sound from the ship, but suddenly, they were gliding away smoothly. She sighed in appreciation.

A steward, who had introduced himself as Pietro, appeared

in his crisp white uniform carrying cappuccinos for them. Marco said something to him, and he disappeared, returning with a glass of water and a vial of tablets of an over-the-counter motion sickness medicine.

"Only take one, or you'll sleep through our adventure," cautioned Marco. "But keep the medicine in case you need more later."

She did as he told her, eager to calm any sickness down.

"Now, eat a croissant. I promise you, though food may not be appealing, it will help in the long run."

At her raised eyebrows, he simply shrugged. "My brother, Nico used to get sick, too. He's since outgrown it, but my mother did everything when we were kids to help him."

Kate bit off pieces of the croissant, chewing slowly. Marco added some fruit to her plate, talking about the yacht, how many crew members it took to sail, and pointed out some landmarks around him. He was a natural when it came to distracting her.

"You seem to know a lot about the ship. Whose is it?" she inquired, taking a tentative bite of melon.

"Another friend. As you can see, there are plenty of ships," he said, indicating the many large yachts in the water. "And I have a lot of friends! I thought we would sail to Capri today. If I knew you suffered from motion sickness, I would have thought of something else to do. If you're feeling okay, we can sail around, and I'll show you some landmarks and the grottos."

Kate reassured him she was feeling much better, and it was worth it to see his relief. He was like a boy with a toy, eager to show it to her. They finished their breakfast, and she saw the island approaching. The marina was bustling with the ferries dropping off visitors and boats of every size were approaching. The yacht passed by and kept traveling slowly around the island. Kate and Marco climbed down a deck so they could be closer to the water. He showed her different mansions, some owned by celebrities or world-famous clothing designers. They sailed around at a very low rate of speed, and Kate almost felt like she wasn't moving. Her stomach had calmed down just as he had promised and she gave him a wide smile, which he returned.

Capri was bigger than she had originally thought. They traveled by grottos and nooks and crannies—all of which Marco knew a lot about. She marveled at the vibrant blue water, which turned different shades of green and turquoise as it traveled near the shore. Marco pointed out an immense white building on the cliff that housed an exclusive restaurant. He said people waited years sometimes for a reservation there.

"They're no happier than we are," remarked Kate.

"What?"

"Oh sorry, just something my father used to say when we were little. He used to not be impressed with wealth," she added so dryly that Marco looked at her closely. He apparently decided not to pursue it, instead pointing out a line of boats. "Are you up to seeing the blue grotto?"

Kate had read about it when she had been doing her travel research. She knew some visitors had written it off as a touristy thing to do, and she eyed Marco nervously.

"We have to go in by rowboat, don't we?"

"Yes, unfortunately, this ship can't make it in the grotto." His eyes glinted at her. "But we can do what we can to minimize the discomfort."

Kate told him she would like to try. Her stomach felt fine, and today was about new things: a short dress, small boats, yachts and everything in between. She was going to see it through. As always, she felt braver when Marco was around. She was safe.

They soon arrived near the Blue Grotto. Marco had made a call, and another boat came to pick them up to wait in line with the other vessels. They reached the area where they needed to transfer to a large rowboat, and Kate and Marco were among the first to board. She was alarmed as people continued climbing onto the rowboat. Did they have a capacity for these things? Marco's firm grasp of her hand calmed her, though. Before entering the blue grotto, the young man piloting the boat told them they would all have to lie backwards as much as possible. Marco's strong arms came around her from behind and drew her down toward his chest. This must have been what he meant about minimizing her discomfort. She was perfectly content to lie against his chest, feeling the strong beat of his heart as they glided through the grotto. She couldn't resist taking out her phone and taking a selfie with him. She then quickly put it away so she could take in the grotto's beauty. Kate gasped—the blues were beyond anything she could have imagined. She had heard stories about how lights manipulated the colors, but she didn't care. It was beyond beautiful, and she knew she would remember this moment forever.

Kate grasped Marco's hands in front of her. She was startled suddenly, remembering how she and her mother were in the same pose in the wallpaper photo she had shown Marco. She was grasping onto him, and the intensity of her feelings rocked her. She felt her heart beating fast. Hopefully if he felt it, he would think it was just the grotto.

The boat slid out of the Blue Grotto just as quickly as it had entered it. Transfers made, Kate found herself back on the yacht with Marco. They began to sail back to the busy harbor.

He looked happily at her. "Ready for lunch? We could have it on the ship, but I thought it would be more fun to see some of Capri."

Kate nodded her agreement, and soon she found herself in a water taxi to the marina. They walked over to queue up for the tram, joining the throngs of tourists to cram into the rectangle vertical bus to ascend the hill. Once again, Marco held tight to Kate, as they stood holding onto a pole, similar to a subway. Disembarking at the top, they walked out to the brilliant sunshine and the stunning view of the sea below. They continued walking hand in hand, past exclusive shops that Kate had only seen on Rodeo Drive. Every designer in the world seemed to be represented. The street was lined with brightly colored flowers in perfectly manicured pots. Vibrant wisteria and other trailing flowers wound down from trellises and contrasted with the stone-white walls. Marco led her to a restaurant where they were seated in the shade outside, overlooking the sea. Kate looked up in wonder at the lemon trees wound through the pergola above her head.

She pointed it out to him, wide-eyed, grabbing her phone to take photos.

"We had to go somewhere to match your dress." He shrugged, smiling.

Looking over the menu, they decided to share several small plates again, this time playfully negotiating. They opted for eggplant rollatini, sun-dried tomato risotto, pan-seared scallops and a homemade bruschetta, bursting with tomatoes and mozzarella. Throughout lunch, they never lacked conversation. Despite the difference in their cultures, they enjoyed similar movies and books. They had both recently binged a suspenseful series about a billionaire and his children competing to run the corporation, and they debated on the cliffhanger.

As they departed the restaurant, Kate glanced around uneasily. She wasn't interested in entering any of the designer stores, feeling like she would be looked at with disdain as Julia Roberts was in *Pretty Woman*.

As if reading her mind, Marco remarked, "We'll go to Anacapri next time. It is very different from this." He waved off the shops dismissively. "So much natural beauty. You'll love it."

Kate was excited about spending time with Marco and seeing that side of Capri. She was still having fun, though, and wanted him to know it. "I'm stuffed. We didn't need the scallops," she said, changing the subject and teasing him because she had lost that part of the negotiation.

"Too stuffed for gelato?"

Kate considered the question, smiling as he pulled her into a nearby shop featuring a wide array of overflowing cans of gelato. After careful deliberation, she laughingly chose lemon. He grinned, finally selecting pistachio. They retraced their steps, eating their cones, stopping often to sample one another's gelato. For one moment, life was simple and so sweet.

Marco begged Kate for another taste of hers—his third, if she counted right. Grinning, she batted his nose with it slightly as she raised it to his mouth.

He grabbed her wrist quickly. "You'll pay for that," he teased, drawing his pistachio cone near to her face.

She shrieked with laughter, fending off his cone, at the same time licking her hand where her own cone was melting. They were going to be a sticky mess at this point!

"Marco!" a voice said sharply.

Tangled up, their gelato cones poised in the air, they both swung around.

Gianna.

eleven

Gianna stood watching them, looking horrified at their antics. She had obviously just exited a designer shop, given the shopping bags she was holding. Kate's cheeks flushed just thinking about how Gianna witnessed them fighting like two little kids.

Gianna was even more beautiful than in the wallpaper photo, wearing a chic, short white dress, her long black hair flowing in a shining wave down her back. Her gold jewelry was a perfect complement to her smooth olive skin. Her gold strappy sandals completed the picture.

Gianna stood silently, looking Kate up and down. Marco had let Kate go so quickly she had almost lost her balance. Kate frowned—so much for his job of keeping her from hitting the ground. She glanced down at her lemon dress, so crisp and sweet this morning, now seemed almost childish—especially combined with tennis shoes. She straightened the neckline with one sticky hand. She knew her hair, which had been blowing all morning on the various boats, desperately needed a brush. She had gelato running down her arm, and her makeup was long gone.

"Gianna," Marco said, inclining his head toward her. He stepped away to toss his pistachio cone in a nearby trash can, wiping his hands and face with a napkin he still held. He then stepped toward her but did not touch her. She approached him, wrapping her arms around his neck and hugging him tightly. Marco's arms stayed at his side, but that didn't seem to dissuade her. She continued to embrace him, turning her head so she could meet Kate's eyes. Finally, she stepped back and began speaking to him in rapid Italian.

Marco turned to Kate, the look in his eyes unreadable. "Please excuse me for just a few minutes."

He stepped back toward Gianna and addressed her in Italian. As they continued their heated discussion, Kate turned around and strolled to the side. She shifted from one foot to another before deciding to go find a restroom. She glanced around, but not seeing anything, she retraced their steps, deciding to go back to the one at the restaurant.

Once inside, Kate looked in the mirror with horror. It was even worse than she thought. Her hair was standing on end like a scarecrow. She used her brush to fix what she could. She washed her hands and face and felt refreshed. She discovered gelato all the way up her arm to wash off. What a mess. She found a hair tie in her bag and gathered her hair back in a high ponytail. At this point, she didn't care anymore. She couldn't compete with Gianna in the looks category, just like she had stopped trying to with Meara. Leaving the restroom, Kate started toward the exit.

"*Signorina*," shouted a voice. She turned to find their waiter running toward her.

"*Signore Rinaldi* left his credit card. I tried to follow you, but I couldn't find you." Smiling, he handed her a black credit card, nodding happily. "Please apologize to him. He is a very important man, and we do not want him upset with us."

Kate nodded absentmindedly, looking at the card. She knew

from Meara that a person had to be invited to have this card. How could Marco afford this? Was he involved in some kind of nefarious activity? Suddenly, Kate's feeling of safety began to diminish.

She walked out to the blinding sun and back the way she came. She saw Marco standing in the middle of the pedestrian street, looking around anxiously. He turned and saw her and hurried over. "Kate! I had no idea where you went! You didn't answer your phone," he snapped.

"I'm sorry—I just decided to freshen up for a minute," she stammered. "Um, here's your card. I ran into the waiter."

"Thanks." He stuffed it in his pocket nonchalantly. He looked at her, his face a careful mask. "Do you mind if we go back to the ship?"

Kate stared at him, the luster gone from the day. She could only nod, a lump in her throat.

This time, he didn't take her hand. He walked beside her, the same stoic look on his face. They made their way back to the tram, down the hill and waited in a queue for a water taxi. Deciding it was going to take a few minutes, she mumbled an excuse and slipped into a nearby shop just to get away from him and the tension for a few minutes. After buying a T-shirt, she joined him as he neared the front of the line, still saying very little. Even more wary now, she was glad for the silence while she worked to untangle her thoughts.

ONCE ON THE YACHT, Kate pleaded a small headache. Marco gave her a measured look but showed her to a large cabin and told her to rest from the heat. He seemed almost relieved to be rid of her.

Kate laid down on the king-sized bed willingly. Though she didn't have a true headache, her head felt heavy. Time away from

Marco and the intensity of her feelings was a relief. She was surprised when she woke up over an hour later—she hadn't intended on sleeping.

Kate explored the room and found a modern, beautiful bathroom with an intricately tiled shower and tub, and amenities laid out on the shelves in baskets. Splashing water on her face, she brushed her hair again and put it back up in a ponytail. She didn't care that her make-up was long gone. She might as well go get it over with. Marco had looked like he was in no mood to continue their day. She grimaced into the mirror, thinking that the ship was probably headed to Positano now if it wasn't already back.

She found him standing outside on a deck, talking on the phone. Turning around, he saw her approaching and ended his call abruptly. His eyes, now hidden behind sunglasses, made it even more difficult for Kate to read his expression. As she approached, he gestured to a table with an umbrella, and they sat. Pietro soon arrived with two frosty glasses of lemonade.

"How is your headache?"

"Much better, thank you," she answered politely. "I'm sorry. I didn't mean to fall asleep. Are we headed back to Positano?"

Marco took his sunglasses off and placed them on the table. He stared at her, his expression unreadable. "I hadn't intended on returning yet. Do you want to go back?"

She studied him and slowly shook her head.

He nodded, looking off into the distance. "I guess it was inevitable that I would run into Gianna again. I had thought they had settled in New York, but apparently, she's back," he added dryly, stating the obvious.

Kate could only nod, her heart thumping. She looked down at her fingernails for something to do. Frowning, she was now regretting that she didn't splurge for a manicure with the pedicure she had gotten.

He was watching her intently. "I'm sorry if it spoiled our day."

Kate thought for a moment. She could take two roads, and she suddenly decided which one was the best.

"It won't unless we let it," she finally said slowly, deciding to stay the course. "Are we sailing somewhere else?"

Marco seemed to let out a deep breath. "It's still pretty warm. How about a swim?" he asked suddenly, as if he was trying to shake off his mood.

Nodding, Kate went back to the cabin to change. She shut the door, taking both swimsuits out of her bag, she laid them out on the bed. Picking up her suit from home, she was tempted. She knew her old standby covered more of her, but it looked worn, especially up against the vibrant blue suit. Scrunching up her old one, she threw it back in her bag. Maybe it was seeing Gianna, but Kate felt like it was time to throw caution to the wind. She put on the new suit, careful not to look in the mirror. If she did, she might lose what little confidence she had.

She threw on the cover-up and headed up the stairs to the back of the ship, where Marco was waiting. Dressed in simple black trunks, his shirt off, she stopped dead in her tracks. She wanted to turn and run back to the cabin. Better yet, she would dive off and swim back to Positano. Her heart was beating so heavily she could barely catch her breath. He simply stole every breath she had. Marco's broad olive-skinned shoulders were smooth, tapering down to his lean waist. His back was to her, but she knew for a fact when he turned around, she'd be faced with his perfect abs. She closed her eyes for a second, preparing herself to show no reaction to the Adonis who was standing before her.

"There you are, slowpoke. Let's go!"

Kate opened her eyes. Yep, she had been right. He was simply perfect—she couldn't look away, as if she was mesmerized. Sighing, she approached him, taking a minute to look around. The ship had anchored near a giant rock that had jetted out near Capri. She placed her sunglasses on the bench and then decided to just get it over with. Unzipping her cover up, she shed that, too. She couldn't look at Marco—suddenly feeling hot and cold all over.

"Katie," he breathed. Touching her face, he looked her in the eyes. "*Bella*. You are exquisite." He slid his hand behind her neck and kissed her lightly. Putting his forehead next to hers for a minute, he simply held her. He drew back, gently touching her cheek. "Your skin is so lovely."

"Marco, I'm so pale! I don't tan—most of the time I burn," she protested.

"I worried about that, *cara*. Did you bring any sunscreen with you?"

She nodded, reaching into her bag. "I never go anywhere without it." The minute she said it, she regretted it. He took over, grabbing the tube and squeezing some into his hand.

"Turn around, Katie," he instructed softly.

She did so, his warm hands sliding down her back. The suit left a great deal of her back bare, and she should be grateful he was assisting her in covering it with sunscreen so she wouldn't burn. The warmth of his powerful hands sliding down her back, however, was almost her undoing. He rubbed her shoulders next and down the back of her arms. She had put her hair up in a messy bun on the back of her head. He squirted a little more sunscreen on his hand and applied it to her neck. Rather than just rub it on, he took his time, kneading her tight muscles. He didn't say anything about what had made her so tense, but it was obvious it was left over from his reunion with Gianna.

"Do you want me to put some on your legs?" Marco asked roughly, breaking the spell.

Kate cleared her throat. "Uh, no thanks. I got those already."

He carelessly tossed the tube onto the sofa. "Let's go for a swim. I like to dive—but if you don't want to, you can use the swimming platform."

When he climbed to the edge and dove into the water in a graceful movement, she was in awe of his lithe movements. She opted to take the safer route, choosing not to do a belly flop in front of him. Once in the water, they paddled around, playfully slapping water at each other. Treading water, Kate marveled at the deep blue water. "I've never seen water this beautiful."

Marco grinned widely at her, then submerged completely. The next thing she knew, he was grabbing her waist. Kate squealed. She swam away from him, and he chased her. They swam several yards out and then raced back to the ship, Marco's long arms making short work of her small freestyle stroke.

Eventually, by mutual agreement, they ascended the ladder and dried off. Kate combed her fingers through her hair, her hair tie long gone. She bent to pick up her cover-up, but Marco's hands stilled her.

He gazed down at her with intensity. "You look great just the way you are."

Kate already felt the sun drying her and slowly dropped the cover-up. She noticed a table with a sunshade had been set nearby with wine chilling and an antipasto tray. The crew was very good about tending to them but staying discreet. She sat down in a comfortable chair and watched as Marco filled her wineglass. "I had a good time today. Here's to many more."

She nodded but looked away from his intense gaze. He was good at ignoring the fact she was here only temporarily.

They made quick work of their snack, talking more about Capri and all the island offered. Pietro suddenly appeared, holding a phone. He leaned over, whispering something to Marco, who frowned but accepted the phone. "Katie, I had hoped to not do any business today, but I have to take this call. I apologize."

She nodded, giving him an understanding look.

He lifted the phone to his ear impatiently. *"Pronto."*

Marco frowned darkly and got up and walked to the side of the boat. He ran his hand through his hair, speaking rapidly in Italian. Kate watched as he talked at length, and eventually she grew uncomfortable. She could tell by his body language he was very upset with whatever he was hearing. He continued to move around the boat, talking and shaking his head. Disgust riddled his face.

Grabbing her bag and coverup, she gestured to Marco, who gave her a thumbs up, pacing now, still talking. She went back to the cabin she had used earlier and longingly eyed the bathroom. A shower would feel good. Well, why not? He was certain to be on the call for a while.

Kate took a longer shower than she had intended, but the water felt great. She felt a little guilty using the expensive toiletries and hoped Marco's friend didn't mind. After her shower, she styled her hair, deep in thought. The bathroom also contained a hair dryer and styling tools—again, better equipment than she owned. She only had limited make-up on hand, but the sun had given her a glow. Not quite a tan, but a little color. She happily looked at herself in the mirror.

Kate contemplated the contents of her bag. She had brought a second dress and a pair of shorts and shirt with her, not really knowing what the day would entail. She decided to put on the dress now, relieved to have an alternative to the one she had been wearing that felt sticky and damp.

She felt better now in the crisp, green floral dress. She put her towels in the hamper and tidied the bathroom. She knew that the large crew would clean up after her, but she wanted to be an ideal guest.

Kate sat on the bed for a minute, her thoughts a twisted mess. The day had unfolded much differently than she expected. It had thrown her some curve balls, and her mind was racing. She heard a ding from her phone.

How's Mr. Hunky?

Kate grinned at Teresa's text.

Hunkier than ever. Kate added some heart emojis.

Where are you right now? I need to live vicariously through you.

On a yacht.

His?

No, a friend's.

Who is this guy?

She stared at the text for a minute. They often joked that Kate was the paranoid one of the two, but she had blindly followed Marco like a puppy dog. Her business was working online, and she was a pro at cyber sleuthing. Something had held her back from searching Marco's name. She knew part of it was that deep down she felt there was something she didn't want to see. Though she trusted him, she could tell he was holding back, and things were not adding up.

Another text from Teresa popped up.

Is he married?

Kate stared at the question for a minute. That had never entered her mind with Gianna in the picture.

No, he was engaged once.

Katie, if you are falling for this guy, you need to check him out.

Kate knew her friend was right. She had been avoiding this all along.

Promise to do so. Have to go.

Kate purposely ended the text exchange. Teresa's questions were rattling her a bit. Biting her lip, she typed his name into the search field of her phone and stopped. It just seemed wrong. It was then she remembered the name she had seen on the folders in the ceramics shop office: Oro Industries.

She reasoned with herself. It couldn't be bad to search for more about the company. In fact, Marco had again praised her work on the ceramics shop homepage during lunch and asked her if she would consider doing a little more work—compensated, of course. She had eagerly agreed, not arguing with him about payment. Of course, she would do it pro bono if it would help him, but she would save that discussion for a later date. She rationalized searching the company was acceptable if it was to find out more about it in interest of redesigning the website.

Kate knew any red-blooded female would have searched him far and wide by now. She told herself it was time and hit enter before she could think anymore. The search engine populated 15,000+ entries on the name.

Frowning, Kate scrolled down. She clicked the first link and began to read.

twelve

Marco snapped his phone off. One phone call had turned into several, and he was regretting even taking the first one. Of course, he had to—things were rapidly developing, and he couldn't leave Sal to make all the decisions.

The news unsettled him. On top of all the issues he was already facing, Sal told him a lawsuit was being filed against the corporation. Frivolous in nature, the claimant had hired a high-profile attorney who was calling in favors to bring even more press to the case that alleged breach of contract under fraudulent terms. In normal times, a lawsuit such as this wouldn't be a big deal, but with the current climate, it could be disastrous. Anxious investors did not need to see Marco's face displayed online with negative headlines.

Sal had pleaded with him to stay on the ship for a few days until things cooled down. Reporters were roaming all over Positano looking for him, knowing he had been there most recently taking care of his uncle's affairs. Alfonso confirmed that reporters made inquiries at the ceramics shop. He alerted Giovanni, as well as other local businesses to say they hadn't seen him in quite a while.

What was he going to tell Kate? He couldn't very well hold her hostage on the ship.

Marco went to his own cabin to shower and change. He assumed she was doing the same thing. He needed to buy some time and think about his next steps. Damn, Lucca. If he would just be reachable! He needed to ensure he had the majority of shareholders in his pocket.

He showered and looked over the expansive wardrobe he kept on the ship for his convenience. He didn't use the yacht as often as he liked, usually loaning it to friends and extended family. He realized how much he was enjoying it today. It allowed him the privacy he so desperately wanted, especially while spending time with Kate. He winced, thinking about how Capri had been a disaster. He knew he had to sort through his feelings eventually at seeing Gianna, but he wanted to enjoy this time with Kate. Now he wished they had just stayed on the ship the entire time, but he had wanted to show her a little of Capri.

Slipping into a khaki-colored pair of shorts and a brown designer polo, Marco put his watch back on and slipped into deck shoes. Staring at his phone, he tossed it on the bed. If Sal really needed him, he would call Pietro as he had done before. He needed to focus on Kate right now and figure out how to get through the next couple of days.

He walked up the stairs, going to the top deck automatically, and glanced around. She was standing at a side rail on the deck below, staring out to sea, her back toward him. Quickly, he joined her, greeting her softly. She turned around and eyed him coolly.

"Marco, isn't it about time you told me who you are?"

MARCO WAS TAKEN ABACK. He had not seen this Kate, her face a neutral mask. She looked beautiful, despite her coolness. Her skin had a glow from the sun, her hair was blowing gently away from her face as the ship glided through the sea. The green of her dress made her brown eyes more vivid— the same eyes that were busy assessing him. Marco stared at her for a minute before gesturing to a nearby table with comfortable chairs. He sat down slowly, his face a mix of emotions.

"Did you look me up on online?"

"Sort of. I searched Oro Industries—I saw that on the website."

He nodded absently.

"You can start at the beginning," Kate prompted.

He stared at his hands, not looking at her, speaking slowly. "It depends on what you think is the beginning. I guess it goes way back. It's kind of a story."

"I have time," she murmured.

He nodded. "I guess it starts with my great-grandfather. He was a simple farmer who grew lemons and olives. He did well, and his only son, my grandfather, took over. He bought more property—around this region and in Sicily. He began producing olive oil and making a few lemon products. Before that, most of the produce had been sold at local markets. He had no education to speak of, but he was extremely smart. He was methodical, too. He grew the business slowly."

"My grandfather had two sons, one who worked hard and one who played hard," Marco said bitterly. "My father—his name was Giacomo—was the one who played hard. He left my mother when I was eight, after Nico was born. I'm the only one of my brothers who really remembers him."

"I'm so sorry." Kate covered his hand with hers, imagining a young Marco broken-hearted at his father's betrayal.

"Giacomo's brother—my Zio Angelo stepped in. He built a house for my mother on the original property—she still lives there today, outside of Sorrento. He ensured we were educated, but he also made sure we learned the business from the ground up. We picked the produce; we worked in the distillery and even in our warehouses. He paid for us to go to university—and I followed up with my MBA at Stanford, so I know your city well."

"I wondered. You speak English so well."

"Yes, my uncle ensured we were comfortable in America, knowing how much business we do there. We are the largest exporter of lemon products to the United States—candles, soap and..."

"Limoncello," Kate added.

Marco nodded, a small smile crossing his face. "Meanwhile, Zio Angelo kept diversifying, adding olive oil. He brought on investors, and he drastically grew the business. But then he made some risky deals—involving people in the community who needed his help. He had a terrible time telling people no. Except me—he was very firm with me—but not my brothers."

At her confused expression, he explained, "Of the three of us, I look most like my father. That is unfortunate, for every time Zio Angelo looked at me, he thought of Giacomo. He worried I had the same characteristics. And perhaps when I was younger, I did." He shrugged.

"When I began to work at the company, Zio Angelo kept me as a junior executive for a long time. He had just recently brought me up to the executive level to teach me what he called 'his way.' He was so happy when I was engaged because he often worried I would become bored and possibly go back to the States to live."

"I certainly gave him and my mother a lot to worry about. School wasn't easy for me and to make up for it, I looked for distractions. When I started at the company, I was bored at the junior level."

He looked a little chagrined. "Some of it was my resentment for my uncle not bringing me up sooner. He sent me to our office in Milan for a time, which was probably the wrong move. The nightlife there is amazing, and I took full advantage of that."

"Katie." He sighed. "I am sorry I was not honest with you, but my past isn't something I'm proud of. I went out with a lot of women, enjoyed the nightlight way too much. I was no saint, and the tabloids loved it." He looked at her closely, gauging her reaction.

At her bland expression, he continued. "My uncle brought me back to Positano for a time and had me work with his old friends in the ceramics shop. He threatened to cut me off and for a time, and I thought of leaving. My brothers were still in school, though, and I could see my mother's disappointment in me.

"I stuck it out—I was the Alfonso of the ceramics shop while he was still going to school, playing *calcio*—football—or what you Americans call soccer. He's quite good," Marco added proudly.

"Alfonso's parents, Enzo and Gina, became like second parents to me. I lived with them and there was something about the way they interacted. My uncle had remained single, my mother never remarried. I had never seen a solid and loving relationship before. I soaked it in, and I loved them dearly. When they died in a car crash, a part of me died with them. It was only then that I learned my uncle had owned their shop—Enzo and Gina had gotten in over their heads, and he had bought it from them, giving them a generous salary—much more than the shop was earning. The store will be Alfonso's some day when he is ready for it," Marco promised.

"Since my uncle's death, I have learned he made investments throughout Positano. It was a different place several years ago, and people struggled. Over the years, our little resort town has grown with tourism. It just seems to grow more popular every year."

Kate nodded. "I have to admit, it was seeing photos online that brought me here."

Marco continued looking at her, still serious. "There is another part I wasn't excited to share, but after today, I feel like

I owe you that. I knew Gianna for years and watched her date several high-powered men and celebrities. It was probably my ego again, but I set out to see if she would notice me. She began to see the value in being with me." He grimaced at the memory.

"My uncle was thrilled. He wanted me to settle down, and Gianna's parents were old friends. He encouraged me, urging me to spend more time and money on her until it became natural that we would become engaged."

He looked off into the distance now, his face a mask. "I don't think I ever loved her. Sure, I was deeply attracted to her. Gianna was an expert at playing it just perfectly. My mother even warned me, but I ignored her. My uncle's approval meant everything to me."

"As I stood at the altar, I thought back to Enzo and Gina— their deep love and respect for one another. My brothers were glaring at me. My mother, sitting in the front pew, couldn't meet my eyes. At that point, I swear I thought about going to find Gianna and telling her we were making a mistake. I felt the biggest sense of relief when her father came to tell me she had left. Of course my pride hurt." He shrugged. "How could it not? The entire town was in the church. The headlines were brutal. Some said I had cheated on her, which was all lies. My uncle was devastated, but for the first time, he said he trusted me, and he knew I hadn't betrayed her. After she left for New York and joined her now husband, the rumors died down. Life was getting better."

"It was then my uncle suffered a stroke." Marco looked down, staring at their clasped hands. "We discovered he had an inoperable brain tumor. We were all with him at his bedside when he died. His last wish for me and my brothers was to have a happy life. He told us his biggest regret was not finding someone to share his life with, that making money became so important to him that he made do with the odd relationship. He called me 'son' before he died. It was the greatest and the saddest moment of my life."

By now, the tears were freely flowing down Kate's cheeks. She reached up and wiped them. Marco gently stroked one errant tear away. She could see the pain in his face so visibly etched. He looked out toward the sea, his face a mask of grief.

"Go on," she whispered.

"My uncle's will stipulated I was now the CEO. He had always meant for me to replace him, but he ran out of time before he could teach me. My mother, brothers and my cousin, Lucca, also own shares of stock."

"When I began to learn about the company, I discovered my uncle's heart had been too big over the years. He had made some poor investments to help people and leveraged the corporation. I have worked hard to rein things in and build up our strongest, most profitable areas. It has taken time, but I thought I was gaining traction. Just when I think things are better, Sal shows me another balance sheet, and I see more issues. Meanwhile, the shareholders are largely my uncle's old cronies. Their confidence in my leadership is shaky at best. That's why Sal said maybe I should take a step back and cool things off while he settles them down. We are set to have a board meeting soon where they will see the changes I've made."

"In the meantime, I am desperate to find Lucca, who is on safari somewhere unreachable. We have people all over Kenya looking for him. With him and my family's shares, we keep a majority interest. I need to know I have those votes."

"What was today's phone call?" Kate asked, determined now to learn all the truth.

His eyes narrowed as he told her about the lawsuit. "Sal wants me to stay on the ship for a couple of days. The last thing the shareholders need to see is me involved in some scandal."

He stared hard at her now. "I've been wondering if at some point you would search online about me."

Kate explained how Teresa's prompting had led her to decide that her own intuition was nudging her to discover more. She told him about seeing the name Oro Industries in the office.

"What does Oro mean?"

"Gold. My ancestors had big dreams." He gave her a bitter-sweet smile. "Katie, I know little is private anymore. I just wanted some time with you so you could get to know me and not the person I was before. I liked you accepting me for who I was without the wealth and the complications that come with me. I didn't want to lie to you. I've been lied to enough in my life— from my father, who said he loved me, to Gianna, who said she loved me. I believed I was doing the right thing."

Marco ran his fingers through his hair again, something Kate had observed he did when he was frustrated. "Things have been so out of control and bleak. I was grieving for my uncle when the company started to unravel. I have been doing my best to make decisions. Some days I feel so unprepared for this," he admitted in a rare show of humbleness.

"Then you dropped into my life, literally right onto the street," he teased. "I know you are here on holiday, and we haven't talked about the future, but I want you to know that I already care about you."

She looked at him, taking a deep breath. "I feel the same way —whatever this is."

Marco grinned, his perfect white teeth in full display. She smiled back just as big, and they stared at one another, not wanting to break the spell.

"Katie," he asked almost impulsively, "would you consider staying on the ship with me for a couple of nights? We could go back to Capri, or tour Sorrento or Amalfi. Whatever you want, just as long as we keep a low profile. You will have your own cabin, and we certainly have enough chaperones," he added, his eyes filled with humor as he gestured to the crew gathering chairs from the upper deck and busy setting up for dinner.

"While I am very attracted to you," he said, drawing out the word *very*, "I'm also determined to take this slow. My life is very complicated right now. I want to treat this—whatever this is—with care."

She looked at him for a minute. "Before I give you my answer, can I ask you one more question?"

His dark eyes pleaded with hers. "Anything."

"What did you and Gianna talk about today?"

Marco's face grimaced. "She and her husband have moved back to Italy to be close to family. She wanted to explain everything, and I cut her off. I just didn't want to hear it right now. I might someday, but I was conscious of you walking away and I was panicking. She asked about you then, and I told her you were just a friend. I didn't want her to know anything about you."

"It was nice of you to say that."

His eyes were wary, showing past hurt. "But we are more than friends, aren't we?"

She looked away and then back at him with honesty in her eyes and nodded. Taking a deep breath before she changed her mind, she answered him, "I would love to stay on the ship with you. I have to warn you I will turn into a pumpkin in a couple of days. That's when I'm supposed to go to the apartment I rented and write. I can't go back on that. It's something I promised myself I would do. It's important to me."

He nodded. "I understand."

Standing up, he smiled at her. "Let's go dine. I think the chef is out to impress you tonight."

Marco casually put an arm around her until they reached the top deck, leading to a cloth-covered table, set with fine china and silver. Several tea lights reflected off the glassware.

"Marco, wait." She stopped before sitting down, turning wide eyes toward him. "I just realized—all my clothes and stuff are back at the hotel. And Giovanni? He will worry!"

"Would it be alright if I asked Giovanni to have one of the staff pack your things? It's not even sunset yet. We can have your case brought down, and Luigi can deliver it to the ship. I can direct the captain to head back toward the harbor."

"You can do that?"

"I can do that." Marco grinned. "Be right back."

He strolled out a few minutes later and sat back down. "Your things will be here soon. And I settled your bill with Giovanni."

At Kate's frown, he continued firmly. "We're not going to argue about it. You are doing me this favor. I know you have precious time here, and it should be exploring the Amalfi Coast —at least by land! Instead, I am holding you captive on a ship."

"Marco, your car? What if it rains?" Kate asked suddenly, remembering how he had left it in the alleyway.

"It's already back at my villa by now. I took care of that, too. Also, I think I definitely have shared my secrets with you today," he said teasingly.

"One last question, though."

Marco's eyebrows rose inquiringly.

"Who's Margherita?"

His eyes glinted at her, full of humor. "My mother."

thirteen

N ow, with their heavy discussion over, Kate tried purposely to keep things light, and Marco followed her cue. They dined slowly, watching the sky light up in oranges and pinks as the blues began to fade. They talked quietly about all kinds of things while she sipped on limoncello, he on cognac. When he admitted he actually didn't like limoncello, she cried with laughter, and he joined her.

They explored the ship, visiting the captain in the cockpit. Kate was amazed at the vast amount of electronics, looking over it with curiosity. The captain was charming, showing her all the controls and teasing her. With a frown, Marco finally pulled her away, and they dipped their heads into more cabins—all large and luxuriously decorated. They walked through several lounge areas, a formal dining room, which Marco said he didn't prefer to use. They walked over the smooth teak floors, down to a game room, which had several board games, a poker table, ping-pong, and the latest electronic games. Marco taught her to play backgammon, and she beat him in a few card games. They teased each other at their attempts at some of the video games, with Kate steering her car into a wall, Marco driving effortlessly.

Kate had texted Teresa back to assure her "Mr. Hunky" was not a serial killer or worse—married! She told her friend she would fill her in later. Kate was going to have to be careful now —she didn't want to betray Marco's story. It was his to tell, but she knew her friend was concerned. She and Teresa had lived through every crush and relationship together. Teresa knew Kate did not give her heart easily, and she agreed to learn more later.

Teresa had simply replied: *Be careful.*

Kate stared at the text. She knew Teresa was right, but she was diving headfirst in right now, and it felt good. Methodical in nature, she wasn't one to throw caution to the wind. But this time she was, and she didn't care.

They spent their first day sailing along the coast, settling off Sorrento, Marco pointing out landmarks to her. They took out the jet skis, racing each other, before Kate pulled back. Marco was much more of a speed demon than she was. He grinned as he bounced over the water. They swam again and lounged in the sun until they got too hot and went to change. They met in a beautifully furnished lounge, featuring comfortable lounges, sofas and chairs, and an oval teak bar in the corner. Kate chose a white chaise to stretch out on and took out her phone.

Marco excused himself to look at his tablet.

"Taking notes?" He looked up amused, watching her typing madly.

She nodded, and he reached over and grabbed his laptop. "Use my computer. I know you have yours, but mine is right here. You could just email yourself."

Kate agreed. She had already emailed herself the notes she had previously taken. She opened the laptop and was happy when she saw his wallpaper was one of the stock photos it came with. She called up her email and sent all her notes. Finishing, she saw he was still busy, so she asked him if it would be okay to work on the ceramics shop's website.

She already had the log-in from the day she had worked on it.

Now she became absorbed in her task, shaking her head at the mess. She cleaned it up even more, organizing the tabs and rearranging photos. She began to re-build the e-commerce portion, so it was more prominent and efficient. It was only when Marco touched her shoulder that she realized how much time had passed.

"Katie, you've been at this for a long time," he said, frowning. "I apologize—I got lost in a series of contracts my assistant sent, and I should have called a halt earlier."

She shook her head, putting up a finger. Several more strokes, and she sat back triumphantly.

"Done!" she exclaimed.

"The whole site?" he asked incredulously.

"Well, not quite, but a lot."

He sat down near her, and Kate shifted so she could show him what she had done. Enthusiastically, she showed him some of the technical elements.

"Katie, remember the wallpaper debacle? I can only understand every third word."

"Oh, Marco. Highly doubtful. You are brilliant." She rolled her eyes. Last night, they had spent some time discussing his corporation. He had been forced to learn so much so quickly. He seemed to grasp a situation very quickly and she was impressed by his knowledge. He explained Sal was his uncle's oldest friend. He had worked hard to bring Marco into the fold and expose him to everything.

"I don't feel brilliant," he said, looking away, his voice with a touch of sadness. "It's overwhelming. It feels good to tell you about it all. I haven't really been able to talk to my family much."

He had explained the family had divided the roles. Even though they had a manager and a fleet of staff, his mother still was active in the daily operations of the lemon grove. It was a very small part of their business anymore, but their mother felt it was the foundation and honored it. The grove offered daily tours, showing visitors how they had once processed the lemons from the centuries-old stone building. They also hosted frequent large dinners in the lemon grove—a popular tourist event, as well as weddings and special events. Nico often was there, traveling between that property and all their properties in Southern Italy and Sicily. Marco told her Stefano was based in Florence but came home as often as he could.

The weight of the family business seemed to be solely on Marco's shoulders, and Kate was grateful he had Sal.

"Let's go enjoy the scenery now that the sun isn't so hot." He said, breaking the mood. They strolled the ship, greeting the crew, who were busy with their chores. The crew members cheerfully saluted them, continuing their work.

Marco had inquired many times if Kate was comfortable—any motion sickness? Was she getting burned? She jokingly told him he was worse than any Italian mother, but secretly, it made her feel cherished. *Cherished.* That was the word she had been looking for when trying to describe her reasoning to Teresa. No man had ever made her feel this way.

"Do all Italian men name their yachts after their mother?" she teased him.

"Smart ones, do," he quipped back, giving her a side grin. "You'll meet her soon. She'll love you."

Kate smiled, feeling bittersweet. The chance of meeting his mother was slim to none. He liked to talk about their future, and she had learned to let it slide. She just wanted to focus on the present.

They dined again that night on the ship, enjoying the quiet time together. Kate had burst out laughing when the steward had brought them pizzas after their appetizers. Marco told her the chef had long expressed dismay that pizza was one of Marco's favorite foods. Marco even had a pizza oven installed on the yacht. He had stopped in to tell the chef he wanted him to make pizza for Kate, because it was her favorite as well. The chef had only rolled his eyes.

"It's still so delicious," she remarked enthusiastically. When the chef appeared, they toasted him, and he accepted it with a slight formal nod. Marco spoke to him briefly in Italian. "I told him tomorrow he can make you all of his best dishes." The chef smiled happily before departing.

They were talking softly, long finished with dinner, when Marco frowned, pointing out the darkening clouds in the distance. The purser came to speak to him, and Marco turned to her. "The radar shows a storm is approaching. The captain has changed course, and we will anchor off Amalfi for now. Let's go inside and hunker down. Don't worry, Katie—this ship is built for powerful storms. It may get a little rocky, but it will be fine. Do you want some medicine?"

Kate shook her head, her eyes wide. She wasn't a fan of storms, especially while she was on a ship in the middle of the sea. She told herself she was being foolish. The ship was almost bigger than her apartment complex. She would be fine.

They entered the theater room Marco had shown her earlier that afternoon. Kate shivered, suddenly feeling the drop in temperature. He left briefly, coming back with a big sweatshirt that was emblazoned with NERD on the front.

"You seriously want me to wear a sweatshirt that says 'Nerd?'" she asked, smiling up at him.

"It's my favorite Stanford sweatshirt," he argued.

At the crack of thunder, she grabbed the sweatshirt. It was warm and cozy and fit her almost like a dress. Kate left briefly, coming back in yoga pants, feeling perfectly comfy. Marco was busy scrolling through the ship's movie and television catalog.

"It smells so good in here," she cried happily. Popcorn was busily popping in a nearby machine. He looked amused at her enthusiasm and handed her the remote. "You choose."

Kate silently marveled at a man who would willingly hand a remote over. She quickly decided on a new action movie.

"No rom coms?" he teased.

"Oh, we'll get to that. But I've been wanting to see this one," she said, deciding she needed more stimulus to forget the storm. The weather had unleashed outside. The ship was steady, but outside she heard the thunder roll. She was glad the theater room was in the center of the ship and windowless, so she couldn't see any lightning. Marco left briefly and came back, wearing sweats of his own with a blue zip-up sweatshirt. She stared at him for a long time. Dressed like that, he looked like he could still be in college.

He mistook her staring for apprehension. "A lot of rain now, but it's fine."

They snuggled on one of the deep couches, happily chomping on popcorn, regardless of the fact they had just finished most of the pizza. The movie was a sequel, and they debated the characters, whether the actors had aged well and if the plot was realistic. The movie was loud, featuring fighter jets and Kate noticed every so often, Marco would turn it up a little. She became absorbed in the movie and was surprised at how much better it was than they had predicted.

Standing up and stretching as the credits rolled, she glanced over to see Marco had shifted, his head lying on the back of the couch. He had fallen asleep. How could he be asleep with all this noise? She remembered how that morning he'd had shadows under his eyes, which likely meant he hadn't slept well.

She stood. Should she wake him? Instead, she covered him with the blanket they had been using. He was lying rather awkwardly, but she didn't want to disturb him.

Wandering toward the outside door, she peeked her head out. The wind had died down, and only a gentle rain remained. The storm appeared to be over. Breathing a sigh of relief, she went back to her cabin.

Once in bed, she found herself wide awake. It had been a wonderful day, but Marco had barely touched her. He hadn't even tried to kiss her. He had treated her almost like a sister. The mixed signals were hard to keep up with. Kate sighed. She was in for a sleepless night herself.

fourteen

Marco turned over in his bed and stared at the ceiling. He had woken up with a start after midnight on the couch, his neck aching. He had glanced around immediately for Kate, but realized she must have gone to bed. Disappointed in himself, he went to bed, only to toss and turn.

Keeping Kate on the ship with him was presenting more issues than he had anticipated. Though the ship was massive, the two spent all their time together. Marco was fighting every urge he had about going slow. He had promised himself and Kate, so that meant mentally putting her in the friend zone. One kiss, one embrace, would ignite his entire body.

Kate had been scared during the storm last night. He had purposely turned up the movie when he could hear the thunder crashing near the ship. He was used to the tropical storms of the region and the spectacular lightning show they presented, but Kate wasn't. He had wanted to hold her and put his arms around her. Instead, he ate three bowls of popcorn, just trying to keep his hands off her.

Marco sat up against the headboard, adjusting his pillows. He picked up his tablet and scrolled through his emails—many from

Sal. Their attorneys were doing their best to squash the lawsuit, and so far, only a small blip had been reported. That was finally some good news.

It was still early, and Kate was probably asleep. He got up and put his workout clothes on. He needed time to think, and he might as well get out some frustration. He headed to the workout room, prepared to tax his body.

But Kate wasn't asleep. As Marco walked through the door, he saw she was on the exercise bike. The video screen in front of her was blasting the workout.

"I want you out of the saddle at a fifty resistance!" shouted the instructor, and Kate rose from the seat, pedaling rapidly.

He raised his eyebrows. Watching her from this view was probably not going to help the situation. Walking over, he cleared his throat, trying not to startle her, but she was too focused. Finally getting near her sightline, he waved. She sat back down suddenly, gripping the bike's handles.

"Oh my God! Marco, you scared the life out of me." She put a hand to her chest. She hit pause on the screen.

"I hope it's okay that I came in here," she added quickly at his frown. "I was exploring and found it, and it seemed like a great idea after all that pizza!"

"Perfectly fine," he assured her, trying to appear nonchalant.

She reached for the wireless headset. "Let me just put these headphones on so you don't have to listen to my instructor."

Marco nodded and walked across the room. Fortunately, the treadmill was facing the window. He got on and turned it up high, running like someone was chasing him. They had to get off this ship, he decided. And soon!

KATE WIPED her forehead with a towel and glanced over at Marco. He was running fast, not even breathing heavily. She eyed his beautiful legs and lean body. She hadn't been totally honest with him. Sure, she could always burn a few calories, but after her sleepless night, she had felt the excess energy she needed to burn. She had missed her bike at home and was delighted when she found one onboard.

She dismounted and glanced over at the free weights, wanting to lift for a few minutes. Marco was not looking at her. She might as well.

She was beginning to regret her agreement to stay on the ship. Marco was acting so strangely, and she wanted the closeness they had when he had told her everything. Now he seemed distracted and distant.

She picked up the fifteen-pound weights and began doing bicep curls. She avoided looking at herself in the mirror. She probably looked like a fright in her workout shorts and cropped top, her hair pulled back in a high ponytail. She had thrown in the clothes in case she wanted to go hiking and was glad she had. They were her old, comfy workout gear, though. How would she have known that she'd be in a workout room with a freakishly handsome man just feet away?

Kate racked the weights. She gave a quick glance at Marco, who was still running, looking outside the whole time, his earbuds in his ears. He didn't even appear to remember she was in the room. Resignedly, she went to shower. "We'll see what today brings," she muttered. She chose not to wave at him or try to get his attention but slipped out instead. It was only after she closed the door, she realized her heart was beating as if she were still on the bike.

~

DIO! Marco thanked God she was gone. Seeing Kate in that tight outfit was almost worse than a bathing suit. The thin fabric skimming her curves was too much. Her flushed face and hair pulled back to show her long neck was sexy as hell.

Marco had focused on looking outside but he was hyper-aware of her every move. When he had glanced over to watch her with the weights, he had almost run right off the treadmill! He got off now, wiping his face with a towel. He began using the weights himself, pushing his muscles to the brink.

He grimaced. It was time to get off this ship.

∾

"LET'S GO ASHORE ON SORRENTO," Marco suggested over breakfast.

Kate looked up, surprised. He had joined her at a table on deck where she had been sipping her cappuccino, wondering if she should wait for him to eat or not. He had sat down just as Pietro was putting the plates before them.

She picked at her frittata, wondering why the sudden change of plans. "I thought we had to stay out of sight?"

"I doubt anyone would imagine I would be in Sorrento. I would love to show you a little of the town."

An hour later, Kate found herself ushered into a speedboat and delivered to Sorrento's marina. Marco wore dark gray shorts, a white polo, and a black baseball cap. The cap made him look years younger, like the sweats had. They disembarked with Kate already enchanted by the rustic charm of the port.

As always, Marco was a wonderful tour guide, taking her through the streets, stopping patiently to let her take photos. He seemed to know every detail, talking about Sorrento's history and how the poet Byron had spread the word, inspiring literary masters, such as Dickens and Tolstoy to visit. Limoncello was born here, he told her earnestly.

They strolled past magnificent hotels and shops that ranged from touristy to exquisite. They passed several outdoor restaurants, already filling up with diners, the smells of garlic and seafood floating through the air. Kate was thrilled that he was again holding her hand, interested in all her observations. Her stomach suddenly grumbled loudly, and Marco laughed.

He led her over to a takeout window, grinning a little. "I thought today we'd try something different. No utensils required." He winked. "These are my favorite paninis. I used to come here just for these alone."

He showed her the signboard and how they could choose to fill the focaccia bread with eggplant, lamb, meatballs, and a few other choices. She chose eggplant, something she loved, but didn't get a chance to eat it often, since Teresa said it tasted slimy. He chose meatballs, and they took their paninis, wrapped in red-and-white paper, to a bench overlooking the busy port. Watching the ships coming in and out and fishermen cleaning their nets, they concentrated on eating. She giggled at his antics of keeping the meatballs inside the bread. That was exactly why she hadn't ordered that one, she told him, glancing at her white jean shorts and the light blue Capri T-shirt she had bought. It was a sure magnet for red sauce!

The paninis *were* delicious, Kate assured Marco, who was almost apologizing for their casual lunch. It was fun to just hang out and not worry about hovering waiters or fancy meals. When she voiced that out loud, he looked at her seriously. "You are unlike any other woman I have dated."

She bit her lip. That sounded bad—she probably seemed so common to him. Glancing down at her outfit, she thought back to Gianna's couture. Looking up, she saw Marco staring intently at her.

"Katie, we have to get off the ship."

fifteen

K ate looked at Marco, her heart dropping to her feet. She was right. He was already tired of her. He probably found her amusing at first, but now was clearly seeing it couldn't work for them long-term.

"Whatever your little mind is coming up with now, it's wrong." Lowering his head, he kissed her hard. "Katie, you're driving me crazy. I want to take this slow, but on the ship, all I think about is what we're *not* doing," he added suggestively.

"I think we should go back to Positano tonight. Alfonso hasn't seen any more reporters. Our attorneys have been working hard at keeping this quiet. I'm sure it's fine." He gave her a small smile, as if he was trying to appear confident.

She nodded, finding herself smiling widely at him. She was relieved all of her assumptions weren't true.

"Why are you smiling at me like that?" He leaned in and kissed her again, slowly and deeply. "You are trying me greatly. I am Italian after all. We are a very passionate people." He arched an eyebrow, pouting.

"I am half Italian. Does that mean I'm only half passionate?" she teased before taking a sip of water.

He gave her a heated look, his voice full of desire. "Something tells me you and I will be like a match to tinder."

She choked on her water, coughing while he sat staring at her, his eyes now amused. Her heart gave a funny little somersault. To hide her flushing cheeks, she stood up, gathering their garbage and throwing it in a nearby trash can. The spell now broken, they continued to stroll through the streets. The town was growing quiet; the heat taking its toll on its visitors. By mutual agreement, they made their way back to the ship to go for one last swim. Playing in the water, it seemed like their bond was back.

Kate took one last shower in the luxurious bathroom and packed up her stuff. It was still hot outside, and she decided to just put her shorts and T-shirt back on. Marco had said they would have dinner on the ship and go to shore at sunset. He had called Giovanni, who was able to provide a room for her last night. Marco had said he would need to go up to Milan shortly and might be away for a few days. Though Kate regretted any time away from him, she also remembered why she had come to Italy in the first place. Except for all the note taking, she was not getting closer to her goal of finishing her novel.

Kate looked around the room one last time, making sure she didn't leave anything. On impulse, she picked up Marco's NERD sweatshirt and stuffed it in her suitcase. She would give it back to him before she left. It was just a little physical piece of him she selfishly wanted to hang on to for just a little longer.

After an exquisite dinner as promised, Kate insisted on going around to each crew member and thanking them profusely. Each seemed intrigued by this American girl who was so gracious and conscientious and thanked her for coming, which Kate found hilarious. She was supposed to be thanking them! The captain kissed her hand until Marco tugged her arm, frowning. "Luigi is waiting."

This time, Marco sat with Kate while Luigi steered the boat. Knowing now how short of a trip it was, her motion sickness was kept at bay. She flashed him a bright smile as they cruised quickly over the waves and edged into the marina. Marco gave Luigi instructions for her suitcase. He promised to get it to the hotel and in the custody of Giovanni.

They walked hand-in-hand down the waterfront, passing brightly lit open-air restaurants, diners merrily eating and drinking against the picturesque sky. Lights twinkled from the hillsides above them, glowing in the evening light. Kate smiled at the sight. She would never tire looking at it.

Marco had put his baseball cap back on, and she noticed he had glanced around a few times, seemingly on edge. The waterfront was packed with people. Ferries were delivering the last of the visitors to Sorrento or Capri for the day. The walkway by the sea was crowded with people enjoying the night. The bells of the church were pealing merrily, and Kate glanced at her watch, confused. It was not the top of the hour, and she pointed that out to Marco. He stopped, as if thinking for a minute. In the distance, she could hear a marching band. He checked his phone for the date and was excited.

"You're in for a treat. It's the feast day of Saint Vito, the Protector Saint of Positano. It's a celebration! I haven't been to it in years."

They went over to a nearby concrete wall that lined the stairs going upward to the town. Marco helped her to jump up and sit on the wall. "Save my spot," he called, hurrying through the crowd.

He returned shortly with two cones of gelato, looking satisfied. Handing both to her, he hopped up on the wall next to her before eagerly grabbing his back. Happily, they ate their gelato, watching the crowds swell. Suddenly, the sea of people parted, and the music got louder. A band marched by, playing loudly.

The drum major gestured for the band to stop almost right in front of them, and Kate turned her head, smiling at Marco.

The band wore bright blue uniform shirts with gold buttons and black pants. Their hats were pulled down on their foreheads, their expressions solemn. Suddenly, she grabbed Marco's arm. "There's Alfonso!" Ridiculously, she waved and waved, until Alfonso, halfway down the row tilted his head once toward her, a smile growing on his face before it was his turn to play his trumpet.

Kate handed Marco her gelato, getting out her phone to take photos. She took as many as she could until the band started to march again, taking the cheery music and Alfonso farther down the boardwalk.

Kate leaned forward to see what was coming next. Four altar boys holding an altar proceeded past, with two priests dressed in traditional robes trailing slowly behind. As they passed, she saw Marco bless himself, kissing his fingers and noticed the others in the crowd did so as well. She took a few more photos discreetly. The music trailed down the boardwalk with the procession, and Kate turned to Marco, excitement on her face. "I'm so glad we got to see that. It was like a real Italian *festa*."

He grinned down at her, enjoying seeing her excitement. She giggled when she saw he had been eating her gelato too, poking him with her elbow. She took her gelato back, but it was melting now, and a big blob fell right on her chest. She scraped it off with her finger, laughing with Marco. She licked her finger before finishing her cone. She shrugged—she would be back at her hotel soon, anyway. Now it was fun to just watch the people in the crowd, who were all enjoying the night.

"There should be fireworks soon."

"That would just be the perfect ending," she breathed, and he looked down at her with gentle amusement.

The band members, now finished, strolled back one by one,

joining their families. Kate watched one man run up and grab his wife, kissing their small baby the woman was holding. They looked so in love. She gave a small sigh.

Before Marco could inquire about her sigh, the first fireworks lit up the sky. The crowd cheered at the colorful explosions over the sea. The colors reflected against the night sky. He put his arm around her, and they sat quietly watching. When the last one fizzled through the sky, the crowds clapped and slowly began to move again, the action over. Marco reluctantly asked her if she was ready to go. Kate nodded, jumping down from her perch and, as usual, clumsily lost her footing. He grinned, putting his arms up to steady her, and it was only natural that he bend in to give her a lingering kiss. She willingly held her face up to him, taking in the magic of the moment.

POP, POP, POP!!!!

Lights were exploding around them. Kate was disoriented. Did the fireworks start back up? Before she could process what was happening, Marco pulled away from her violently and the dark expression on his face alarmed her. She had never seen him this angry.

She glanced around and saw they were being swarmed by photographers, snapping as many photos as they could. Shouted questions in Italian and English swirled through the air. Marco grabbed her by the arm, hauling her up the stairs. The photographers followed for a bit, but they had already gotten their shot. They soon tapered off. Marco continued running, pulling her behind him. It wasn't until they got halfway up the hill that Kate, clutching her side, begged him to stop. He slowed, glancing around. The haunted look on his face told her he hadn't even been aware they were no longer being followed.

She gasped, taking in large gulps of air. What a time for a reminder that she needed way more cardio time.

When Marco looked at her impatiently, she nodded, knowing

he was anxious to get up the hill. Without a word, they turned on to the street toward her hotel, finally entering the front doors. They went to the front desk, where the night manager greeted them, Giovanni long retired. Marco barked an order at him, and the man left quickly, returning with Kate's suitcase. Marco grabbed it and headed for the exit, Kate running to keep up with him. "Where are we going?"

"I need to get you someplace safe," he replied curtly. They ran across the street to the alleyway where he had left his Alfa Romeo—what seemed like weeks now. In its place was a sleek, modern black sports car. He stowed her case and helped her in the car—continuing to glance around. He got in, and the car roared to life. They drove up the hill, the car handling the turns with ease.

"Now will you tell me where we are going?" she asked louder than she had intended. She knew he was very upset, but she truly didn't appreciate being manhandled out of the hotel as if she was a piece of luggage as well.

"To the lemon grove."

Kate glanced at him in alarm. "The lemon grove? You mean your family's estate? I'm going to meet your mother? Dressed like this? With a stain on my shirt?" She knew she sounded hysterical, but she couldn't help it. She gestured at her shirt and shorts. "Marco, please, let's talk about this," she wailed.

Maybe it was her tone or that he was just starting to breathe again, but he pulled over at a scenic area turnout. Keeping the engine running, he turned to her. "I am sorry, Kate," he said stiffly. "I thought we were safe, and then I got caught up in the celebration and your joy of watching it. I didn't think there were still any reporters lurking about. But shortly, your photo—*our* photo—" he corrected, "is going to be splashed all over online. The tabloids are now going to want to know more about you, and they will find you if you remain in Positano. The lemon grove is private and protected. And yes, though it's a large estate, you'll find our home to be comfortable. My mother prefers it that way."

Kate eyed him apprehensively. There was just enough light coming from the car's complex dashboard that she could see his stern expression.

"So tonight, I'll stay at the lemon grove, and then I'll go to the apartment I rented."

He didn't acknowledge her remark. Looking at her steadily, he told her it wasn't a long drive, and then pulled the car back onto the road.

If things were normal, Kate would have enjoyed the drive. It was a beautiful night, and Marco was a safe driver, easily handling the powerful car. The sumptuous leather seats surrounded her, and she looked out the window at the inky night sky and lights that became less and less as they traveled toward the country.

Finally, he turned onto a gravel road. He swiped a card next to the reader, and a big iron gate opened for them. The car shot through, up the road about a mile, before coming to some outbuildings. Marco continued up a paved road now, before finally pulling up to a circular drive. A picturesque fountain stood in the middle, ringed by flower beds. The nearby expansive cream-colored house was surrounded by a wide terrace. Kate took in the numerous arched windows, all rimmed in black, lights blazing. Window boxes were abundant and a little wrought iron balcony was in the center of the house on the top floor. She was startled by its warmth, despite the size.

Kate suddenly knew this was home for Marco. He simply wanted to come home.

~

MARCO SIGHED as he put the car in park and pushed the button to shut it off. He knew he had bullied Kate into this, but he was so upset with himself. Their privacy was now compromised. Every tabloid would try to discover her identity. They would dig up anything they could about her. God forbid, she had anything bad in her past. His anxious investors would think he was back to his old playboy ways and would wonder what he was doing with this American woman. Looking over at Kate, who was staring apprehensively at his family home, he knew in his heart she had nothing to hide. She was hardworking and loved her family deeply—even with their differences. She had mentioned Teresa and a few friends who were her people—those she counted on. Marco desperately wanted to add himself to that list. To think that he could be the person she counted on the most would mean so much. Right now, his life was a hot mess, he reminded himself. Tonight had proven that. He had inadvertently dragged her into his drama, and he couldn't forgive himself.

"Let's go in," he told her, rougher than he had intended. At her look of apprehension, he took a breath. He knew enough about women to know most liked to be dressed appropriately when meeting someone's family—and Kate had made that clear. He thought she looked adorable in her white shorts and T-shirt, but he knew she wanted to be dressed differently when meeting his mother.

He tried to adopt a patient tone. "Katie, I know this isn't ideal, but I promise you it will be alright. I'm asking you to trust me."

She nodded hesitantly, jumping out of the car before he could come around.

Marco retrieved her suitcase from the trunk and led her to massive mahogany front door. He let them in quietly, not sure if his mother had gone to bed. He hadn't wanted to call her, just in case.

"Well, well, well, our fearless leader is home."

Marco turned his head and rolled his eyes. Grabbing his brother, Nico, he gave him a fierce hug. They had parted on such bad terms, with Nico shouting that he didn't want to have anything to do with the corporation. Just let him tend to the farms Nico had insisted.

Standing before them in jeans and a worn T-shirt, Nico was a little shorter than Marco. He broke out of his embrace, punching him a little. It was always like that with Nico. They fought, and then his little brother instantly moved on. He loved that about him, knowing that Stefano was more likely to hold a grudge. No matter what, the three brothers were as close as they could be, despite their differences.

"Nico, where's Mamma?"

"She's in bed. One of her headaches." Nico looked past Marco inquiringly.

"This is Kate," Marco introduced her, putting his arm around her gently.

"*Buonasera*," Nico greeted her softly, kissing her on each cheek. He looked back at his brother, and Marco understood his confusion. Kate did not look like his usual type. Though she was beautiful, she was also authentic. Standing there with her casual clothes, messed hair, and no make-up, Kate almost looked like a college girl.

"Are you hungry? Mamma went to bed early, and I just made some paninis."

Marco frowned. "Where's Maria? Is anyone taking care of Mamma?"

"I am taking care of Mamma," Nico told him distinctly. "Maria had to go be with her daughter."

"Our housekeeper's daughter is having a baby," Nico told Kate politely, giving Marco a quick glare at his lack of manners. "Is there anything I can offer you, Kate?"

Kate suddenly looked exhausted. She simply shook her head.

Marco looked at her closely. He definitely had damage control to do.

Picking up her bag, he gestured toward the wide staircase. "Katie, I'll show you to one of the guest bedrooms," he murmured.

"Goodnight," she called softly to Nico, who grinned at her. She trailed behind Marco, up the stairs and down several hallways, until he entered a bedroom, flicking on a light.

The expansive room featured white, gray, and neutral colors. Plush carpet extended throughout the room and a large bay window featured upholstered seating, with soft white curtains blowing gently from them. It was a restful room, with paintings of Positano on the walls.

"This room has one of my favorite views. I think you will enjoy it. Why don't you take a long bath or a hot shower and go to bed? We can talk tomorrow, *cara*," Marco told her gently. He knew instinctively there wasn't anything he could say tonight. They both needed to go to their corners and then see what the morning brought. He gave her the lightest of kisses and left her standing in the middle of the room, looking after him with an uncertain face.

When he descended the stairs, Nico was nowhere to be seen. He walked into the expansive kitchen to find his brother now standing at the island eating a cannoli—a specialty of his mother's. Marco always marveled at how his youngest brother seemingly ate night and day.

Nico began firing questions at him in Italian. Marco pulled out a stool, accepted the beer Nico handed him, and told him the whole story. It felt good to confide in him. He left out certain parts of the story, fiercely protective of Kate's own personal life, but Nico got the gist.

When Marco had finished, Nico sat grinning at him. "My big brother is finally in love."

Marco frowned at him darkly, assuring him that wasn't the

case. He admitted he had feelings for Kate, but love? They weren't there yet; he explained. Nico just continued to look at him smugly. The more Marco talked, the bigger Nico's grin became.

Nico finally began to laugh. "Wait till Mamma hears."

sixteen

K ate sat on the upholstered window seat, looking at the lemon grove that extended well into the distance. Bright light filtered into the room. She leaned her head against the glass, wondering if she should go downstairs. She had actually relaxed in the beautiful room last night, but had woken up disoriented until the events of the previous night came flooding back.

Kate's phone sat in her lap but she had purposely avoided picking it up. Now she stared at it with trepidation, deciding that searching for the photos of them could wait. Stretching, Kate glanced at the time and realized she probably should make a move to go down and meet Marco's mother. The last thing she needed was his mother thinking she was some lazy woman who was expecting room service or something.

Kate eyed the clothes in her suitcase. She had wheeled it into the large walk-in closet last night but hadn't unpacked it, since she would be leaving for the apartment today. She picked through her clothes, now a crumbled mess. Digging deep, she drew out her white jean capris and a lavender sleeveless blouse. Smoothing them out, she was relieved that they weren't too wrinkled. Debating, she realized it was probably the best choice, given the state of her other clothes. Then again, should she choose a dress? Shrugging, she acknowledged her place: She was an American woman who would soon be back at home and out of Marco's life. It was doubtful his mother would be too invested. Besides, the outfit looked perfect for being out in the country. She put on her white tennis shoes and brushed her hair out, leaving it hanging around her shoulders. She had taken a quick shower before bed, and it looked alright even though she had not fussed with it too much. A little light makeup, a small pep talk to herself in the mirror, and she was on her way, treading softly downstairs.

Kate glanced around, but the house seemed . . . empty.

"*Buongiorno*?" she called tentatively?

Crickets.

Kate found a note propped up against a tray of pastries on the immense island. In his bold, slanted handwriting, Marco told her he and Nico were called to solve a problem in the distillery and would be back as soon as they could. His mother's migraine was no better and she was going to rest in bed for the morning. He added they would hopefully be back by late morning.

She wandered around the beautiful kitchen. It had a rustic farmhouse style but featured marble countertops, and modern stainless-steel appliances. Two ovens were against one wall, a massive stove against another. She marveled at the subzero refrigerator and walk-in wine cellar.

She smiled when she saw another of Marco's notes on the cappuccino machine with instructions on how to operate it. Reading it carefully, she got a painted ceramic cup from the glass cupboard and made herself one. She brought her cappuccino to the table. She would have a pastry later if her stomach handled the cappuccino.

She saw another note from Marco propped up against a laptop.

We made the news. If you want to get it over with, take a look.

He had drawn a small heart on the note, which gave her heart a small bump. She put her head on the table for a minute. Finally sitting up and squaring her shoulders, she opened the laptop. The browser was open already to a webpage and her eyes widened. Pushing the cappuccino aside, she moved the laptop closer. Two pictures of them filled the screen. The first one was him kissing her, her arms winding around his neck, his hands nestled on her hips. The second was him pushing her through the jostling cameras.

It was worse than she thought; she groaned out loud. The only redeeming factor was that she was turned in such a way that the stain on her T-shirt was not obvious. She gave a hysterical giggle. Her casual outfit and her messy hair was sprawled all over the news. She did not look like someone who would be dating the CEO of a major Italian corporation.

Kate automatically hit the translation button and began to read. Two words jumped out—*billionaire* for Marco and *mistress* for her. Slamming the computer shut, she felt her cheeks flushing. *Mistress*? They had to be kidding.

Then the other word hit her. *Billionaire*? She knew he was wealthy...

She sipped her cappuccino, lost in her thoughts. The worst part was her family or friends could see it, though it wasn't likely to make news in the States. Suddenly, Kate's phone buzzed.

Meara.

Was it a coincidence Meara was calling her? She let it go to voicemail, staring at her phone as it sat on the table. She waited for the ping of the voicemail, but there wasn't one. A few minutes later, her text tone went off.

Call me ASAP.

"Well, I won't," Kate said rebelliously to the deserted kitchen. She knew now Meara had somehow seen the articles. She wasn't about to justify the situation to her sister. Sighing, she opened the computer and read the entire article.

Two cappuccinos later, she felt she could run a marathon. She should have known her limits, but today seemed like a good time to keep the caffeine coming. She had read several articles she had found open on Marco's browser. They all were repetitive, reveling in his checkered past, his broken engagement, and the pending lawsuit. Some brought up the death of his uncle and hinted of a corporation in turmoil.

Kate finally got up, automatically taking her cup to the sink and rinsing it out. She looked at the clock, wondering what she should do. She didn't have the concentration to write, that's for sure. She felt like she could run around the property several times over.

Now standing at the island, chomping on a pastry, she figured Marco and Nico would be back before lunch and would probably be hungry. There was no sign of their mother. Should she go check on her? That could be incredibly awkward, bursting in on an elderly Italian woman in her bed. She checked that idea off her list.

Kate opened the massive refrigerator doors and looked at the array of colorful vegetables and fruit. It was fully stocked with all kinds of fresh produce, proteins, and cheese. She glanced at the doorway and thought for a minute. She walked slowly out of the kitchen toward the massive entry hall and grand staircase and listened intently. No sounds came from upstairs.

Shrugging, she grabbed an apron she found in the bulging walk-in pantry. Kate went to the refrigerator, grabbing ingredients and setting them on the counters. She found a big pot and a cutting board and knife and set to work at the island.

～

"MAMMA?" Marco called as he came into the house. Anxiously, he entered the kitchen, Nico following him, busy texting on his phone. "Lunch smells delicious!"

Taking another deep appreciative breath, Marco called again for his mother. No answer. He looked at Nico, who briefly glanced up from his phone, and shrugged. "Stefano might be here."

Lifting the lid of the pot, Marco looked at the colorful soup bubbling on the stove. He then saw two loaves of bread baking in one of the ovens. Closing the oven door, he left the kitchen. He would go find Kate and see what she did with her morning and check on his mother.

Treading lightly upstairs, he went first to his mother's suite, concerned they had left her for so long. She never wanted to be bothered when she had a migraine, insisting that rest and quiet was the only thing that would make them go away. He had brought her some water and pain medication before he had left. Walking into the darkened room, he saw his mother was fast asleep, her breathing even. He backed out and quietly closed the door.

Next he went to the corner guest room where he had brought Kate the night before. The bed was made, and the room was tidy, but no sign of her. He took the stairs two at a time, re-entering the kitchen, but was met with Nico still on his phone. Marco's heart thudded. Had she somehow left?

"Mamma's asleep. I don't see any sign of Stefano. Maria must have come by and made lunch. But where's Katie?" Running a hand through his hair, he heard a dog bark. Max. The foreman of the property had an aging Golden Retriever who roamed freely and often sunned himself outside the house, providing great company to their mother. Marco walked out the French doors to the massive covered terrace. Various patio furniture was spread out on its stone floor. Down at the end, at a built-in bench, sat

Kate curled up typing away on her phone. Max sat next to her, as if he was protecting her already.

Marco called out, so he wouldn't startle her. "Hey!"

She looked up quickly. "Hey yourself."

He strolled toward her, trying to read her expression, smiling slightly. "I didn't mean to be gone so long. I'm sorry. We thought it was a small problem at the distillery. Turned out it was a bit more major, and it was, how do you say—all hands on deck?"

Truth be told, he was a coward this morning. He could have let Nico handle the emergency, but he had gone, too. He needed to put some space between him and Kate, especially after seeing the news articles. Even weaker, he had left it for her to see and absorb. He figured he would be better off if she saw it while she was alone and had some time to process it before he returned. He looked at her now tentatively.

She gave him a small smile. "That's okay. I got caught up in my notes and drank just a wee too many cappuccinos." She chuckled. "Oh, and I got to meet this one." She bent down to stroke Max, who looked at her adoringly.

"Massimo," he informed her, bending over to pet the dog's head, who dutifully licked his hand. "We call him Max. Did Maria stop by?"

"Nope." Kate stood up, stretching.

"She's very excited about her new grandchild. But I wish we had someone else to fill in. Mamma doesn't like to have a lot of staff in the house. There are so many people already on the property. She's content with Maria and the groundskeepers, but I wish she would accept more help."

Kate nodded, but before she could respond, her phone's alarm rang.

"Whoops, timer," she called, brushing past him.

Kate ran into the kitchen, waving to Nico who was sitting at the table on his phone. She washed her hands quickly before grabbing oven mitts from the counter, and took both loaves out of the oven, setting them on nearby cooling racks.

Turning around, she glanced at Marco, who had trailed after her. "Phew. That was a close one. I should have set the timer a few minutes earlier."

"You did all this?" His eyes widened, waving at the stove and bread.

"Well, yes, I didn't perform surgery or anything." She laughed. "I just took my anger out on some vegetables and pounded some dough. The result is minestrone and bread."

"*Dio*." Marco rolled his eyes. "Will you ever stop amazing me?" Wrapping his arms around her, he kissed her soundly, not caring about his brother's presence. Taking a deep breath and smelling the aroma, he joked, "Maybe you need to be angry more often."

A throat clearing had Kate shooting out of his embrace. Only it wasn't Nico clearing his throat. In the doorway, behind Marco, stood his mother.

seventeen

Oh my God. Did she and Marco seriously have the worst timing in the world?

Kate eyed Marco's mother cautiously. Kate knew she had been conjuring up a stereotypical Italian mother out of a movie. She had imagined a shorter woman with gray hair, maybe in a bun and, of course, wearing an old-fashioned dress and possibly an apron.

Instead, Marco's mother was a slender woman who was a few inches taller than Kate. Her black hair had wisps of silver and was pulled back in a simple ponytail with a clip. She had on black pants, flat sandals and a crisp white silk blouse. Her gold watch and heart-shaped necklace accessorized the look. She was elegantly styled with minimal fuss.

Marco turned toward his mother, carefully keeping his arm around Kate. "Mamma." He slowly released Kate and then walked over to embrace his mother, asking how her headache was.

His mother responded that she felt fine, but weak, her eyes directed at Kate in quiet appraisal.

"Mamma, I'd like you to meet Kate Malone," he said formally.

Kate was flustered. "*Buongiorno Signora Rinaldi.*"

"*Buon pomeriggio,*" Marco's mother corrected softly. Kate glanced at her watch and groaned inwardly. Yes, it was afternoon.

"My name is Margherita," said the older woman, approaching Kate and giving her a kiss on each cheek. "My friends call me 'Rita.' You may, too, if you like." Her black eyes, so like Marco's, were kind.

Marco ushered his mother carefully over to the big farmhouse table next to the open-style kitchen. He took the laptop off and put it aside, carefully easing his mother into a chair.

"I'm not a hundred," she admonished him. "It was only a headache."

"Kate made lunch," Nico spoke up. "And I'm hungry."

Kate's cheeks flushed. It had seemed a good idea. Looking over the contents of the refrigerator, a soup had seemed like a natural idea. What was she thinking, cooking Italian food for Italians in Italy? This is a story she would eventually joke about with Teresa, but right now, it could prove painful.

"That's very nice of you," Margherita said graciously. Marco smiled and came to Kate's side. "I'll help you serve." She glanced at him quickly before walking over and handing him a serrated knife to cut the bread. Nico joined them, grabbing plates and utensils to set the table.

Kate carefully ladled the soup into the white porcelain soup bowls that were in one of the massive cupboards. Marco and Nico delivered them to the table while she went to the refrigerator and retrieved a giant wooden salad bowl. She had made a salad as well, using vegetables that appeared to be right out of a garden. She had made her mother's favorite dressing, and lightly tossed it into the salad. Nico came to get it from her with a big grin.

Everything on the table, Marco carefully held her chair out. Kate was just sitting down when she thought of something. "Oh, do you have any parmesan?" she asked and then immediately looked embarrassed. "That was just about the stupidest question you can ask an Italian family." She rolled her eyes—she might as well admit defeat. To her surprise, everyone laughed. Nico grinned at her and came back with a giant slab and a hand-held grater. He went to each person and grated some on top of their soup.

Kate's admission had seemed to break the ice, though, and the brothers explained the morning's emergency and what they had done to resolve it. Margherita listened intently, smiling at her sons.

Meanwhile, Kate was inwardly panicking. She hadn't even tasted the minestrone before she had put it in the bowls. She had made it often with her nonna, and it felt like comfort food to her. Maybe that's why she had assembled it today. She was definitely in need of some comfort, especially right now.

"*Buon appetito,*" Margherita said, as she picked up her spoon. Kate held her breath as they all took the first spoonful.

"*Delizioso!*" exclaimed Nico, the first one not to hold back.

Marco agreed, looking at her proudly. "It's delicious, Katie."

His mother nodded, continuing to eat. "Where did you learn to cook like this?"

"I had an Italian grandmother." Kate explained that her mother had been of Italian descent—Sicilian actually, she clarified. Her grandmother was the only one of her grandparents who had lived long enough to see Kate and her sister grow up.

"She died when I was sixteen." Kate looked down, a rush of memories coming over her. Marco's hand slid over hers briefly.

"What else did she teach you to cook?" Margherita inquired, clearly more intrigued by the cooking than anything.

"Oh gosh, a lot of things. Bread, some pastas, eggplant, a few chicken and lamb dishes. Pizza," she said pointedly at Marco, who grinned.

Kate thought back to how she stood at her nonna's elbow, carefully writing the recipes on notecards. It was difficult given that her grandmother cooked by instinct and often added an extra pinch of something. She still had the little box with the recipes. Occasionally, she looked through them, but she mostly knew them by heart now.

"I still can't make her sauce or meatballs." Kate sighed.

"Really? I will show you how I make mine," Margherita offered, her eyes lighting up.

Kate looked down, not wanting to be rude. Finally, she smiled. "That would be wonderful, but I'm leaving today, so there really isn't time."

MARCO DIDN'T SAY anything at Kate's insistence she was leaving, not wanting to have the discussion they needed to have at the table. Fortunately, Nico seized the opportunity to remark how wonderful the bread was, grabbing his third slice before coming up for air. He had a talent for always keeping things light, and Marco looked over at him, thanking him with a subtle nod.

They discussed a few more details about the farm and then mentioned the corporation's big shareholder gala would be in just over a week. It had to be a carefully orchestrated night, Marco explained to Kate. "Everything has to be perfect." It was going to be built around the annual shareholder meeting where he disclosed all the changes he had made and wanted to make.

Kate nodded, standing up to clear their dishes, and Marco helped her. "Leave them in the sink. We need to talk," he quietly instructed.

He led her outside. They walked the length of the terrace,

and Kate looked out at the lemon trees as far as she could see. "Can we take a quick walk before I go?"

"Katie, I need you to listen. Don't say anything. Just let me finish. You saw the articles?" At her nod and grimace, he continued.

"I was hoping you would. I figured I would be out of the way if you needed to throw something." He touched her arm, running his fingers down to her hand, which he squeezed. "I didn't know some vegetables would be murdered or I would have stayed."

Kate elbowed him in the ribs. "That's not funny. Mistress? Are you kidding me? Just because I kissed you? My father might read that!"

Though she was trying to joke about it for Marco's sake, she remembered Meara's unanswered text and phone call. "I know it wasn't your fault, and of course, I don't blame you. The last few days have been wonderful—an adventure. But it's time for me to leave," she stated firmly.

"That's just it. I don't think you should. Nico and I talked about it today. The articles didn't name you. It's just a matter of time before the press figures it out," he said grimly. "Reporters will find you wherever you are and hound you. I can have a security team assist you, but I know that would bother you."

He met her questioning eyes steadily. "Stay here. As you know, I am going to Milan for a few days. Mamma is a little lonely, I think. Zio Angelo used to be here with her, and it's a big farm and operation. There's a lot of people, but it isn't the same. She's busy and will give you plenty of space. You could write here. Imagine sitting here with this view, writing on the terrace," he said persuasively.

"Marco, I can't say yes. What will your mother think? Oh my God, she hasn't even seen the photos!" Her eyes widened with alarm. "She's going to think I'm some tart after her son."

He raised his eyebrows. "Tart?"

"That's what my father would say," she retorted glumly.

"Well, there's one way to find out. Let's go talk to her." He put his arm casually around her, gently pulling her into the house before she even had time to argue.

Margherita was still at the table, her phone out and a calendar nearby. "There you are." She looked at them over her readers. "Just looking over the schedule for the next couple of weeks. It's going to be busy. The season is taking off."

"Mamma, we need to talk to you," Marco began.

Margherita's head snapped up. She took off her glasses and put her phone down. Marco went to retrieve the laptop, opening it to one of the articles. He carefully placed it in front of her. Gesturing to Kate, he helped her sit down next to his mother at the table.

Watching his mother scrolling with no expression on her face, Kate was impressed. She had to give it to her—Margherita was made of tough stuff. Finally, she clapped her hand over her mouth, giggling.

"Mamma!" Marco grumbled, clearly exasperated.

"*Dio*, Marco, I thought it was something horrible. This is nothing." She waved at the screen dismissively. "You scared me!" She pushed the laptop away from her. "So, some rags publish some lies. Who cares? I certainly don't. You'll be yesterday's news in no time. They'll move on to someone else quickly."

"Mamma, you don't understand. The board is already nervous about my tenure. Things like this matter to them, especially given my past." He stared at Kate, who was now focused on her hands.

"The past is the past." Margherita shook her head. "When you have suffered loss like we have, things like this do not matter. The board this, the board that. They reap the benefits of you and your uncle's work. My work! I am sick of them!"

He laughed despite himself. "Mamma, I think I'm going to

have to lock you up during the shareholders' meeting. You might be tempted to say all this!"

Kate almost giggled at the idea. She would love to see this woman go off on some of these entitled shareholders.

Meanwhile, she realized Marco was quickly explaining his idea to have Kate stay and write rather than go to the apartment she rented and be met with curious reporters.

"But of course, you must stay," Margherita said gently. "It will be fun, Kate. *Per favore?*"

Kate looked at the identical pair of black eyes staring at her anxiously.

"Okay." She exhaled. "I'll stay."

eighteen

As usual, Marco had seen to everything. He explained to the rental agency she would not be picking up the key to the apartment. He didn't tell her he had paid for the two weeks demanded because of their cancellation policy. Kate suspected he might have, but when she questioned him, he simply shrugged and changed the subject.

Maria stopped by that afternoon. Looking more like Kate's idea of an Italian mother, she sailed in with a burst of Italian, her hands waving as she told them about the birth of her granddaughter. "No name yet." She sniffed, changing to English. "In my day, we named our children after our parents—it was a system that worked."

"That's why Italian families have the same four names." Margherita joked, lowering her voice so Kate could hear. "I broke that tradition for a reason!"

Maria bustled around the kitchen and got ready to head upstairs with her cleaning tools.

"Maria, *per favore*. You don't have to be here today. Go be with your daughter and her new family," Margherita told her kindly.

Maria brightened. "I'll just clean the upstairs and be on my way. I can quickly make something for dinner."

"Clean the upstairs if you insist," Marco said, walking in. He had left the room to make some calls. Now he went over to Maria, dropping a kiss on her cheek. "I'll make dinner!"

"You can cook?" Kate blurted out. She had never thought about Marco being very self-sufficient.

"Of course, I can," he said proudly. "Mamma insisted her sons know how to cook, clean and do laundry. If you need anything washed, just let me know," he teased.

That would be a cold day in hell that she would ask him for that! She winced and shook her head.

Kate's phone buzzed again with a text from Meara.

Where are you? I need to speak to you!

Kate sighed.

"Is there something wrong?" inquired Margherita, seeing Kate frowning at her phone.

"Oh, it's nothing, um, Rita." Kate felt a little weird calling Marco's mother by her nickname, but she had insisted. She walked over to the doors leading to the terrace. "I think I'll go make a call."

Kate didn't meet Marco's eyes, which had narrowed. She knew what he was thinking—the entire time they had been around one another, she had never broken away to make a call.

She went outside and stood on the deck. Just because Meara was summoning her didn't mean she had to respond. Still, Kate worried that Meara would call their father next and possibly rile him up. He would be the last one to read an international tabloid, but she would like to be the one to tell him about Marco.

She hit the call button before she had time to think too hard. Looking over the magnificent vista below, she found a calm washing over her.

"Katie, what the hell? Why haven't you called me sooner?" blasted Meara.

Kate suddenly felt the calm disappearing. "Hi to you, too," she said softly.

"Fine, hi. Now can we cut to the chase? *What* are you doing with Marco Rinaldi? Katie, there's so much you don't know. He is a player and I mean *player*. Like with a capital P. Way out of your league. I'm sending our corporate jet for you. It can leave out of Naples. I can have a car pick you up to take you..."

"I'm not going anywhere," Kate interrupted. "Meara, I know more than you think. Marco has been upfront with his past. I know all about it."

"I highly doubt you do."

"I'm not a child. Everything's okay—seriously. Look, I'm not thrilled about the photos and the articles either. But it's not what it looks like."

Meara sighed. "I know you think I'm trying to boss you around, but I really want to help you."

Kate was happy to hear that. Sometimes she craved having her sister in her life. They hadn't been close for so long. In typical Meara fashion, though, she spoiled it by continuing, her tone now disapproving. "Can we just agree that sometimes you're just too romantic? He's not the guy for you. Can you just trust me for once?"

"What about you trusting me for once?" Kate repeated angrily. And then she did something she had never done before, quickly ending the call before she said something she would regret. She wanted to scream. As usual, Meara destroyed her self-confidence, making her feel like she was a naïve teenager. Meara had often teased her when they were younger, as she picked up Kate's stash of romance novels. "These will get you nowhere," Meara had said dismissively.

Kate sighed, thinking about it. It had always been that way, and things weren't going to change.

"Everything okay?"

Kate turned around, forcing a smile on her face.

Marco was leaning against a pillar on the terrace, his hands in his pockets, his handsome face studying her. He was still wearing jeans and a T-shirt that he had been wearing earlier. It took years off him. If Meara could see this Marco, maybe she would understand there was more to this billionaire than just the headlines.

"You know, Katie, you don't have to tell me." He studied her face as he walked closer. "But I'd like to think we're friends like we said we were. I've shared with you my secrets—things I don't know if I've ever said out loud."

He stopped before her. Reaching out, he gently combed a piece of her hair behind her ear. "Such beautiful hair." He looked gently at her.

Suddenly, Kate wanted to unburden her heart. "It was Meara. She saw the articles," she told him flatly.

"And she was calling to warn you against me," he said matter-of-factly.

"Well...yes. She said...it doesn't really matter what she said," she stammered nervously, looking away.

"It's probably all true what she said." Marco gently put a hand to her chin, forcing her to look at him. "I told you I'm not proud of my reputation." He regarded her intently, not waiting for her answer. "Do you want to leave, Katie?"

She met his eyes then, searching their depths, trying to find an answer.

"No, I don't," she finally said, shaking her head. Suddenly, it was important for her to show Marco that she believed in him. He had demonstrated nothing but kindness and thoughtfulness. And yes, he had lied to her, but she understood why, and he had more than made up for it. She knew the articles had brought back painful parts of his past, and he probably didn't want to be splashed across the internet kissing her either. Before she could start thinking about that new plot twist, he leaned over and kissed her tenderly, his hands on either side of her face.

Raising his head, he looked unsure, as if he wanted to say more. Finally, he smiled at her. "Come on, let's go in. You can have a glass of wine and talk with me while I expertly make dinner," he promised smugly.

nineteen

K ate sat on the counter, sipping a full-bodied burgundy. She was amused watching Marco's frenetic movements around the kitchen, grabbing things haphazardly. He wasn't the most efficient cook, but what he lacked in technique, he made up for with his enthusiasm. Music played from a nearby speaker, and she relished this time with him. Margherita had gone upstairs to answer some emails, and Nico had disappeared.

With an apron tied around his waist, Marco was intently cutting olives. He had proudly shown her the can of Oro olive oil. She had noticed the wide array in the pantry and had surmised it was the family brand. She hadn't had time to study the label. Now she picked it up, reading about the family on the back. It talked about their olive farms in Sicily and the proud tradition of the Rinaldi family.

Marco had gone quiet, lost in thought.

"Everything okay?" Kate repeated his own earlier question.

"Sorry. I was just thinking about my call with Sal. Earnings still aren't where they should be. It's puzzling to me. I've done everything I can think of. I've cleaned up some of the more unprofitable sides of the business. I've trimmed the budget where I could without losing valuable employees. I need to look over things again, but it's just not apparent to me. I feel like I've read all our contracts a dozen times."

"I might be gone a day or two longer than I want," he added, not looking up, focused on cutting the olives.

Kate frowned, but by the time he looked up, she had resumed a poker face. She didn't want to appear needy. As it was, she was still unnerved by being foisted on to his mother. Margherita had reassured her they would have a good time together, but Kate would have her freedom to pursue her writing.

"Sal says he has more financial data to show me," he continued.

She watched him, lost in thought. "I wish I knew a little more about your corporation. I mean, not that you'd expect me to or even want me to," she blurted, anxious for him not to think she was prying.

"I would like you to know more, too." He looked up, smiling. "I was serious before when I told you it's difficult for me to confide in many people. It would be nice to be discuss some of this with you."

Kate jumped down from the counter.

"Where are you going?"

"I'm doing what I'd normally do if I want to know more about something or somebody," she called over her shoulder as she went to pick up the laptop that was still on the table.

∼

"MARCO, THIS WEBSITE IS REALLY CONFUSING." Kate scrolled up and down, frustrated. She had spent the last fifteen minutes trying to make sense of it. Without looking up, she continued to go through the tabs and links—some of which were broken.

Marco joined her on a stool at the island, refilling her glass and setting his down beside it. She pushed the laptop so that he could see it. "I'm sorry if I'm being blunt."

"No worries there. To be honest, I'm not sure I've ever even looked at it."

She suddenly had the urge to get her fingers on it. "Would you let me redesign it for you?"

He shook his head. "You are supposed to be working on your novel. We are a big corporation. If you start on this, it's going to eat up all your time."

"What if I promise I'll only work a couple of hours a day on it? If you don't want me to, that's fine—I mean, I'm not trying to back you in a corner."

"Back me in a corner?" Marco shook his head with a grin. "You did that a long time ago," he said quietly, not explaining what he meant.

"Okay, let me text our IT manager and get the log-in information and tell him I've hired a consultant," he teased.

"Consultant? I'd like a better title, please," she pretended to protest. "I'll put it in my contract."

He rolled his eyes. "More contracts."

MARCO DISHED up the Pasta Puttanesca, a dish composed of garlic, anchovies, and tomatoes. The real star of the dish was the large amount of olives Marco had so carefully diced. Kate helped him carry it, as well as a salad, to the table outside, where they could enjoy the beautiful views of the vast property. Nico had surfaced right when the pasta was ready—a special talent he had perfected, Marco joked.

He looked at his mother's big smile and suspected Kate's presence was responsible for at least part of her happiness. He frowned a little. His relationship with Kate was becoming deeper and more complicated. He wasn't sure where this was going to go. He had avoided commitment his whole life, and when he finally had attempted to make one, it had exploded in his face.

Rationally, he knew Kate wasn't like Gianna in any way. He trusted her. *Dio*, he had just given her his website's log-in information! Every moment he spent with her, he became more enchanted.

He was frustrated—they needed more time together. He wished with all his heart he didn't have to travel to Milan, but he needed to get to the office and focus. Plus, he needed to consult with Sal. He still did not understand the true picture of the corporation's challenges. If he stayed here looking at spreadsheets and contracts, he wouldn't be able to concentrate the way he should.

Looking at Kate smiling at him as she carried the slab of parmesan, he realized he needed to get to Milan—and fast! When she looked at him like that, all he wanted to do was pick her up and take her some place to be alone.

He sat down and listened as his mother and Nico were intent on talking about him as a young boy. "He was so naughty." Margherita was laughing. "It's a wonder Giacomo and I even had more children."

At the mention of his father, both men looked down. His mom looked wistful for a minute, lost in her memories.

Kate seemed to sense the sudden shift. "What kinds of things did Marco do?"

"There was the time he and his friend skipped school and tried to take one of the fishing boats out for a day at sea." Margherita rolled her eyes. "Of course, they got caught. I almost had a *poliziotto* take him to jail for stealing, but he told me he couldn't put a ten-year-old boy in jail. It might have taught him a lesson." She frowned at Marco with mock severity.

"The problem was he was always so cute. I would take one

look at him and would melt. He knows how to use those eyes." She giggled at the memory.

Kate nodded, smiling understandingly.

"I will show you some photos later," Margherita promised.

"There will be no photos, Mamma. Put away the photo albums." It was Marco's turn to roll his eyes. "Kate and I have a trade agreement on things such as this. We will need to negotiate the showing of any photos—especially embarrassing ones."

Kate grinned, obviously interested in seeing photos of Marco as a child.

Marco then noticed Kate's plate. She'd been busy pushing the pasta around, not eating much. He was worried Meara had gotten to her. He knew there was more to the sisters' relationship than Kate had originally confessed to him. The dark cloud had lifted when he had distracted her in the kitchen, but it would likely come back. Hopefully, it wouldn't fester while he was gone. Having too much time to think might not be good for either of them right now.

"We'll clean up. You take Kate for a walk," his mother was saying, getting up from the table. She stopped and gave him a quick kiss. "Dinner was delicious."

Marco led Kate out to the front terrace. Max immediately got up, coming to lean against her legs.

"Oh, can we take him?" Kate begged.

Marco whistled, and Max didn't need any additional invitation. He bounded down the stairs with them, trotting alongside as they walked up the path. The sun had not set yet, but her automatic lights were turning on, illuminating their way. He told her about the lemons—Amalfi lemons were only grown in the fifteen towns of the Amalfi region. They were sweeter than a regular lemon and almost double the size of what she was probably used to. Marco pointed out the stone distillery in the distance that his grandfather had built, but explained primarily the limoncello was made in a factory in Rome. Still, they bottled some in the distillery for tours and in honor of their ancestors.

Spotting a nearby golf cart near one of their sheds, Marco told her to jump in, and Max hopped in the back as if he did it every day. The industrial-sized golf carts were used throughout the property by the groundskeepers, event staff and caterers.

Marco took her a fair distance up another hill to show her the event space, and Kate marveled at the custom kitchens and indoor and outdoor venues. He told her about how they had attracted a well-known chef to the property after the tour dinners grew too big for his mother to cook for them. She still liked to help occasionally, but she now teased it was a young person's sport.

"Come on. I want to show you something else." Marco pulled her along, grabbing her hand.

They got back into the golf cart, and he drove down a path and then up another road, which was lit by twinkling lights on the nearby trees. The sky was a soft pink and orange, and she whipped out her phone, trying to capture a few sunset photos.

Parking at the top of the hill, Marco grabbed her hand, and they walked to the back of the cart. Sensing his place, Max jumped down to go sniff the nearby bushes. Stepping up to the seats on the back of the golf cart, they sat watching the sky darken in silence.

Kate swung her legs back and forth, feeling truly content for the first time since before the reporters had mobbed them. She didn't mind the silence and loved feeling the warmth of his arm against hers. She longed to put her head on his shoulder.

"You didn't eat much at dinner," he remarked, gazing at the sky as stars began to appear.

Kate shrugged.

"Are you still thinking about your call with Meara?"

"No, not really. I should probably check in with my dad, though."

"I've noticed you haven't really talked about calling him."

Kate looked down at her hands clasped in her lap. "It probably seems strange to you. Your family is so close."

"Mamma likes you." He nodded. "Nico does too—he's comfortable around you. He's shyer and quieter than all of us. Someday you'll meet Stefano. He's different from me and Nico." Marco shook his head. "I often wonder how all three of us came from the same parents, but it is probably because Mamma always had a way of making each of us feel like we could be our own person."

Kate nodded. "That's important. I wish my dad knew a little more about how to do that. I know he loves me very much," she trailed off.

"Do you come up here often?" She jokingly asked, wanting to change the subject.

He smiled. "I used to. I haven't for a while. This is my property."

At Kate's confused look, he explained. "Mamma gave us all a large plot of land on the property when we were younger. It is ours to do what we want with. I thought of building a house— not a house I would live in, but more of a retreat—a place to come to when I need to escape. Maybe a place for a wife and kids," he added softly. "I never started on it because I haven't really needed it. I have my place in Milan and one in Rome and, of course, Positano."

"And your yacht."

"Yes, and the yacht. But there's something special about this place."

"It's home," she said simply, and he nodded.

They looked at each other for a moment. This was their last night for several days, and he wanted to leave on a high note. He elbowed her teasingly. "Okay, secret-trading time. I'll start. I think I already owe you one from earlier. The story Mamma told you? That wasn't the first time." He chuckled. "Frankie and I

169

used to skip school and steal fishing boats all the time. That was just the time we got caught." He grinned mischievously.

Kate giggled, imagining a young naughty Marco.

"Your turn," he coaxed.

Looking at him directly, she thought back to their dinner, her stomach rumbling. "I really, really hate olives."

Marco threw his head back and laughed.

twenty

K ate got up early, eager to start the day. Not knowing what the house routine was, she grabbed her computer and headed downstairs. Should she make her own breakfast? Wait for Margherita? She frowned. She forgot to ask Marco.

Her frown turned to a smile when she thought back to last night. After admitting her violent dislike of olives, Marco insisted on bringing her back to the house to get something to eat. He built her an enormous sandwich of salami and cheese and even grilled it, saying if she was going to have a sandwich on his watch, it better be an Italian panino. It had been delicious, she remembered. He had made her laugh, sharing more stories with her while she ate.

Afterwards, Marco had led her back outside and down the terrace stairs to show her his mother's garden. The winding paths were cleverly lit and even in the dark, Kate could see and smell all kinds of flowers. She gasped when, at the end of the path, they reached a breathtaking pool. Marco had simply shrugged. "Swim when you want."

They had ended their walk outside on an aging wooden swing with his arm around her and her head on his shoulder.

She could still smell his cologne, and the warmth of his body felt so good. She could have stayed like that forever. They had grudgingly climbed the stairs to go to their respective rooms when they both acknowledged they were exhausted, and Marco had to leave before dawn. He had given her kisses that she would remember for a long time. Finally, he had reluctantly forced himself away and thrust her into her room, his eyes telling her how much he wanted to stay. Earlier, he had apologized profusely about leaving, but Kate reassured him she would be fine with false bravado. She didn't want him to worry, but truthfully, she was feeling a little awkward.

Rounding the corner into the kitchen, Kate saw a note propped up against the cappuccino machine. Marco knew it would be the first place she would head. She grinned, reading it. He wished her good morning and told her to help herself to whatever she wanted to eat. He explained his mother was an early riser and would likely be out meeting with staff in the morning. Maria usually came around lunchtime if she was going to work that day.

Kate looked at how he had signed it—with a strong M at the end and his silly little malformed heart. That made her smile while she brewed her cappuccino and grabbed a croissant in a nearby basket.

Kate took her computer out to one of the tables on the terrace. She couldn't wait to get her hands on Oro Industries' website.

Three hours and another cappuccino later, Kate sat back, rubbing her neck. She had spent the last several hours just learning the site and looking at some of the old files that were now hidden in the administrator's section. She found a vast amount of old material that probably needed to come off the site. Feeling a little nosy, she glanced around before she downloaded some files and opened them.

Marco was right. The numbers from the past years compared

to some earnings she had found, even in the more recent reports, were way off. Even more puzzling was that some of their former companies appeared to have been very profitable. Why had Marco sold them?

She chewed her lip. This was really more of Meara's arena. Kate wished she could reach out to her sister with some questions. Obviously, Meara was not a fan of Marco's and besides, this wasn't Kate's information to share. She just wished she was more knowledgeable about the financial side of things. She had always excelled at writing but could barely make it through her finance courses. She probably wasn't even reading things correctly.

Lost in thought, Kate didn't even hear Margherita until the older woman appeared in front of her carrying tall, frosty glasses of lemonade.

"*Buongiorno*, Kate. I hope you like lemonade," Margherita said with a grin. "It's a mainstay on a lemon farm."

Kate gladly accepted it. "Wonderful, thank you."

"How's the writing going?"

Kate felt herself flush. She hadn't written one word, but she didn't want Marco's mother to fret about that. "Uh, slow, but good."

"Do you want to keep writing or would you like to take a break?"

Kate raised her eyebrows. "What do you have in mind?"

The answer was a big smile from Margherita.

TWO HOURS LATER, Kate and Margherita finally sat down at the farmhouse table. They had exchanged their glasses of lemonade for a crisp pinot grigio and they toasted each other. Bubbling on the stove was a big pot of meatballs and sauce, or "sugo," as Kate's nonna had called it.

Through trial and error, Margherita had helped Kate tweak her nonna's recipe. The sauce still needed more time to simmer, but the early results were promising. Kate whipped out her phone and began typing notes.

Margherita nodded as Kate explained she'd better capture what they had changed. She put down her phone to thank the older woman. She truly enjoyed Margherita. After years of not having a mother, Kate realized she had missed hers more than she had wanted to admit. Those feelings were bubbling up within her.

Margherita looked at Kate and saw the unshed tears. With the instincts of a mother, she patted Kate's hand. "What was your mother like?"

That was all Kate needed for the floodgates to open. Margherita got up and returned with a box of tissues, her face distressed. "My dear, I didn't mean to upset you."

"Oh, it's okay." Kate sniffed. "Really, it wasn't you. I guess I've been thinking about my mother and my nonna a lot while in Italy. You've been so kind—it just made it all come to the surface." She gave a small smile and began to tell Margherita all about her mother—how beautiful and funny she was. How she was devoted to her husband and children. She told her about all they had done together and how devastated they were when her mother was diagnosed with cancer. Kate described the last years of her mother's life briefly, not wanting to dwell on them. Margherita continued to pat Kate's hand through it all, squeezing gently.

"Your mother must have been so proud of you." Margherita nodded, smiling.

"You know, I think she was," Kate acknowledged. Suddenly, her heart felt a lot lighter.

～

NICO'S mere presence did a lot to keep the evening light. He had a way of making the most mundane chore into a story. His eyes lit up when he talked about farming and how they used no pesticides—similar to organic farming in the United States, he told her. He discussed studying the effects of climate change on the crops and the need to adapt. He clearly was a sponge, soaking up research. He told her about the various symposiums he had attended and how much more he felt he needed to learn.

After dinner, he took Kate on another ride around the property, which differed vastly from Marco's tour. Nico showed her small details, stopping to point out improvements they had made, his vision for expansion and other details. He talked about their other farms in the region and in Sicily, and Kate was just beginning to understand the vastness of their operations. He stopped and let her play with some of the baby goats they kept on the farm, laughing as the mama goat chased her. Kate hopped back into the golf cart with a shriek.

That night, Marco called her just as she was getting into bed. She had been hoping he might call and had just given up when she saw his name appear. He sounded exhausted and apologized for not calling earlier. She gave him a summary of her day but chose not to say anything about the website. She needed more time to absorb what she was discovering. Marco didn't ask either, seemingly preoccupied. He apologized several times when he was forced to yawn.

"You should go to bed," she suggested softly.

"I *am* in bed." He teased gently. "Just talk to me a little while longer, Katie. It helps relax me."

So she launched into more detail, exaggerating their attempts to replicate her nonna's sauce. They had eaten it for dinner, and it was really close, Kate told him excitedly. She could hear the happiness in his voice when he told her how pleased he was she'd had a good day. Eventually, she could hear his breathing get quieter.

"Goodnight, Marco," she whispered.

"Hmmm," was all she heard. She smiled and hung up. Two hours later, she was still staring at the ceiling. She punched her pillow in frustration. Just talking to Marco had stirred her up so badly she was now tossing and turning.

Switching on the light, Kate grabbed her computer and went back to the website. It really was a mess. There was no e-commerce for any of their products, relying only on wholesale. There wasn't even a list of where consumers could buy the products. She had to scroll down and click through several tabs to even find information on tours of their lemon or olive farms. She found other companies that didn't even seem to fit in with their brand. She suddenly realized the website was a symptom of the problem. Marco's uncle had continued to take on new businesses without updating the marketing efforts of the ones they had. The website almost seemed like an after-thought—something designed with an off-the-shelf-product. Kate rolled her eyes just thinking about it. She went to search for social media and found nothing.

"No social media presence at all," she said out loud, shaking her head. She wondered how she could broach this with Marco. She didn't want him to think she was criticizing him, and he was already so overwhelmed. She only wanted to help. Pushing her laptop off her lap, she laid back down and thought about it. It was the early morning hours before she finally closed her eyes.

twenty-one

Kate settled into the household routine, and the days soon were filled. She was able to write in the mornings, but then often found herself investigating the website. She still had made no changes to the site, realizing that she would be forced to explain to Marco that it couldn't be salvaged. He would need to invest in rebuilding a whole new website. She started saving the things she downloaded to one of the thumb drives she had found in her computer bag. She wasn't sure what she was going to do with the material, but she saved it just in case.

Some afternoons she helped Margherita, who had shyly asked her if she was interested in seeing some of the event planning. Kate willingly expressed an interest. They went up to the event space, with Margherita introducing her to the staff. Kate met Luciano, the chef, and Bella, the event planner. Margherita was careful to let them do their jobs, but it was clear she wanted things done a certain way. She was a stickler for details, often going out to the long tables set under the many pergolas of lemon trees and rearranging centerpieces or dishes. Bella happily took copious notes. The young girl was obviously taking the opportunity to learn from the experienced woman.

177

Nights were spent dining outside and sometimes Kate went for a quick swim, either by herself or with Nico if he was home. He liked to tease her, and she soon found out they shared a love of board games. He was wickedly smart, beating her at Monopoly twice, laughing as he counted his money. Some nights, they rode around the property, or she helped him in his beloved greenhouse, where he showed her his cherished exotic plants. Nothing for sale, he told her. Just for his own enjoyment. She knew he was probably obligated to entertain her, but he generally seemed to like her company.

She ended each night with a phone call from Marco. Some nights, their talks were better than others. More than once, she hung up with a frown. He tried to push his frustration and stress aside, but she could tell it was right there on the surface. He didn't seem to want to share much about what was going on, answering her curtly before softening and pleading to hear more about her day.

One night, Marco was in surprisingly good spirits. The lawsuit had been dismissed, he told her triumphantly. His attorneys had effectively navigated it quickly through the courts and it had no basis, as he had believed. He told her what was surprising was that he discovered that someone was covertly paying the press to cover it—someone with deep pockets. He believed the claimant did not have access to those kinds of funds.

"We aren't even sure how they could pay for such a prominent attorney. I'm just happy it's over. I didn't want you to get your hopes up, but the reporters have become disinterested. I doubt there are any left in Positano. I hope you will still stay at the house, though," he added slowly.

Kate agreed to stay. At this point, she wouldn't find any lodging anyway during the busy season. She had booked her own accommodations well in advance. She didn't discuss with him about returning home, but they would need to talk about it soon.

One afternoon, Marco had called to go over final details for the shareholders' dinner with his mother, who put him on speaker as she took careful notes. Kate tried to busy herself on her laptop, not wanting to seem like she was eavesdropping.

"Is Katie still there?" he asked.

Margherita smiled, taking it off speaker and handing it to Kate. After a quick greeting, he remarked tiredly, "Katie, I imagine you'll need a more formal dress than you have with you to wear to the shareholders' gala."

Kate was instantly annoyed. "Well, I might if I was invited," she answered coolly. This was the first time he even mentioned her presence there.

"Of course you're invited," he snapped. Taking a breath, he said evenly, "I would very much like you to be there. It will be my first shareholder's gala as CEO, and I want you by my side."

She held her breath. The shareholders would have seen the photos of the casual American woman kissing their CEO. They would have read the innuendoes in the press. A feeling of vengeful pride rose inside her. She wanted to prove she was better than what they thought of her and that drove her to agree.

"I would love to, Marco," she said now warmly. "But how can I get a dress?"

"Sergio will find someone to drive you into Positano," he told her, referring to the farm's operations manager. "You should be able to find something there, and just tell them to charge it to me," he added dismissively.

Kate rolled her eyes. Did he know her? She chose not to argue, given his abrupt mood, and hung up soon after, deep in thought.

In fact, just to prove her point, Kate bought several things at the lemon grove's gift shop later that day. She was delighted with the quality of merchandise—it wasn't the usual mass-produced tourist products. Rather, Kate found high-quality candles, linens, paintings and hand-painted ceramics in addition to the family's products. The young woman working at the gift shop had no idea Kate had any connection to the family and was friendly, explaining it was important to the Rinaldi Family not to just sell their wares, but to showcase local artisans.

When Margherita saw her bag, she frowned, telling her they would have given her anything she wanted. Kate put her arm around the older woman, telling her how much they had already done for her. On the way home, Kate got in the driver's seat of the golf cart, after noticing the tired lines around Margherita's eyes. When they got home, Kate suggested that Margherita rest. She agreed, climbing the stairs slowly. Maria had left dinner on the stove and when Kate heard Nico arrive, she began dishing up.

Coming into the kitchen, he glanced around. "Where's Mamma?"

Kate told him his mother had gone to lie down and that she was a little concerned. Nico bounded up the stairs to go check on her. "She's asleep already," he told her, coming back into the kitchen. "It's too much for her, Kate. This business is going to kill us all," he added bitterly.

Kate handed him a plate, and the two took their meal outside. Nico was strangely silent while eating, lost in thought.

She looked at him thoughtfully. "Are you happy, Nico?"

He dropped his utensils, pushing away from the table. "Of course not!" At her surprised expression, Nico apologized immediately.

"I'm sorry. I'm letting my anger get the better of me. That's more like Stefano than me," he said, chagrined. Kate realized just as she had needed an ear the few days before, Nico did, too. He seemed to choose his words carefully, describing how much travel he had to do and how he was required to be in the office in order to manage supplies, staff and complete the paperwork required by the government. He just wanted to work in the soil, he told her. He wanted time to become more educated. Marco wouldn't hear of it, saying he knew the business too well and it would be too hard to replace him.

Nico turned honest eyes toward her. "Stefano isn't happy either, overseeing the products," he told her flatly. "And Mamma, she works and works. She should be enjoying life."

Kate looked at him, her eyes softening. "Have you talked to Marco?"

"A few times." He sighed. "At first, we were silent. We all grieved for our uncle. We knew Marco was under a lot of pressure, and so we did our jobs and stayed quiet. Now it has become hard on all of us. I have talked to him. Stefano has talked to him. But Mamma, she won't. She doesn't want to let him down." he shook his head sadly.

He looked at her seriously. "We could sell all of it. It is worth billions. We could even keep some of the property. What is money if we are all chained to this corporation? What is the good if it sends us all to an early grave like our uncle?"

He was looking at Kate now contemplatively, raising his eyebrows. "Perhaps you could talk to Marco."

She gave a helpless laugh. "Nico, no. I can't involve myself in your family business that way. That would be way above my pay grade."

"Pay grade?" He looked at her, clearly confused.

"I'm just teasing. I just mean that it isn't any of my business."

Nico put his head in his hands. "That's too bad. I was hoping you would make it your business."

twenty-two

The next morning, the sun was up and shining brightly, which helped Kate shake off Nico's dark mood from the night before. She had just made herself a cappuccino when Margherita entered, without a sign of her past tiredness.

Kate made Margherita a cappuccino as well, and then joined her at the table.

"Rita, I need a dress," she blurted. "For the shareholders' gala."

Kate had been up the night before, worried about finding something just right. The gala could be one of her last nights with Marco. Not only would it be special, but it would be *his* night as well. She wanted to look perfect.

"Well, of course you do, dear. I'm sorry I didn't think of it sooner."

"Marco said Sergio could find someone to drive me to Positano and I could look there."

Rita rolled her eyes. "He's such a man. Positano has beautiful shops, but you need something very special, Kate. I think you should go to Capri to shop," she said. "They have the best designer boutiques. You will find something perfect there."

Kate tried not to show Rita the panic she was feeling. Her suggestion was so innocent—she probably did not have to worry about money for so many years. It didn't occur to Margherita that Kate couldn't afford a designer dress or she might assume Marco was paying for it.

"Is it alright if I ask Sergio to find someone to take me this morning? If I need to catch a ferry, I should go early."

Rita got out her phone. "Of course. Let me call him for you."

It was Sergio himself who soon brought the big black sedan around the driveway, pulling up to the front door and getting out quickly to open a car door for Kate. He was an older man, with beautiful soft brown eyes, still sporting a full head of hair that was slowly turning gray. He moved with a quiet competence and a gentleness Kate found charming. She had enjoyed meeting him earlier that week.

Kate waved goodbye to Margherita, who was standing on the wide terrace, slowly petting Max's head. After he helped Kate in, Sergio went up to the terrace to say a few quiet words to Margherita. She had her head to the side, looking shyly at him. Kate watched with interest. She had seen that look earlier this week when Sergio was in the office. There was something between them, and that made Kate happy.

On the way to Positano, she sat lost in thought. Sergio spoke to her a few times about her travels, and she answered him absentmindedly. In her head, she was busy calculating her savings account. She would need to spend considerable money on a dress, but she rationalized that she had saved money this past week not paying for any lodging or food.

Soon, they were pulling into Positano. Sergio checked the ferry times for her and promised to pick her up in the late afternoon. If she wanted to come back sooner, he gave her his phone number, sending her off cheerfully.

Kate walked down the hill, stopping often to take photos. She breathed in the sweet-smelling air and marveled at the town again. She had felt sad to leave it without warning, and it felt great to be back.

As she passed the shop where Francesca and Allegra worked, Kate saw Allegra putting out the big lemon candle for the day. Allegra gave her a friendly wave. Kate slowed her steps, unexpectedly getting an idea. Before she could question it, she entered the shop. Both women greeting her warmly, inquiring how she was.

Kate gave them a wide smile as well. She decided to venture in to ask them for ideas. While she trusted Margherita's opinion, these women were younger, expertly dressed, and might have a better idea of what kind of dress she should look for and where she could shop. She explained she was on her way to Capri to look for a dress for the annual shareholders' gala.

"The thing is, I don't know what to wear. It's at the lemon grove, and that seems casual, but the event sounds more formal," she told them.

The two women nodded.

"You need our help," Francesca stated.

"And we can help you. You came to the right place. We are experts," boasted Allegra.

They quickly gathered their purses and told a younger woman working there that they would be gone for the afternoon.

"I can't take you away from your work," protested Kate.

Allegra was already linking arms with her. "Of course you can. Do you think we can resist shopping? This will be fun!"

Kate wanted to make something clear before they departed. "I should probably tell you." She bit her lip. "I'm on a budget."

The two women looked at each other and laughed.

Francesca was the first to speak. "You are dating Marco Rinaldi, and you are on a budget? But he could buy you the whole boutique if he wanted."

"He's not paying for it," corrected Kate. "I am."

"Ahhh." Allegra nodded, a funny look crossing her face. "I

still don't understand, but we will do as you say. We will find you the perfect dress...on a budget."

They left the shop and headed down the ferry and were pleased they didn't have to wait long before one pulled up. They walked on deck with the throngs of tourists headed to Capri, talking and laughing. Kate found the two women had great senses of humor, playing off each other. She couldn't help but giggle at their stories about Positano and its people.

The ferry soon pulled up to Capri, and they disembarked, working their way through the crowd and up the same tram Kate had taken with Marco. Seeing Gianna that day and the memories of her humiliation flooded back to her, and she could feel her cheeks burning. Allegra asked if she was feeling okay.

Kate smiled reassuringly. "Perfectly fine." She stubbornly pushed the memories to the back of her mind. She was determined to have fun.

~

KATE SOON LEARNED SEEING Capri with Francesca and Allegra was a completely different experience. The two flitted from shop to shop, whirling through racks and rounders with practiced ease.

"Rags," proclaimed Francesca rather loudly in one shop, tossing a dress back on the rack. Kate glanced around uneasily, putting a finger to her lips.

Francesca grinned and grabbed Kate's hand. "Let's keep going, Allegra," she called.

After several shops, Francesca stopped and pointed to a boutique, finally looking more animated. "This is a good one. Lots of options. It is actually a local designer, so these are more unique dresses."

Kate entered the shop and looked around at the perfectly dressed women, all adorned with fine jewels. Francesca and

Allegra, who were also dressed exquisitely, blended right in. Kate looked down at the red-and-white-striped sundress she had donned for the occasion. She felt frumpy now, standing next to these women who seemed so effortlessly chic.

Francesca and Allegra began thoroughly investigating the shop, speaking to each other in rapid Italian. Kate half-heartedly pushed hangers around, glancing at a few price tags discreetly. Her eyes widened.

Francesca began speaking excitedly, quickly sweeping her long blond hair behind her and beckoning Allegra over.

"You found it, Francesca." Allegra nodded proudly.

Together, the women held up a dress for Kate. It was a long silky, draped gown that at first looked strapless until Francesca held it out and Kate saw it had a wide swath of material that formed a simple halter neckline. The back was fairly non-existent, dipping low. But it was the color that was striking—it was the most vivid blue Kate had ever seen.

"It's beautiful," she breathed.

"Go try it on." The women pushed it at her. They summoned a salesperson, giving her instructions.

Alone in the dressing room, Kate looked at herself in the mirror. She had to admit, it *was* beautiful. It fit her like a glove. It seemed this dress had been in this shop waiting just for her. Stepping out of the dressing room, she confidently walked up the stairs to a little area in front of several mirrors. She twisted and turned, looking at it from every angle. The fitted bodice hugged her curves. The side slit went halfway up her leg, just enough to give her room to walk. Both women swarmed her, high-fiving each other.

"*Perfetto*," they both said with such excitement that even the shop ladies looked amused.

After much admiration, Kate reluctantly went back to take the dress off. She had put off looking at the price tag and finally she took a deep breath. The amount was much steeper than she had feared. She emerged from the dressing room with the dress on the hanger. Finding her new friends, she whispered, "Francesca, this isn't affordable."

Francesca grinned smugly. "It will be." She strode confidently to the front counter, dress in hand. Kate watched Francesca, beautiful in her tight cream-colored dress and strappy sandals. She addressed the woman in Italian, gesturing with her hands, turning and pointing at Kate. Kate heard "Rinaldi" at one point. She looked away. This situation had gone off the rails but she didn't know how to stop it.

"You can buy this dress for half price." Francesca returned to her triumphantly.

Kate looked at her, shocked. "But how?"

"Shh." Francesca gave her a quick look. "Just pay it and let's get out of here."

Kate obediently handed her credit card over to the shop owner with an apologetic smile.

WALKING up the hill with her garment bag, the women began intently discussing shoes. Kate told them she already had a pair that would work. She had thought about it last night when she had been worrying about what to wear. Before her trip, she and Teresa had gone shopping, and on an impulse, Kate had bought a strappy pair of black sandals with glittering rhinestones. Teresa had teased her, saying they weren't the most practical item, but Kate had thrown them in anyway, her mind full of romantic nights. She hadn't worn them after her spectacular fall. Even after her ankle was better, she eyed the cobblestones suspiciously, not wanting to take a second tumble. She had thought about wearing them with Marco, but there hadn't been the opportunity. The heels would bring her up to his shoulders, she realized dreamily.

Francesca stopped abruptly, demanding to see what they looked like. Kate quickly searched for them online, finding them still on the store's website. She proudly showed the women a photo. Proclaiming them *"perfetto"* also there was nothing else to do but go eat. Kate had insisted lunch was on her, and they headed to a spot at the top of the hill.

Sitting at the outdoor table with its wide umbrella, Kate gazed at the beautiful view of the sea below. They ordered a bottle of wine and toasted to their success. After the waiter took their lunch order, Kate took another sip, smiling at her new friends.

"Francesca, how did you convince her to discount the dress?" Kate bit her lip, hoping she wanted to hear the answer.

Francesca shrugged. "I told her you were wearing it to the Oro Industries' shareholders' gala as the guest of Marco Rinaldi. I reminded her that press are invited to it as well. That dress— her design—will be posted on social media within minutes."

Kate stared at her in horror. "You mean, *me* in that dress will be pictured?"

Francesca grinned. *"Esattamente!"*

KATE ENJOYED lunch with the two women. It made her realize how much she had missed her friends. Despite their different cultures, they found they had a lot in common. All of them were working jobs they weren't really passionate about. They were all single, and they traded horror stories of some of the worst dates they had been on, laughing until tears came to their eyes.

Francesca asked how she had met Marco, and Kate told them the hilarious story of her falling and then him carrying her up the stairs to her hotel. Allegra leaned on her hands, pretending to swoon. "So romantic." She giggled.

Clearly, they adored Marco and seemed confused when Kate asked for their contact info so they could stay in touch. They questioned why she was not considering staying in Italy with the prospect of continuing her relationship with Marco. Kate didn't want to explain, not before she and Marco had even talked. The two Italian women exchanged looks, but typed their information into Kate's phone.

Francesca stared at her, eyebrows raised. "Men like Marco Rinaldi seldom come around."

Kate opened her mouth and closed it again. She nodded and then signaled to the waiter to bring their bill, deciding to remain silent.

Returning to Positano, they stayed on the top deck of the ferry again, and Kate enjoyed seeing the town come into view as the ship slowly approached. The colorful houses lining the hills were a welcoming sight, and she felt a sense of belonging she couldn't quite explain. She departed from the women with kisses and hugs and climbed the hill, holding her garment bag.

She thought briefly of going to see Alfonso, but when she looked at the time, she worried Sergio would already be waiting. She was right—he was there, smilingly helped her into the car. She was soon back at the house, toting her bag in the front door. Margherita was coming down the massive staircase and greeted her excitedly. She turned around immediately to shoo Kate upstairs, insisting she try on the dress. Kate grabbed her shoes quickly and got dressed in the bathroom to make her grand entrance into her bedroom, where Margherita sat waiting.

"Oh, Kate, *bella!* You look lovely," exclaimed Margherita.

Kate beamed at her. Margherita had been so kind, and now she gave her much-needed confidence. She bit her lip. "Are you sure it's appropriate for the occasion?"

"Absolutely *perfetto*," came the quick answer. *Perfetto* seemed to be the chosen word, and so Kate breathed a sigh of relief.

She gave the older woman a quick hug before going back to

the bathroom to change and go downstairs to join her in the kitchen. They began evaluating the contents of the refrigerator, with Margherita naming possible dinner ideas.

"How about fish?" asked a voice from the doorway.

"We don't have any," Margherita answered, almost automatically. Turning quickly, she closed the refrigerator door. "Stefano!" she cried.

Kate looked up to see a man who resembled Marco. He was dressed in a dark business suit, even taller than Marco, but slighter, and his hair was clipped shorter, his face more chiseled. He was now setting two bags carefully on the island.

Coming around the island the opposite way was Marco, also dressed in a dark business suit, a bouquet of red roses in his hands that he now presented to Kate. She looked up to see his tender smile. His eyes were wary, almost as if he wasn't sure what kind of greeting he was going to receive.

"Marco! I didn't expect you." Kate was a little embarrassed that their first greeting was in front of his mother and brother, but she couldn't resist his kiss, leaning up eagerly. Still, they kept it brief. The promise in his eyes to continue later made her heart flutter. He kept his arm around her, as if it was the most natural thing in the world.

"Katie, this is my brother, Stefano," Marco said formally.

Stefano walked over to her, gently kissing her on each cheek. "I've heard much about you, Kate." He smiled. His face transformed, making him appear more relaxed than when he first walked in.

"It's nice to meet you." She grinned back at him, pleased to meet Marco's other brother. Marco's arm tightened around her, and she looked up at him happily. She was so glad he was back.

Stefano turned away. Shrugging off his jacket and rolling up his sleeves, he proclaimed he was going to cook.

"Stefano made me stop at two fish markets before he was satisfied with the quality of the sea bass." Marco complained. "I was in a hurry to get back," he whispered to her, and she blushed under his intent stare.

"While Stefano cooks and catches up with his mother, why don't you two go out to the terrace?" suggested Margherita with a glint in her eye. "I'll put these beautiful roses in water, Kate."

Marco grabbed two glasses and a bottle of wine and ushered Kate outside. They walked to the end of the terrace, and he put everything on a table before grabbing her and tugging her over to the side of the house. She wound her arms around his neck as he kissed her hungrily, finally taking a breath and sliding his lips up her jawbone, his hands running up and down her sides.

"Oh, Katie. It's so good to come back to you," he whispered, putting his forehead next to hers. "I missed you. I was so worried you would be upset with me for not coming back sooner." He stroked the side of her face, kissing the spot where he said her dimple was. She had been doubting this dimple fixation, making faces in the mirror. She had yet to see this mysterious dimple.

"Enchanting," he murmured.

Kate reached up and kissed him impulsively.

"Do you know that's the first time you've kissed me on your own?" His eyes glinted with amusement.

She beamed at him. Now that he was right here in front of her, she couldn't stop hugging him. "I'm just so happy."

He gave her a few more sweet kisses, before he finally let her go. He led her over to the table, pouring them each a glass of wine. He shrugged out of his coat, putting it on a nearby chair, looking at her inquisitively. "What did you do with your day today?"

"I went shopping, and I found a dress for tomorrow night!"

Marco smiled at her enthusiasm, and she continued, describing her day with Francesca and Allegra. She left out their inquisition about their relationship. "We had so much fun."

"I wish I could have taken you. I would have loved to watch you try on dresses."

Kate giggled, putting out a hand. "Oh Gawd! No! I'm not one of those women who drags a man shopping. That's the worst! Besides, I only tried on one."

His eyes widened. "Why only one?"

"There weren't many in my price range," she explained honestly, without thinking.

He looked exasperated. "I said I would pay for it!"

"Marco, you're not buying my dress," she argued. "I'm perfectly capable. Your mom says it's beautiful, and I'm excited about it. Just be happy." She grabbed his hands.

He continued to frown at her, and she changed the subject. "So, not to talk business, but I have been waiting to discuss your website."

"Must we talk about it now? I would rather hear more about your day and what you and Mamma have been up to," he commented wearily.

She stared at him, knowing he was tired, but it seemed like forever that she had been waiting to talk to him about the website. "Let me just show you a couple of things, and then I'll put my laptop away. I promise—just for a few minutes. I'll be right back."

Marco nodded, sipping wine, as she ran into the house to grab her laptop. Stefano was busy at the stove, the island littered with ingredients and bowls. Margherita was chatting easily, and Stefano answered with short replies.

Kate quickly re-joined Marco. He was sitting looking out over the view, lost in thought, the sleeves of his white shirt rolled up, one polished Italian leather shoe crossing the other.

"Dinner already smells delicious," she remarked as she sat down near him.

"Stefano is an amazing cook." He lifted an eyebrow. "He will sadly put my puttanesca to shame."

"Well, if his sea bass dish doesn't have a million olives, he's already ahead of you." She teased, and he grinned back.

After loading the website, Kate pointed out a few things to Marco. Scooting his chair closer, he began to nibble at her neck, sending thrills down her spine. Finally, laughing, she pushed at him until he grudgingly agreed to pay attention. He grabbed his glasses out of a suit pocket and studied the screen. Kate showed him some issues she had found, including how difficult it was for visitors to find any information about any of their properties.

She showed him how many clicks it took to find his products and that there was no e-commerce on the site. "There's no way consumers can buy your products."

"We've focused on wholesale—they're in stores and restaurants. We're the largest exporter—at least with all of our lemon products." He shrugged.

"Well, even if you aren't set up for retail, people don't even know where to buy them. But you should probably think about what it would take to sell to people directly as well."

He stared at her, but she could tell the wheels were turning.

"Think of your website as a reflection of your company," she continued. "This shows a dated and disorganized company." Kate was busy scrolling through the site and didn't notice the look of sadness cross his face. She was used to being straightforward with clients and didn't think twice about it.

"The other thing is, I see no social media presence at all. People aren't going to sit around wondering about your products or tours—or any of this. They aren't going to think about going to your website. You have to get in front of them. Oh, and the search engine terms are non-existent."

Marco sat back and ran his hand through his hair. "Can you fix all this, Katie?"

She turned and looked at him now, instantly feeling remorseful. In her excitement to show him her thoughts, she hadn't chosen her words carefully. She realized she had just lobbed more pressure on Marco, and he was already feeling overwhelmed.

She smiled gently at him. "I could. But you need more than me. This website isn't even structurally sound."

At his confused look, she tried to explain. "Think of a house. There's really no foundation for this site. Someone needs to build a better, stronger platform that can handle all the things we just talked about. And then there's the continual upkeep. You need a team."

"We have a team," he remarked dryly. "I guess not a very good team, though."

"Well, maybe no one has told them what to focus on. Technology and consumer habits change frequently. It is difficult to keep up."

Marco stared at her long and hard. "Katie, what if you moved to Italy and came to work for me? You could head up the whole thing. I would pay you three or four times what you make now, and you could live for free!"

She looked at him, stunned.

"Dinner is served!" yelled Stefano from the door leading into the house.

Saved by the dinner bell. Kate stood up quickly, trying not to meet Marco's questioning gaze.

MARCO WATCHED KATE THROUGHOUT DINNER. She had looked at him earlier like he had lost his mind. He hadn't meant to blurt out the job offer. She was so brilliant and knowledgeable, and he trusted her. If she came to work for him, he knew it would get done, and it would get done right. He had appreciated her openness with him, even if he was already at the end of his rope.

He should not have made such a radical proposal before they had talked about their relationship or even the possibility of a future commitment if they lived in the same country. He shook his head, ready to bang his head against the table. He knew enough to know his idea might just send her running. Though he didn't know where they were heading, the idea of Kate going home made him physically ill. Still, he wasn't sure he was ready for a personal commitment right now. He tugged on his collar, just thinking of it. What woman wanted to be offered a job, though?

Stefano had teased him about his feelings for Kate on the way to the house, especially when Marco was driving at a breakneck speed. He had shrugged it off. His life right now was in turmoil after inheriting a far greater mess than he first realized. Sal had spent the last several days trying to show him more of the issues until he had finally called a halt to it.

"Let's get through the shareholder meeting, and then we'll start attacking these other problems," Marco had finally barked out in frustration. Sal had pressed him to decide, even presenting him with options to sell some of their companies. For once, Marco had held his ground, saying he needed time to think. He was finding it virtually impossible to juggle all the corporation's challenges and Kate. Whatever this was with her couldn't have come at a worse time.

Kate turned and smiled at him, and he realized he had missed a family joke. Nico had arrived and now his two brothers were intent on telling more embarrassing stories of his youth. Their mother was smiling and looked radiant—she was always happiest when the family was all together.

Marco watched Kate joking with both of his brothers, who already seemed under her spell. Nico especially had grown close to her—often teasing her and now putting an arm around her shoulders.

"Nico, you can stop manhandling Katie," Marco said a little more roughly than he intended, slapping Nico's hand away.

The chattering stopped, and Nico looked at him, his eyebrows together. "What's with you? Kate and I have spent a lot of time together. She likes me, even though I beat her every night at Monopoly."

"You cheat and you know it," she joked, sending Marco an anxious look.

Marco smiled a little despite himself, listening to them argue over Nico's complex Monopoly strategy. It was stupid of him to be jealous of his little brother. He realized Nico and Kate had been making memories all week while he was knee-deep in contracts and earnings reports. It bothered him and he tried to shake it off.

"Let's have dessert outside," he suggested, pushing away from the table.

DESSERT on the terrace had turned into a prolonged family event with a big plate of cannolis. It wasn't until much later that Marco found himself alone with Kate. His brothers had hung around purposely frustrating him. Finally, they had left, snickering a little, as his mother shooed them upstairs like teenagers.

Now they were finally alone, and Marco wrapped an arm around Kate as they leaned on the terrace rail, looking over the hills. "Tell me about your dress, *cara*," he said softly.

"It's the most amazing color of blue with a halter neckline..." she answered absently before blurting, "Marco, did you mean what you asked earlier?"

He didn't have to question what she was referring to. Obviously, the subject of her working for him was on her mind. He stared down at her, his expression unreadable. "I never say anything I don't mean."

"There's a part of me that would love to say yes."

"But..." He raised his eyebrows, looking at her intently.

She looked away from him, biting her lip. "I think it would be the wrong move for me. I can't explain it. The timing is just off. I need time to figure out what I want to do when I grow up." She gave a small laugh—continuing her habit of making small jokes when she was nervous. Swallowing hard, she looked up at him earnestly. "I want to find something I love doing."

"But you are so skilled. I saw what you did with the website for the ceramics shop and everything you said this evening makes sense," he argued. "You are very smart. If you don't want to work at Oro Industries, you can always be a consultant," he teased.

Kate gave him a small smile. "For a long time, I enjoyed it, but I'm not passionate about it. I just sort of fell into it after my mother died and then never had the nerve to look for something else. I feel like there's more out there for me. I have a few contracts to get through when I get home, but then I have to figure it out." She shrugged. "That's why I came to Italy. I wanted to challenge myself, write a novel and do something different."

He stared at her, sliding a piece of hair behind her ear and gently touching her face. "Katie, I admit offering you a job was desperation on my part. We have to talk about our future. Do you intend to go home and forget about us?"

She stared at him for a long minute, choosing her words. "Of course not! How could I? Marco, you mean a lot to me. I care about you. But all of this," she said, waving around her, "is just overwhelming to me. I'm afraid of getting swallowed up by it all. I think my time in Italy has made me realize I have to figure myself out. If we have a chance, you're going to have to be patient."

"Patient is not something I have ever been called," he remarked dryly. "I more than care for you, Katie, but I can see this is not the time nor the place for this discussion," he said roughly, dropping his hand from her face, and then running a hand through his hair.

"Marco," she began tentatively.

"No, let's just table this for now," he interrupted abruptly.

"Tomorrow is the gala. Let's get through that and spend some time together afterward."

Kate looked at him apprehensively. She wanted to continue discussing this, but he was probably right. She knew the next day's events were weighing heavily on him, and she had already pressed him once tonight. He walked a few steps away, staring off into the distance, not looking at her.

"Hey," she said softly, coming up behind him and putting her hand on his back, wanting a connection with him. Turning to look at her, she saw his masked expression. She could tell he was withdrawing from her. Almost reluctantly, he put an arm around her and looked like he was about to say something.

A sudden shout of commotion came from inside the house. They both turned from where they were standing at the end of the terrace.

Nico was leaning out of the French doors. "Marco, you're not going to believe this!"

Another man emerged, heading toward them. Even from a distance, Kate could tell he was incredibly handsome, moving with confidence and a big grin on his face.

"Lucca!" Marco exclaimed.

AS LUCCA APPROACHED and Kate was able to see his face in the evening light, she opened her mouth in shock. Marco had never told her that the mysterious cousin he was trying to find was none other than a world-famous actor. She had seen all his movies. The movies he appeared in were guaranteed immediately to become box office hits. She gasped despite herself.

Marco turned his head, taking in her reaction, before walking toward Lucca.

"*Mio cugino*," Marco said warmly, wrapping Lucca in a big

hug. Marco fired questions in rapid Italian, and Lucca grinned, answering.

Suddenly, it was Lucca that turned to her. Smiling widely, his white teeth gleaming against his olive skin, he looked every bit the movie star. He was tall and lean, his jet-black hair styled perfectly in a short cut that many men had tried to emulate. He had a perfect five o'clock shadow, which seemed to accentuate his strong jawline. His piercing blue eyes—a trademark on the big screen—glinted at her in the evening light.

"*Buonasera, signorina*," he said softly, kissing her on both cheeks, lingering for a moment.

"*Buonasera*," Kate repeated automatically. She knew she should snap out of it, but she was spellbound. She had not expected this turn of events, and she couldn't help but stare steadily at Lucca.

Marco's eyes narrowed. Walking back to Kate, he put his arm around her possessively. "Katie, this is my cousin Lucca. Lucca, my girlfriend, Kate." Kate turned and looked at Marco quizzically. He had never used that term before.

"I read all about it, *cugino*." Lucca teased.

"Not everything you read is true," she interrupted, frowning. *Mistress*.

"Believe me, I know that," he said seriously.

Marco looked at him, exasperated. "Lucca, I tried everything to find you. Our private investigators came up empty! I left messages for you everywhere."

"I'm sorry." Lucca looked contrite. "I needed to get away and have a break. Completely off the grid," he added. "I have a lot to talk with you about," he said uneasily.

Kate suddenly felt like an intruder. She should let the cousins catch up. Lucca was looking at Marco intently.

"I've got some writing to do. I think I'll go up and get a little work done," she remarked.

Marco raised his eyebrows. "Are you sure?"

"Definitely. It was nice to meet you, Lucca." She smiled widely at him.

They walked down the terrace and went inside the kitchen. Stefano was warming up food, and Nico was opening a bottle of wine. Margherita was setting a place at the farmhouse table. It was obvious the family was going to gather. She made her excuses and left the kitchen, slowly letting go of Marco's hand, and climbed the stairs alone.

twenty-three

Marco's cousin is Lucca Delarosa

Kate stared at her phone, waiting to see how long it would be before Teresa replied to her text. She giggled when the response was immediate.

Whaaaat with a wide-eyed emoji. *Are you going to get to meet him?*

Already have. He's very cute.

Just cute?

Well, he's not up to Marco's level of extreme handsomeness, but he IS cute. Kate added a laughing emoji.

She could only imagine Teresa's face right now. Kate had waited until the next morning her time to text, knowing if she did the night before she would never get to sleep. Teresa had a million questions, and Kate patiently answered all she could.

She was glad she had waited until morning. Last night Margherita had popped her head into Kate's room, asking if she had all she needed. Kate looked up from her computer where her cursor sat blinking on a blank screen and smiled at her.

She invited Margherita to sit down and could tell the older woman had wanted to leave her sons and nephew to talk.

Margherita gladly sat in a nearby chair, explaining that Lucca was the son of her oldest brother, and Delarosa was her maiden name. She laughed, sharing how Lucca and Marco were the same age and would get into so much trouble as kids. Lucca's family had moved up north when he was a child, she told Kate. Then his parents went through a trying divorce. His mother had moved back to America, taking her son with her. Margherita's brother had been devastated. It had only been in recent years that father and son had forged a better relationship, she said sadly. Lucca visited in the summers and Zio Angelo, despite not being related to him, had felt a kinship with the boy. He eventually gave him shares of stock to get him started in life. Lucca's acting career had taken off with his first movie, and he never needed to be involved with the corporation.

Kate soaked in the information. When Margherita had left, Kate immediately grabbed her phone and began searching for articles about Lucca. She was so curious and had never read much about him. Even after searching for a time, she was no wiser about him personally. He seemed to have been able to keep most of his life private and very little was public about his upbringing or his parents. Most of the articles talked about the many women he had dated and his glamorous life. She finally laid her head down on the pillow, thinking about all the questions she had for Marco.

She would have to wait with those questions, though. When she had gone downstairs that morning after disengaging from Teresa, the family was all dressed and ready for the day-long shareholders' meeting. The men were in suits, even though the meeting was being held at the farm. Margherita had told her that Zio Angelo had added a boardroom in the back of the event space years ago. Since then, it was tradition that the shareholders' gala be held on the property

Marco made a cappuccino for her, and though he inquired politely about her night, he was visibly stressed. She stared at him, thinking how handsome he looked in his dark blue tailored Italian suit. His tie was a somber gray against his white shirt. He looked every bit the powerful CEO.

Stefano had cooked a big breakfast for the family, but Marco had eaten little, pushing his food around his plate. He got up suddenly and brought his plate to the sink. Kate smiled, watching him. She noticed that no matter how wealthy the family was or how many staff worked for them, they always tidied up after themselves. She was sure Margherita had drilled that into them. Joining him with her plate at the sink, she asked softly, "Can we go outside for a minute?" Grabbing his hand, she pulled him out to the front terrace.

Now that they were alone, Kate wasn't sure what to say to help calm his obvious nerves. She desperately wanted to help him. She watched as he tightened his tie and anxiously looked out at the view.

She stood behind him and put her hand on his back, rubbing the fine fabric of his suit jacket. "Marco, you've got this. I have every confidence in you. You're the leader of this corporation now, and you have done everything you can these last several months."

He turned to look at her, his face unreadable.

She continued trying to reach him. "Your family will be there supporting you. You're going to do great."

"What about you?" he asked coolly.

"Well, I'm not a shareholder, so I can't be there," quipped Kate.

Leaning up, she gave him a small kiss. He reached his hand behind her neck, under her heavy mane of hair. Marco deepened the kiss, taking his time. "Just as long as you are here when I get back," he said in a low growl.

She nodded, her eyes widening from the kiss. She gave him a hug, pressing her face against his fine linen shirt. She could hear the steady beat of his heart, and she wished they had more time together. She turned at the sudden movement, and together they watched the line of black sedans enter through the gate below, slowly making their way up the hill.

It looked like a funeral procession. She glanced at Marco, who was growing more tense, his back rigid, his hands flexing.

"We have to go. I am sorry you will be alone most of the day," he apologized stiffly.

"I'll be fine! It will take me a long time to get ready for tonight anyway." She hoped she sounded convincing.

His family began coming out the front door, talking loudly to announce their presence. Marco gave her one last steady look and kissed her hand, slowly letting go of it. Quickly, he ran down the stairs to join his family. They climbed into two black luxury sedans and departed, leaving Kate still standing on the terrace. She looked over at Max, who had been sleeping nearby. Now the dog was sitting, looking at her solemnly.

She exhaled a long breath. "I know, Max. I guess it's just you and me for the day."

THE TRUTH WAS, Kate didn't have much to do. She picked up her computer and began to write, but after trying for over an hour, she disgustedly shoved it aside. She made a small sandwich for lunch, finding she wasn't hungry. Now the afternoon dragged on. She was out on the terrace, absently petting Max, who sat beside her chair. They listened to the hum of the landscapers tending to the garden. She drank a glass of lemonade, wishing she had secretly put some kind of recording device in the boardroom. She was dying to know what was occurring.

She thought about going upstairs to rest, but she knew she wouldn't be able to relax. Plus, Maria was busy cleaning the upstairs levels. She had arrived just after lunch, excitedly showing Kate dozens of baby pictures on her phone. Kate had politely gushed over them, but her mind was elsewhere. Now she stayed on the terrace out of Maria's way, lost in thought. Kate was happy the whole family was together. They had looked united and determined when they had left, and she knew they would rally around Marco.

Suddenly, she felt an overwhelming amount of homesickness wash over her. She hadn't really thought much about home, rather than her texts with Teresa. Pulling out her phone, she realized she wanted to hear her father's voice.

"Hi, Dad."

"Katie, girl, there's my long lost half-Irish daughter," he said. He and her mother had always joked about it—she called her daughters half-Italian, and he would call them half-Irish. They used to tease about which part was which.

"Everything okay, pumpkin?

Kate winced. When Meara was born, she was long and thin like a zucchini and earned the name "zuki." Then Kate arrived as a round, chubby baby and was unfortunately nicknamed after a round squash.

"Yes, Daddy, everything is fine. I just have been really busy, and I know I haven't been great about checking in."

"That's okay, that's okay," he readily assured her. "Hey, my daughter is calling all the way from Italy," he shouted at the pub.

Kate looked at her watch. "Dad, it's not even eight a.m. Who is there?"

"What?" he shouted.

"Dad, go in the kitchen," she yelled.

She could hear the noise getting a little quieter as her father walked into the back. Now the background noise was plates and glasses clinking.

"I started offering breakfast," he told her cheerfully. "It's been a big hit. You'll see soon for yourself."

"That's great, Dad. But that means you're working even harder." She frowned, worried about him. He already seemed like he lived at the small Irish pub.

"That's okay, Katie. Keeps me out of mischief."

They talked for a few more minutes, but Kate could tell he wanted to get back to the pub. He insisted the call was costing her a fortune, not understanding that she had an international plan.

"It's fine, Dad. But I wanted to tell you I'm not sure yet when I'm coming home."

"Okay, pumpkin. Keep in touch," he added, distractedly. "Love you, honey."

"Bye, Daddy. I love you." Kate looked at her phone, frowning. She wasn't sure if he had even heard her as the line went dead.

Kate went back into the house. She would rest for a while and then get dressed. There was a cocktail hour before the long dinner. Margherita had warned her dinner would go on for hours. She slowly climbed the stairs and wondered what tonight would bring. She looked at her phone and wished she had reminded Marco to text her during a break.

MARCO TAPPED his water glass with his knife again. Finally, the noise in the room subsided. The morning's session had stretched on, and he had given everyone a longer break for lunch, admittedly because he was stalling. They had a lot of material to go through for the afternoon. Sal had not wanted him to present as much information as he was, but he had insisted.

"We can update the rest of this information later," the older man had argued tenaciously.

Marco was insistent. "No, I'm just putting it all out there once and for all."

Marco grabbed the remote, and the doors swung back on the giant screen. His assistant, Dominick, had traveled down to help him. Handing him the remote, Marco waited for the screen to light up with the afternoon's presentation.

Marco stood. Taking a sip of water, he walked near the screen and began to talk. He looked over at his mother, who gave him a discreet smile. The morning had been all the good news. Now he was going to present the bad news.

Standing tall and forcing his tired shoulders back, Marco discussed the lower earnings and the even worse forecasting. He continued to talk, despite frequent interruptions. Often, he had to call the meeting back to order. These older gentlemen warily watched him, clearly sizing him up. Stefano sat stared straight ahead, his face a stern mask that did not portray any emotions. Nico was busy making notes, but Marco suspected he was doodling. Lucca occasionally nodded, as if trying to encourage Marco.

Meanwhile, Sal sat staring at him, his lips pursed, his eyebrows together. Nervously, he glanced around the room and then his eyes would return to Marco, narrowing slightly.

When Marco got to the last slide, he began to breathe again. Whatever happens now, happens. He nodded to Dominick, who clicked the slideshow off.

Silence greeted him.

After a few seconds, a burst of Italian filled the room. Everyone was shouting questions. Two of his uncle's friends were red-faced, yelling at each other, then him. It was chaos. Marco put his hand through his hair. He looked over at his mother, who was not so subtly trying to tell him to get the room in order. He knew she could do it without even raising her voice. They would have no respect for him if he let her. Marco shouted over them to be quiet. One by one, he agreed to answer questions but only if they all remained calm.

Hours later, Marco was exhausted. The boardroom was empty except for his family. Sal had left abruptly to go "smooth things over." He was clearly upset. Marco's mother looked at him with gentle concern. "It could have gone worse," she soothed.

"No, Mamma. I don't think so. Admit it." He ran a hand through his hair as he paced the room. "They chewed me up and spit me out. Those old geezers want their money, and they won't stop until they get it," he said disgustedly. "There is no loyalty. There certainly is no patience."

"They gave you sixty days," Nico offered, trying to stay positive.

"Sixty days! *Dio*, what am I to do in sixty days?" shouted Marco, throwing up his arms. Taking a deep breath, he continued more calmly. "The family doesn't even have the majority any longer. Zio Angelo was insane—what was he thinking, giving some of his shares to Sal? He gave away the majority without telling all of us!"

"The last few years were very hard on him," Margherita said sadly. "I think his health was failing even then. Perhaps I should have done more."

"No, Mamma, all of us could have stepped in. I was too busy having a good time. I thought we would have more time with him. Just as I was ready, he became ill," he said bitterly. "Thank God at least Sal will vote with the family."

Margherita stared at him for a minute, looking like she wanted to say more. Giving her head a small shake, she stood up instead. "Let's go down to the house and change for the gala. We can't keep going around in circles. What's done is done."

Marco slumped down at the table. "You go ahead. I'm going to check in with Sal, and I'll be down in a few."

The family slowly left the room, glancing back at him. They knew he just wanted to be alone. "He needs time," Margherita reassured them quietly as they traveled to the house.

~

MARCO TOOK out his phone and stared at it for a minute. He knew he only wanted one thing. Pressing Kate's contact, he waited for her to pick up.

"Marco! I've been waiting—dying, in fact! How are you? What happened?"

Marco smiled sadly. It made him feel good that she asked about him first and not the corporation. "I'm alright, but it was a disaster," he told her flatly, mentally re-living the accusations some of the men had thrown at him. "I have sixty days to come back with better news and a plan or they will try to vote me out."

"But how..."

"I'll explain later," he interrupted. "I was just anxious to hear your voice and know you're okay."

"I'm fine. But Marco..."

"We'll talk about it tomorrow. Tonight will be better. I promise I will shake this mood off. I want tonight to be special with you. I'll see you soon," he said quietly before hanging up.

KATE HUNG UP THE PHONE, staring at it. Things were worse than she thought. She heard a soft knock on the door, and Margherita came in, looking like she had aged ten years since the morning.

"Oh, Rita, Marco just called me. It sounds like it didn't go very well. How can they vote him out?"

Margherita sighed and sank into a nearby chair. Looking at Kate sitting on her bed in her bathrobe, she said. "You haven't started to get ready yet?"

"I was just going to get in the shower. It won't take me long—believe me! Rita, tell me!"

The older woman began to talk, going over the high points first. She then explained the transfer of stock they had learned about recently.

Kate looked at her, stunned. "Marco never told me."

Margherita shrugged. "He discovered it quite by accident recently. He probably didn't want to burden you further. The good news is that I think Sal will vote however we tell him to, so there's nothing to worry regarding Marco's removal, but there will be consequences. The minority shareholders will not back down. They will make his life miserable until they get some better news."

Margherita nervously wrung her hands in her lap. "I stopped by because I wanted to tell you something. I hope you won't be upset. You can't sit with Marco tonight. I am so sorry!" She blurted.

"Oh well, that's okay." Kate nodded, trying to keep her face neutral. The family must have thought it best to put her in the cheap seats now, given the disastrous day. Lucca had mentioned the press photos of them last night, and it had brought back all the anxiety of what the board would think about Marco's judgment. She was a random American woman who would need some explanations.

"No, it's not okay, but there's nothing I can do." Margherita looked at her steadily. "There's a decades-old seating chart, and the table is set according to executive officers, shareholders and their guests. I am afraid I had to sit you farther down the table. But I tried to make up for it, readjusting a few people down with you."

"Margherita, I'll be fine," Kate rushed to reassure her. She knew Margherita would never hurt her on purpose. "We better get dressed." She smiled gently at Marco's mother.

Margherita looked clearly relieved. "I'll see you soon." She closed the door softly, not seeing the tears that now appeared in Kate's eyes.

twenty-four

K ate looked in the mirror one last time. She had taken a
long shower, her mind lost in thought. Using the luxurious Italian products, she admired how well they worked on her
skin.

She blew her hair dry next and then took the curling iron she
had found in the drawer. Curling her hair the way her hair stylist
had once shown her, she stopped to evaluate the results.

Kate added a bit more make-up than she normally wore. She
slipped on her dress next, careful not to get any makeup on it.
Sitting down in a chair, she put on her shoes, admiring them
again. They really were beautiful.

Kate went over to her travel organizer that was on the
dresser. She had only brought with her a few pieces of jewelry.
She didn't have a necklace that would work with the dress, so
she just wore her mother's small diamond hoops. She purposely
added the bracelet Marco had bought her from the street vendor.
She didn't care that it was an inexpensive piece of costume
jewelry—it brought a flood of memories that helped boost her
sagging spirits. She understood why she couldn't sit with Marco

but couldn't help feeling melancholy—it was supposed to be their night. That news on top of his disastrous day felt like an ominous cloud.

She gave herself one more nervous appraisal in the full-length wooden mirror that was propped over in the corner. She picked up her phone, checking the time. Teresa would be at work. She wished she could video call her and get her opinion. She needed some confidence right now, and her friend always knew what to say.

She then remembered Francesca had put her contact info in Kate's phone. "Who better than Francesca? Kate knew she definitely wouldn't mince words.

Francesca's beautiful face came on the screen, her blond hair pulled back. She had on a casual top and was on the waterfront walking.

"Kate! Tonight's the big night!"

"Allegra! Allegra!" Francesca yelled. "Hold on just a minute. Allegra is buying a gelato."

Kate laughed as Allegra soon appeared with a cone in her hand, and the two studied Kate, their heads pressed together.

"Hold the phone out," Allegra instructed.

"Okay, now put the phone up against something and back away." The two women studied her from every available angle.

"*Perfetto!*"

"You need lipstick, though," Allegra added, taking a bite of her gelato.

"I know! I'll put it on before I go." Kate promised. Truthfully, she was hoping Marco would kiss her when he saw her and the last thing he needed was lipstick smeared on him. The women chatted for a few more minutes, but Kate glanced at the clock and apologized that she had to go.

"*Buonasera.*" Kate waved happily at her new friends and ended the call.

Kate felt much better at their warm praise. She quickly added her lipstick to the pearl clutch Margherita had insisted on loaning her and descended the stairs.

Marco was standing in the expansive entry hall waiting for her. He had changed into an elegantly tailored dark gray suit, crisp white shirt, and a bright blue tie. The tie was almost exactly the same color as her dress. Kate wondered how in the world he had matched it so quickly. She smiled then—Margherita.

Marco was watching her walk down the stairs, and Kate stepped carefully. One misstep in these high heels and she knew she would roll down like a bowling ball, landing at his feet. The thought of her doing that made her almost giggle, and when she looked up, her eyes sparkled.

"*Bellissima*. Katie, you look so beautiful." He grinned widely at her. "I don't even want to touch you. I feel you will disappear if I do." He grabbed her hands, his head tilted.

"There's something missing. I can't put my finger on it." He put a finger up to his face in thought.

"I haven't put on my lipstick."

"No, no, it's not lipstick." Marco grinned.

"I know what it is. It's this." He reached for a velvet jewelry box he had placed on one of the entry hall tables. Kate stared at the box as if a snake was going to jump out at it. She looked warily up at Marco.

"Open it, Katie," he commanded softly.

Kate turned the gold handle on the black velvet box, and it sprang open. Inside was a stunning diamond necklace. The diamonds were in a rope, intricately woven and glinting brightly from their pure white satin nest.

"Marco," breathed Kate. "It's gorgeous."

"Turn around," he instructed. She looked at him again, her eyes wide. He returned her stare, stubbornly.

He took the box from her, taking the necklace out. She obediently turned around, still in shock. Picking up her hair, he easily clasped it. She could feel his breath on her neck, and she shivered at his closeness. She dropped her hair and went to the nearby mirror and swallowed the gasp. It was absolutely breathtaking. Marco came up from behind her, his heated gaze meeting hers in their reflection. She leaned against him, breathing in his cologne. The room was suddenly heady with intensity. Kate swallowed hard.

"We clean up pretty nice," she quipped. At Marco's startled confusion, she chuckled. "I'm sorry. I always make bad jokes when I'm nervous."

Kate fingered the necklace. Slowly, she met his eyes in the mirror. They looked at each other intently. "You know I can't accept this."

He shook his head. "You can and you will. Please, Katie. Give me this one opportunity. Accept this small present."

The precious gems twinkled back at her. She thought back to what he had told her about Gianna, and now she wondered if he thought he had to give her expensive gifts, too. She opened her mouth and closed it again. Finally, she said softly, "Marco, I know you're had a tough day, so I won't argue. We can talk about it later. For tonight, I'll wear it."

His eyes instantly lit up. He turned her around. Glancing down, his smile grew. Picking up her wrist, he fingered the bracelet. "My first gift to you," he murmured. "Such an inexpensive trinket, and yet you wear it tonight along with diamonds." He shook his head, smiling slightly.

She reached up and gave him a quick kiss. "It doesn't matter what it costs. It's from you. That's all I care about."

He gave her a long, searching look, smiling slightly. Finally, he gave her his arm. "Let's go, *cara*."

∾

"WHAT DO you mean she's not sitting with me?" Marco exploded at his mother.

"Shhhh," Kate shushed him, anxiously glancing around. They were sipping prosecco during the cocktail hour, moving through the crowd, greeting the guests. After Marco made introductions, the guests eyed her warily, but were polite, most asking her how her holiday was and what she thought of Italy. Kate was so enthusiastic about their country, and after a while, most smiled and told her stories about their respective towns or regions. Kate soaked it all in, smiling up at Marco.

It was their first outing as a real couple in front of people. It felt wonderful to hold on to Marco's arm, and she found it comforting when she looked up to find him smiling down at her. She felt confident about her dress, and from the gaze Marco was giving her, he liked the way she looked, too.

When they had first arrived, they posed for a few photos. Marco had explained they invited a couple of the more trusted reporters from financial papers to come to the gala, generating publicity for the corporation. She had felt shy initially, but his firm arm around her had given her confidence.

They continued to work the room when Margherita approached to tell Marco it was almost time for the dinner gong. The guests would leave the carefully decorated indoor lounge to go out to the formal dinner. She again apologized to Kate for the seating arrangement, and that's when Marco erupted.

"I told you where everyone was going to sit," Margherita reminded him gently.

"That was before I even met Kate. I thought things would have changed."

Margherita frowned, pointing to her ring finger. She spoke to Marco in Italian, something she usually refrained from doing out of politeness to Kate. Kate glanced away, sipping her prosecco. Marco had been very tense the moment they had arrived, and this wasn't helping. His mother obviously was trying her best to smooth things over. Finally, he turned to her, regret and almost sadness on his face. "Katie, I'm so sorry. There's nothing I can do. But Mamma says she has seated you next to Sal. You will enjoy speaking with him."

Kate nodded and let him escort her to the table outside. She gasped when they went through the wide doors leading to the outdoor venue area. Tables had been stretched together to accommodate the massive party. Above them, lemon trees were interwoven in a pergola, lemons hanging down among fairy lights. Round, clear lights hung down closer to the table, and green and white floral centerpieces in woven baskets had been placed all the way down the table. White linens and intricate white porcelain place settings sparkled, the freshly polished silver gleaming. Wineglasses glinted from the tea lights that were seemingly everywhere. Greenery in white Italian ceramic pots surrounded the table with even more fairy lights twinkling all around them.

Marco looked amused at Kate's reaction. He led her to her chair about halfway down the table where they found a place card with her name written in calligraphy.

Suddenly, Marco frowned, but Kate didn't see what he was looking at.

"I'll see you in a while." She squeezed his hand, longing to reach up and kiss his frown away. She smiled a little—that would certainly give the shareholders something to talk about. Seeing her smile, Marco returned it, albeit grudgingly. He helped her with her chair and went to the head of the table to take his place.

"*Buonasera, Signorina,*" said a silky voice. Kate turned to see a shorter older gentleman. His balding head was shiny, and his gray and white mustache twitched as he looked at her smugly.

A shiver she didn't recognize ran up her spine. She listened as he introduced himself as Sal, Angelo's oldest friend and now Marco's mentor, he boasted. He talked about himself at length without even taking a breath. He told her about how he managed the company when Angelo had gotten sick, and how he had been there all along, especially after Giacomo left. There was something about when he said Giacomo's name and later, Marco's—that made his upper lip almost curl.

Her eyes narrowed. "I'm sure you have been a big help to Marco."

Sal nodded, his face smug. "He is young. Too young for this responsibility, so I have helped. Unfortunately, the board has recognized his deficiencies as well."

Kate took a sip of her wine. He sounded almost happy about Marco's potential demise. She had imagined the man who Marco had waxed poetically about to be kind and thoughtful. Eyeing him, she let him continue, not interrupting. This was going to be the longest evening of her life.

"Well, well, well, look who won the lottery!" exclaimed a voice on her left. Kate turned to see Lucca sitting down next to her.

"You won the lottery because you get to sit next to me?" she asked sweetly.

"No, sweetheart. I meant you won the lottery because you get to sit next to me," came Lucca's arrogant reply.

Kate and Lucca laughed before he quickly looked across her.

"*Buonasera*, Sal," he nodded politely. Sal greeted him curtly and turned to the woman on his right to speak with her.

"He hates Americans," whispered Lucca conspiratorially. "I'm one almost by default now. Don't worry, he'll leave us alone."

Kate looked up and saw Marco gazing down toward her. She gave him a small smile and was rewarded with one in return.

As the first course came out, Lucca talked to Kate about his travels and his upcoming film. She listened as she ate the blood orange salad the waiter had set before her. Its tartness, along with black pepper and green onions, created flavors that burst in her mouth. The food kept coming. *Pasta alla Norma* followed, a penne pasta mixed with local ripe tomatoes, eggplant, basil and salted fresh ricotta.

Kate was already full when she was served the next course of a lemon granita to cleanse their palate, she was told. She dutifully ate, listening to Lucca, asking questions now and again. She knew he was trying hard to make her feel comfortable. She glanced up toward the head of the table several times, repeatedly seeing Marco's frown. She gave him a bright look before turning back to Lucca. She sensed he was unhappy with her. What did he expect her to do? Ignore his cousin?

Lucca was silly and mischievous, and during the next course of *entrecote di manzo*—a grilled steak accompanied by potatoes, he whispered to her tidbits about the various shareholders, doing impressions and making her stifle her giggles. He had a great sense of humor, and Kate was enjoying her time with him. She had long forgotten he was a famous movie star. She looked at him the same way she did Nico—an entertaining brother of sorts.

It was only when they were served the tiramisu that Sal turned back to Kate. "When are you returning to America, *Signorina?*"

"My name is Kate."

"Yes, Kate—you are headed home soon?" Sal's eyes were guarded, but she could see an underlying gleam.

Kate stared at him uneasily. She weighed telling him the truth that her time was coming to an end, but for some reason she wanted to make him squirm. "I may stay here indefinitely," she stated, eyeing him over the top of her wineglass.

Sal's eyes narrowed, and he was about to say something when Lucca interrupted.

"Kate, are you going to eat your tiramisu? If not, I will."

Kate playfully slapped him on his arm. "Touch that tiramisu, and your acting days will be over," she threatened, taking a big bite. Lucca laughed, stretching an arm over her shoulders.

~

DESPITE DESSERT BEING EATEN, dinner stretched on with fruit, nuts, and cheese. Moscato, amaro, and limoncello were served. Kate wanted to get up and walk around, but everyone seemed content to sit and converse. Sal attempted more questions, but Kate fended him off. She turned even more toward Lucca, hoping that her body language would infer to Sal that she really didn't want to talk anymore. Part of her worried about her behavior, knowing that Sal was so close to Marco. She couldn't explain what it was, but Sal gave her the creeps.

"Lucca, are you single?" she asked suddenly and then flushed. She really hadn't meant to ask that. Her mind had been on her texts with Teresa. Not wanting him to think she was prying, she added teasingly, "I might have a friend or two."

Lucca grinned at her mockingly. "I am definitely single," he said, his eyebrows waggling. "If you want to dump Marco, we can leave tonight."

She shook her head, giggling. "You are really something."

"My cousin looks like he wants to come down here and slug me," Lucca whispered. "I am having an extremely enjoyable time!"

Kate rolled her eyes. Marco had been scowling at them during most of the dinner. There was a rebellious side of her coming out. Maybe it was irrational annoyance from being sat halfway down the table from him. It could also be the wary glances from the shareholders or Sal's constant questions about her departure. She wasn't flirting with Lucca—he was her lifeline right now and she was seizing it.

Lucca whispered a few more things in her ear, most of them

naughtily describing some of the women's attire. Kate couldn't help but burst out laughing, shushing him.

"Dinner has concluded," Marco said quietly behind her. Kate shivered at the steel in his voice. She hadn't even noticed his approach. She turned apprehensively to see his calm face, but she knew him well enough now to see the shadow of anger in his eyes.

twenty-five

K ate stared steadily at Marco before nodding and standing. Lucca stood as well, and she thanked him profusely for being a wonderful dinner partner. Lucca's eyes filled with mischief. Reaching over, he gave her a big hug, kissing her on each cheek.

Kate untangled herself, and Marco grabbed her hand and led her back inside. An older couple hurried over as if they had been waiting for the opportunity, and Marco spoke with them abruptly in Italian. Kate felt their eyes on her speculatively, appraising her from head to toe.

It was only after she squeezed his hand that he glanced at her. Reluctantly, Marco introduced the couple. They nodded politely, asked her a few perfunctory questions about her stay, and then turned back to Marco. They resumed speaking in Italian, and this time, their conversation was clearly heated. Kate could feel even more tension creeping into Marco's body.

"Marco," Kate interrupted. "My headache is getting worse."

He turned to her, instantly concerned. "Katie, I had no idea. *Mi scusi.*" He explained her headache to them, quickly ushering her out. He opened her car door before running around to the driver's side.

"I didn't know about your headache."

She gave him a small smile. "My head is fine. I was just trying to get us out of there. Who were those people?" she asked, a feeling of dread coming on.

"Gianna's parents."

"Well, that was like the cherry on top of the evening, right?"

Marco nodded grimly. Starting the car, he began the drive toward the house. Kate snuck a look at him as he drove steadily down the winding path, saying nothing. Anxious to fill the silence, she discussed the dinner, the food, and the table. "I've never seen anything like it."

He murmured a few replies, and she grew silent. Was he mad at her? Really? She spent the better part of the night away from him. On the way out, she had to meet the people who would have been his in-laws. She shuddered, thinking how she was stared at, frowned upon, and felt like a fish out of water the whole night. If it hadn't been for Lucca, she would have had a horrible evening. Looking down at her lap, she thought back to the hope she had felt about their big evening together, and swallowed the lump that came to her throat.

Her thoughts were interrupted by Marco pulling roughly up to the house. Always the gentleman, he came over to help her out and escort her up the stairs.

"Let's stay outside," he suggested, pulling her around the wide terrace toward the back of the house. "The others will stay and make excuses so we can talk."

In another time, that promise would have normally thrilled Kate, but now, as she watched him rip off his tie and throw it along with his jacket on a nearby chair, she could tell he was upset. Kate nervously sat down, studying her hands. Marco flopped into another chair and watched her with narrowed eyes.

"And now you can tell me what you and Lucca were having so much fun about."

~

MARCO WAS TRYING to control his anger. He had spent the entire night watching his handsome, famous cousin make Kate laugh, whispering in her ear and putting his arm around her, stroking her shoulders.

He couldn't believe it when his mother had reminded him about the archaic seating chart. He had thought many times about this night. It was the bright light in his otherwise stress-filled and anxious days. Tonight was going to be about presenting Kate to his family and friends as an important person in his life. He knew they hadn't had a chance to decide what was going to happen next. She had said she wanted to go back home, but he was convinced he could persuade her to come back to make her life in Italy. Could he ask her to move to Italy if he could never bring himself to get married?

Seeing Gianna's parents tonight was indeed the finale to the evening. He grimaced, remembering how he wanted to tell them what he thought of them, especially after the information he had discovered over the last week. He frowned. That reminded him there were things he needed to speak to Kate about, but it seemed their timing was always off.

Marco's emotions were all over the place. He already knew he was being irrational, but he couldn't stop himself. He knew deep in his heart he never loved Gianna. Now, he wasn't sure he could love someone truly, as he thought back to Alfonso's parents, Enzo and Gina. Their love had been so bright, so strong.

Kate wasn't like Gianna, though. She was giving and humble, brilliant and funny. She lit up a room without even realizing it. He was drawn to her, but he purposely held himself back. He realized the woman of his thoughts was now looking at him like she wanted to murder him.

"You're seriously angry at me because I was having a good time? Lucca is funny. He made jokes, and I laughed. I couldn't sit with you, so I wasn't supposed to have a good evening, is that it?"

Marco continued staring, the muscle moving in his jaw. He had spent the whole dinner watching Lucca and Kate, their heads together. They had looked more like a couple than he and Kate did. Suddenly it came to him, that same feeling of humiliation—that he was losing a woman to another man again.

Kate stood and went to lean on the railing, her back to him, clearly upset. Getting up, he came over to her. He tried to take a few deep breaths to calm himself. Running his hands down her arms, he realized she was getting chilled. He grabbed his jacket and came back, putting it gently over her shoulders.

Marco spoke, his breath near her ear. "I wanted to do that ever since you came down the stairs. Katie, there's no back to this dress!" He spoke with mock severity. "It's been killing me."

Kate giggled a little, and Marco breathed a sigh of relief. Turning around in his arms, she looked up at him intently and he brushed his lips softly with hers.

"Forgive me? When I saw how much fun you were having with Lucca . . . I guess I wanted it to be me," he admitted, putting his forehead against hers. There was so much they needed to say.

She nestled into him, and he hoped it was a sign she was forgiving his behavior. He pulled back, looking at her inquisitively. "I guess I expected you to talk to Sal more."

Kate gently pulled out of his arms, adjusting his coat closer around her. Looking at him, she suddenly looked uneasy. "Marco, you said Sal was your uncle's best friend, right?"

Marco nodded. "Yes, and my father's too. They trusted him implicitly."

"Do *you* trust him?"

He looked at her, confused. "Of course, I do. I don't know

how I would have made it through these past months. He has done everything for me. I would be lost without him."

Kate turned and walked over to the table, her mind deep in thought. She sat down, drawing the coat even closer, almost protectively, avoiding his eyes. Finally, she spoke. "I got a really bad vibe from him."

His eyes narrowed as he walked back and sat down in a chair facing her. "A bad *vibe*?" He scoffed.

"Okay, maybe that's the wrong word," she admitted, looking at him now earnestly. "But I didn't like him. I'm not sure I trust him."

Marco waved his hand dismissively. "You spoke with him for how long tonight? How can you draw conclusions based on a small dinner?"

"I guess you can say my superpower has always been assessing someone's character. My parents always said that about me. I can sense things, and my instinct just tells me Sal is not sincerely looking out for you."

Marco shook his head in disbelief. Now wasn't the time to tell her that Sal was not her biggest fan, either. Despite never having met her, the older man had warned him this new alliance of his would not end well. Sal had talked about the effect of an unknown relationship with an American woman on their share-holders. He had pestered Marco all week, telling him that Kate was distracting him at a time he needed to focus. Marco had put it down to just fear of the unknown or possibly not wanting to see him humiliated again. He had been certain when Sal met Kate he would be charmed by her like his family was. He could tell by their body language tonight that it had been a disastrous first meeting.

She was looking at him, biting her lip. "Marco, we haven't had a chance to talk about what I found on the website."

He looked at her, astounded. "You want to talk about business now?"

Kate stared down at her hands. She then looked up with pleading eyes. "I know it's weird. But we just never seem to have any time. It's not about the website, but what I *found* on the website."

He looked at her questioningly, and so she continued talking quickly. "Webmasters often store older documents on the site in case someone needs them. Someone tells them to update a document, and so a webmaster will slide the old document into the administrator's section—so it's not public anymore. It's a common habit. Someone might want that document someday, or maybe there will be some reason to pull it back. So they just hide it and move on. I found all kinds of these old documents on the site—earnings and reports. I looked at some of them, and they don't make any sense."

He studied her with narrowed eyes, and said roughly, "I've seen all those. Sal and I have been going over those documents for months. But you're right, there's a lot of things that don't make sense."

"Marco, I wonder if Sal isn't being upfront about some things. Look, I'm not an expert in all this financial stuff, but I know what I saw. Things just don't seem to add up—I can't put my finger on it without knowing more."

He put a hand through his hair. "*Dio*, where is this coming from? I don't understand how you can meet a man for a few hours and then accuse him of somehow trying to sabotage me or worse."

Kate was still avoiding looking at him. She finally sat up, as if getting the strength to continue. "Maybe you should talk to your family. If you don't want to hear it from me, ask them what they think. In fact, you should talk to them about a lot of things," she blurted out.

He eyed her steadily, his eyes now becoming slits. "What does my family have to do with this? You've known them for what—ten days?"

Kate visibly swallowed hard. "You're right, I haven't known them for very long. That could be why they confide in me. I've heard how unhappy your brothers are in their positions. And your mother...well, she's tired. She might like this time for herself at her age."

He shook his head in disbelief. "To do what?"

Kate gave a slight shrug. "I don't know, travel, have adventures. Fall in love."

"Fall in love?" Marco shouted incredulously at her. "My mother is perfectly happy. She has always worked hard and believed in this company. And I would never let anything harm her! I have always protected her. Especially since my father left. Don't you think I'm doing all of this for them? I thought you, of all people, would understand that."

Marco walked back to the railing, turning his now rigid back to her. He looked out at the vista below. Finally, he spoke in a cold voice. "Kate, I'll have to ask you to mind your own business. I respect what you told me earlier about the website and how it needs to be updated, but now you need to leave the rest alone. You are saying things about Sal and now my family that are just not true."

She sat trembling and addressed his back. "You're right. I probably shouldn't have shared with you some confidences your family has trusted me with. I've spent a lot of time with Nico, very little with Stefano and, of course, your mother hasn't said a negative word to me. They were simply my observations," she added, sadly. "But...I will tell you one thing. And that is I do not trust Sal."

He turned around now, staring at her hard. "He doesn't like you either," he snapped. "No offense, Kate, but you've told me you're not well-versed in financial matters. I think you are out of your league. If your sister, Meara, was telling me this, I might think twice."

Shock, embarrassment, and finally anger washed over Kate.

She felt the blood rush from her face. Standing, she shook out her dress, taking his coat off and gently placed it back on his chair.

She looked at him now, her eyes glinting in the evening light, her tone dangerously quiet. "You're right. You are with the wrong woman."

THE NEXT MORNING Kate stared at her clothes hanging neatly in the walk-in closet. Maria had laundered all her clothes since she had been here, dutifully pressing everything so it looked brand new. She looked down at the crumbled blue dress she had thrown on the floor in a temper last night. She kicked it now with her barefoot, feeling the mortification that had cut her so deeply last night.

She considered her other clothes. What does one wear post-fight? Not choosing anything, she walked out of the closet and sat down on the bed, lost in thought.

Last night, she had left Marco on the terrace after his outburst. He hadn't even tried to stop her. She had taken a hot shower, scrubbed what was left of her makeup off, and dropped into bed. Surprisingly, she had fallen into a deep, dreamless sleep. Today, her face, white and puffy, stared back at her in the mirror.

Kate reached up to rub her temples. Comparing her to Meara had felt like a physical slap. Words had simply left her body. She knew she needed time and distance. Could it be that their relationship had simply run its course? The Marco of last night was not the man she had come to know. She felt out of her depth suddenly. He had been right—this world was not one she was used to living in.

Tears filled her eyes. Would there be a time someone didn't compare her to Meara? For Marco to do so was the last straw.

Worse yet, Kate had woken up to a barrage of texts from her sister—all of which she couldn't even bear to look at right now.

She bit her lip and wondered what she should do next. The thought of facing him this morning filled her with anxiety—especially with his family around. She didn't know what time they had returned from the gala. She hoped with her whole heart they had not been there to hear her discussing them with Marco. She knew it was none of her business. She had simply grown fond of them and wanted them to be happy.

Kate needed time to sort everything out in her head. The past few weeks were a heady mix of excitement, happiness, and stress. Last night, she probably shouldn't have brought up any of it, especially Sal. She knew it was tough for Marco to hear negative things about a man he considered a cherished adviser. She had felt so strongly, though, and she trusted Marco as someone who respected her opinions—heck, he kept telling her he did. She had been wrong. He had blown off her feelings about Sal, using a condescending tone as if she was a naïve little girl.

She dressed slowly, finally choosing her white jeans again, and a casual green top. Hoping the whole family was sleeping in, she crept down the stairs and found Maria busily wiping the marble counters.

After Kate's greeting, Maria told her the family had to go to the boardroom again. Marco had called an emergency meeting of the majority shareholders to *strategize*, she told her, taking considerable time to sort out the word. Kate nodded, relief washing over her. She went to the cappuccino machine. There was no note. That spoke volumes.

She sat down absentmindedly at the table without making one. Maria brought her a piece of the frittata that had been sitting on the island.

"Stefano got up early this morning to make this." She patted Kate's arm, leaving her in the kitchen by herself. Kate picked up her fork slowly and took a bite. It was delicious, but she pushed it away. Her stomach was in knots, and her head was swirling.

The doorbell rang, and Kate wondered if Maria was going to answer it. She could hear the vacuum going somewhere in the house and doubted she had heard the bell. Kate walked to the massive mahogany front door, pulling it open, expecting it to be Sergio or one of the staff. Instead, standing at the door looking ready to do battle, was her sister.

twenty-six

Meara stood on the terrace, dressed in a dark blue skirt and jacket, staring at Kate with flashing eyes, her body tense.

"Let me in, Katie. We need to talk." Meara pushed past Kate, walking into the entryway, her high-heeled sandals clicking on the wood floor.

Kate closed the door. Leaning her head against it, she sighed. She had wondered if the last twenty-four hours could get any worse. Now she had her answer. Meara was standing there, assessing her with raised eyebrows. Kate turned and gave her sister a quick kiss and a stilted hug—their usual greeting.

"You didn't answer any of my texts."

Kate looked chagrined for a second. "I'm sorry. It's been busy."

"I know. I saw the photos." Meara shook her head in disbelief. Glancing around, she asked, "Is there somewhere private we can talk?"

Kate shrugged. "It's all private. We are the only ones home, except the housekeeper. Emergency board meeting."

Meara looked relieved. "Good."

Kate ushered her sister into the kitchen. "Cappuccino?"

At Meara's nod, Kate made her sister a cup and one for herself as well, giving her time to get her thoughts together. She carried them over to the table, and they stared at one another.

Meara took a sip. "Wow, that's really good."

"I don't think you came all this way to try my cappuccino," Kate said dryly.

For once, the ever-confident Meara seemed uneasy. "Fine, let's cut to the chase. You know I've been against this relationship from the start."

Kate opened her mouth. Despite being angry with Marco, she was not going to let her sister disparage his reputation. He had treated her with nothing but respect and kindness—except last night, that is. She almost tasted the bitterness in her mouth. Worse yet, she couldn't even tell her sister why she was angry with him. "He's not who you think he is."

Sighing, Meara reached into her purse. "I didn't want to have to do this, Katie. Please believe me." She slid a few pieces of paper over to Kate, her eyes almost looking at her with pity.

Kate stared at the pages warily. Taking a breath, she unfolded them. Photos of Marco stared up at her. Except Marco wasn't alone. He and Gianna were at an outdoor café. In one shot, they were talking earnestly. In the other, they were laughing. Kate looked at the next page. This one was even worse—the photographer caught them deep in conversation, their heads were close as they looked at something on his phone.

Kate felt a giant lump in her throat. She looked up at her sister, tears forming in her eyes. "How . . .?"

Meara grimaced. "Private investigator, of course. I had Marco followed when I learned he was with you. Most of the time, he was at home and then back at the office in Milan. Then last week he traveled to Rome, and that is what he was doing." She indicated the photos.

Kate felt numb. She hadn't even known he was in Rome.

During their nightly phone calls, he had not said a word about it. She couldn't believe it, but the proof was right in front of her.

Meara eyed her steadily. "My car is waiting. Come with me to Rome, Katie. I'm working in Italy for a bit. You can stay at my corporate apartment there as long as you want." Meara ran a hand behind her neck, looking down at her cappuccino. "I know we have our problems, but I did what I thought was right. I didn't want to see my baby sister hurt—not again."

Kate grimaced. Despite how close they were in age, Meara always referred to her that way. Meara trying to control her life had always been their constant issue. This time, Kate didn't feel rebellious. She looked at her sister, eyeing her warily, and she suddenly felt gratitude.

"I'll go pack."

KATE RAN AROUND HER ROOM, gathering her small number of belongings. It would be awful if she forgot something. She could hardly call Marco and tell him to send it on. She yanked her suitcase from the walk-in closet and opened it, grabbing clothes from the hangers and the dresser drawers. As she bent to put the clothes in the suitcase, she saw Marco's NERD sweatshirt. She had totally forgotten about taking it from the yacht. She fingered it for a minute and, after making a quick decision, she piled her clothes on top of it.

Grabbing her makeup bag and her toiletries from the bathroom, she swept them in her case. She took her computer and placed it on top before shutting her bag. With everything packed, Kate glanced around one more time at the beautiful room. As she went down the hallway, Maria came out of a bedroom, duster in hand, and immediately saw her suitcase. "*Signorina* Kate, where are you going?"

Kate impulsively hugged the older woman. "Maria, you never told me what your granddaughter's name ended up being."

Maria smiled, a proud look in her eyes. She got out her phone, swiping to show Kate a photo. "Katarina," she proclaimed. "I had told my daughter about the nice American girl with *Signor* Marco, and she liked the name."

Kate felt the odd tug on her heart and hugged her one more time. "*Grazie*. Thank you for everything, Maria. My sister just arrived, and I am going with her." Before Maria could ask any more questions, Kate picked up her suitcase and ran down the stairs.

Meara was now in the entry hall, looking around. "Some house," was all she had to say.

Kate nodded absentmindedly and told her she would be out in a minute. Meara grabbed the suitcase almost as if she were afraid Kate would change her mind.

Kate went to the back of the house and into the luxurious office Marco had shown her when she had arrived. He had told her she could work there if she wanted. The big masculine desk dominated the room, and a leather sofa and matching chairs were positioned nearby. Kate had never worked in there, finding it too distracting to be surrounded by Marco's things. She sat down at the desk now and grabbed a notepad and pen. She quickly wrote a note to Margherita, thanking her for her hospitality. She explained her sister had arrived and wanted her to travel with her. It was too good of an opportunity to miss to spend time with her. She put the note in the envelope and then carefully wrote Margherita's name on it. Opening drawers, she found a larger envelope and wrote Marco's name. She deposited the thumb drive she had made of all the hidden files on the website. Reaching into her pocket, she carefully pulled out the diamond necklace, staring at it. She did not know what Marco had done with the box, so she just slipped it into the envelope as well. She looked at the crumbled photos

Meara had brought with her and shoved them in before sealing it.

Kate sat and looked at it. Was she being too dramatic? She didn't know anymore. She just knew she wanted to go. Suddenly very fatigued, she forced herself to get up. She laid the envelopes on the entry hall table in front of the mirror she and Marco had admired themselves in. It was less than twenty-four hours ago. How had things turned upside down so quickly?

She took one last glance around the beautiful home and closed the door gently. A big black luxury SUV was waiting with the engine running. Kate felt relief when she jumped in the back where Meara was waiting, and the driver pulled away. Her heart was beating out of her chest. She hadn't been sure what she would say to Marco if he appeared before she left. She just had no words.

The car headed out of the big wrought-iron gates that were now open for visitors to the lemon grove. It wasn't until they approached the highway and took on speed that Kate felt like she could breathe. She saw signs for Positano and considered telling Meara to have the driver drop her off there. She knew with a heavy heart that it wouldn't be the same. Her beloved Positano with her new friends would not bring her the same joy. Besides, someone would tell Marco, and he might come to find her. He would probably feel obligated to explain that he and Gianna were back together. She couldn't bear that one last talk with him when he would ultimately say goodbye and that it had been fun or something similarly trite.

Kate dug in her purse for her sunglasses and found a vial. Pulling it out, she saw the motion sickness tablets Marco had given her. She sat staring at the vial and memories flooded through her. How could a medicine container make you suddenly realize how much in love you were? Katie choked back a sob. She was head over heels for this man. She had played it down even in her own mind, almost knowing from the first it would not end well. Kate felt the pain of a million tiny needles attacking her heart. She had never suffered from panic attacks, but she felt like she was having one now. She struggled to breathe.

Meara had opened her tablet and began working. "Are you feeling sick, Katie?" She pointed at the medicine. "There's water in the cooler over there.

Kate simply nodded but put the vial back in her purse. Better for Meara to think she was just getting sick and not that her heart was breaking in two. She closed her eyes, pretending to sleep to avoid her sister's prying eyes.

The trip to Rome took no time at all. Kate actually did sleep for a time, the smooth car soothing her. When she woke she was surprised to see them gliding up to a hotel. Meara explained the top floor was an apartment her company kept for the executives. Kate nodded, uncaring. All she wanted to do was fall into bed. She had turned off her phone when she had gotten in the car and decided not to turn it back on until at least tomorrow. She needed a break.

They walked through the lobby and headed for the elevators. Meara used her keycard and they ascended to the penthouse apartment which opened to an expansive living area.

Meara asked her if she wanted anything to eat, and Kate shook her head, her stomach in knots. She told her sister she just wanted to go take a shower and rest. Meara nodded again, eyeing her closely. "Katie, I did the right thing."

Kate looked at her sister and impulsively hugged her. It was then the sobs overtook her. After a minute, Meara's arms came around her, and she held her.

twenty-seven

Marco hauled himself out of his infinity pool at his villa on the hilltop of Positano. Drying off, he sat on a nearby chaise, looking at the town at his feet. He felt like a caged animal, and the long swim had helped. He breathed in the quiet, having dismissed the household staff in his desire to be alone with his thoughts.

He had never been more furious in his life than when he came home to discover Kate's note. Not even a note, he realized bitterly, but an envelope. She hadn't even had the decency to write anything to him. When he saw the photos of him and Gianna, he had winced. His anger then turned to himself. He knew right from the start he should have been honest with Kate about it. He had kept it to himself, thinking it was better to have the conversation in person. Deep down, he knew he had stalled, wanting to make sure they were on solid footing. He had intended on telling her when he returned, but one thing happened after the other—Lucca, the gala and then their fight. Still, it hurt that she simply left without even giving him a chance to explain. He deserved that, at the very least.

Marco got up slowly, walking back into his house. Getting a bottle of water out of his massive refrigerator, he glanced at a counter, spotting the jewelry box with Kate's necklace in it. He had taken it out of his briefcase to put in his safe but then had simply left it lying there. Now it chastised him as well—a reminder of what he had lost. He couldn't return it, nor could he ever see another woman wear it. He had it designed by his private jeweler and had traveled to Rome to pick it up so he could ensure it was exactly as he wanted. He had been so excited to give it to her. Instead, she had looked more alarmed than appreciative. That was the problem, he realized. He didn't have a clue how to reach her. He had thought giving her presents would prove he was serious about her.

When the family had returned to the house late that morning, Maria had run down the stairs as fast as her short legs would allow to say Kate had gone. He had instantly sprinted up to her room to see for himself, completely in disbelief. It was only after his mother read Kate's note that said she left with her sister that it hit him. "She doesn't even want to be around her sister," he shouted.

His brothers and Lucca had quickly disappeared, leaving a disappointed Margherita to try to talk with him. He had shrugged off his mother's attention, wanting to be alone, and soon left for his villa. He needed to get away from everyone's looks of pity. Poor Marco, they probably thought. Once again, a woman left him.

He looked out the floor-to-ceiling window at the winding streets and the colorful houses. Dozens of memories were exploding in his head—he and Kate toasting with their pizza, buying her the sandals, eating their gelato, her face watching the festa—the memories he now held close to his heart.

Marco leaned his forehead against the glass. He had acknowledged he was deeply in love with Kate. He realized he had been all along. He had acted like a besotted teenager, inventing reasons to keep her close. He knew the reporters would have left her alone after getting the initial information about her, but he purposely wanted to keep her at the lemon grove and near him and his family. Yet, despite everything, he had intentionally held back. He hadn't wanted to analyze his feelings. Why else did he want her to move to Italy? What an idiot he was! He had offered her a job. A job. Who does that? Apparently, he did, he grimaced.

When he had flung her sister's financial prowess at her after the gala, he had instantly wanted to take it back. He didn't want to hurt Kate for the world, but somehow the pressure of the entire last few weeks rolled up with her upsetting words about Sal brought up old wounds from the past. He felt stupid and not good enough.

Despite their trading of secrets, he hadn't told her one of the biggest ones to affect his life, and now he probably never would. Marco had not only had a hard time in school as he had told her. He had been virtually illiterate for several years. Growing up in a country school on the Amalfi Coast, no one had thought about learning disabilities. First his father and then his uncle reproached him to work harder. His mother had gently coached him, trying to help him with his homework. After his father had left, Margherita had hired many tutors. All quit because they couldn't deal with the angry young man. It was only as he got older that it was finally discovered by a young teacher that he not only needed glasses but had a vision disorder. He had worked with a specialist on exercises to train his eyes to track properly. Some days, when his eyes were tired, he still struggled. Ultimately, his grades improved, but only after Marco spent the next several years doing nothing but studying. He had worked hard at University and was thrilled when he was accepted to Stanford. He didn't tell Kate that's why Stanford meant so much to him. It was the pinnacle of all his work. It was the first time in his life he felt smart and successful.

In a moment of clarity, Marco now realized all of his feelings of insecurity from his youth had resurfaced over the last few months. In his new role, he fought daily against the humiliation that washed over him, suggesting he wasn't smart enough for the job.

Pulling out his phone, he checked it for the hundredth time. He had tried calling Kate almost immediately when he got back to the house. When it had gone directly to voicemail, he realized she probably turned her phone off. Last night, after a few glasses of whiskey, he had sent dozens of texts. Probably not the smartest thing, but he was desperate to see her, talk with her. Kate had told his mother she was traveling with Meara. Was there a possibility they were still in Italy?

Marco knew he should return to Milan, but Positano made him feel close to her again. The sixty-day deadline the shareholders imposed was like a giant clock ticking, but he acknowledged he needed time to get himself together. He hadn't even taken any time to grieve for his uncle, and now he had lost Kate. Marco sat down in a nearby chair and scrolled through the photos he had taken—all their silly selfies. He smiled, his finger touching his phone, as if he could stroke her face. Squaring his shoulders, he knew he had to get a hold of himself. He would try to find her.

Several phone calls later, Marco was no closer to finding her than he was when he started. He had called Francesca, who had checked with Allegra. Neither had heard from her since the night of the gala. He called Alfonso on the off chance she might have called to say goodbye. They all seemed confused why he wouldn't know where she was. He told them very little, only that she was traveling with her sister.

Marco decided to call the private investigator firm his company used. Obviously, that's how Meara had been able to get those ridiculous photos taken of him and Gianna. He stopped himself before hitting the button. What if he found her, and she still didn't want to see him? It had to be on her terms. Or did it?

He went back to his texts. They had been delivered. He had no idea when Kate would read them. He squared his shoulders and started sending new ones.

twenty-eight

Kate sat back in her chair, completely stuffed. She couldn't believe how much breakfast she ordered and then proceeded to eat it all. She was sure the young man who brought it up thought the breakfast was for two. She had impulsively ordered three cappuccinos as well.

She sighed. Was it bad she had devoured everything when she was heartbroken? Weren't people supposed to waste away to nothing when they suffered from heartache?

She sat staring at Rome, literally at her feet. She hadn't noticed last night in all her misery the breathtaking view from the apartment. Opening the door, she went out to the balcony, gazing at the dome of St. Peter's sitting majestically in the distance.

She had woken up to a note from Meara with instructions on how to order room service and her driver's phone number, in case Kate wanted to go anywhere. Meara had suggested a few places for her to start her sightseeing and said she had a late meeting and probably wouldn't be home until after dinner.

Kate wanted to see some of Rome, but she knew she had to do something first. She opened her computer to search for the photos of the gala. Sure enough, there was the photo of her and Marco posing. Kate tried to take a step back and look at them clinically. She loved that gown, and she had to admit the necklace *was* breathtaking. One photographer had captured her looking up at Marco like a lovesick teenager. Well, who wouldn't? The man was drop-dead gorgeous. Even in the photos, he radiated charm and sexiness.

They looked happy—that one moment frozen in time. Kate stared at it for a few minutes, willing herself to hate him, but she couldn't. She couldn't let the unhappiness taint this memory that was so special to her. She had thought he'd come to care about her. He'd said he had. Did he change his mind after seeing Gianna and then just faked it for the gala? Was that what he was telling Gianna's parents when they confronted him?

Kate leaned her head back against the sofa cushion. She dug her phone out of her pocket and hit the power button. She watched as the missed calls and messages started stacking up. At a glance, she saw she had ones from Marco, Margherita and Teresa. She read Teresa's first.

How's Mr. Hunky?

Katie, I saw the photos. Oh my God, you look so beautiful and so happy.

Katie, are you okay? Have you eloped? Don't I get to be a bridesmaid?

Okay, now you're worrying me.

I'm coming over if you don't answer me! I'm getting on a plane! Hello?

Kate glanced at the time. Teresa was probably at work, but she didn't want her to worry anymore.

I'm sorry. Phone was off. Long story, but I'm okay. I'll be coming home soon, and I'll tell you all about it.

Kate's phone rang, and she jumped but wasn't surprised to see Teresa's photo.

"You're not getting out of this with just a text. What is happening? Where is Mr. Hunky, and what are you doing?"

Kate swallowed the lump in her throat. "Oh, Teresa. It's a mess."

"Do you want to tell me about it?"

Kate let out a deep breath. All the pent-up emotions of the last two days seemed to overwhelm her. "I want to tell you everything, but do you mind if we wait for a few days? I'm so tired, and I just can't even talk about it right now."

"Are you coming home soon?"

"I think so," Kate answered tentatively. "I may stay in Rome and try to write. Only, I'm not sure how much I can really focus. It might be easier to get out of this country so I can forget him."

"Do you think you can?"

"No," Kate admitted softly.

"You should at least get out and see something," her ever-practical friend pointed out.

Kate agreed and promised to keep in touch. Hanging up, she sat and stared at her phone. She wasn't up to reading the messages from Marco or Margherita yet. She was very curious what Marco had to say, but at the same time, reading his words of an apology or the news he was back with Gianna would be too painful. Picking up her purse, she grabbed the key card Meara had reminded her to carry and headed out.

THE DAYS UNFOLDED the same way for Kate. Meara left before she even got up and came home as Kate was getting ready for bed. They barely had an opportunity for a conversation.

Kate had taken a tour of St. Peter's on her first day. She sat alone on a bench against the wall in the Sistine Chapel, oblivious to the surrounding crowds. She stared up at the vivid colors on the ceiling in wonder and somehow found peace in the tremendous artistry. Finally, she had left, wandering slowly down to the Trastevere neighborhood, known for its restaurants and shops. She stopped to have a delicious piece of goat cheese and artichoke pizza.

Pizza.

How can a food even remind you of a person? He's even ruined pizza for me, Kate thought glumly, staring at the piece on her plate. Forcing herself to keep busy, she walked the streets. Crossing the bridge, she wound through the Jewish Ghetto, taking in the scenery, the food stalls, and the people enjoying themselves.

The next day, she toured the Colosseum but felt alone in its vastness. She tried to listen to the tour guide who described its history so intensely. Kate found her mind wandering and trailed behind the tour group. Later, she stopped at the Trevi Fountain, watching the people jostle each other to throw a coin over their shoulder in the clear water. She sat alone, with people all around her, never feeling so lonely in her life. Families posed for photos, couples shared gelato.

Gelato.

Kate sighed. There he was again.

Despite those small reminders, Kate felt better wandering the streets of Rome, watching the visitors enjoying the city, chic women balancing the cobblestones on their high heels and young drivers riding motorbikes haphazardly in the streets. It was a large, busy city, and Kate took her time, seeing bits and pieces, her nose buried in a guidebook she had bought, teaching herself the history of the many landmarks.

She had answered Margherita's text, which simply asked if she was alright. Kate told her she wasn't, but she would be someday. Margherita simply answered with a heart emoji.

Kate still hadn't read Marco's texts. Every day, she received more. She swiped them away and moved on, too miserable and depressed to think clearly.

After grabbing a quick lunch, Kate walked back to what had become a familiar spot in front of the Pantheon. Its piazza was always busy with tourists dining at nearby restaurants and visitors sitting on the stairs of the Pantheon or its neighboring fountain. A few tourists approached Kate with their phones out to take their photo. As she was handing a phone back to a mother, she saw a man clad in a dark suit, strolling through the piazza in the distance. Marco! Before she could stop herself, she ran toward him, not knowing what she was going to say once she reached him. Her heart hammered against her chest. She couldn't stop herself—she had to get to him. Suddenly he stopped, waiting for a woman to join him. As Kate got closer, she realized with crushing disappointment that he wasn't Marco. In fact, he barely resembled him except for his similar sunglasses. She was truly losing her mind.

Walking slowly back to the Pantheon, she sat down at the fountain. If that *had* been Marco, what would she have even said? She opened her phone and took a deep breath. It was time to read his texts. She needed closure. She would just read the bad news and respond so he would stop texting her.

Ten minutes later, Kate sat back, holding her phone, tears rolling down her cheeks. His texts ranged from long apologies to frustration to sadness. He told her he had a good explanation for the photos of him and Gianna. He asked her to contact him. The last text was simple.

"*Per favore, Katie!*"

Despite still being angry about their fight, Kate realized she believed him. She didn't know why he met Gianna, but she knew for certain it was innocent. No matter what their differences, Marco wouldn't cheat on her. The clarity of that hit her like a ton of bricks. How stupid she was to immediately assume the worst. She was feeling so low about herself after his comparison to Meara, she had instantly accepted the photos as proof of something nefarious. Kate felt an overwhelming sense of remorse.

She should have stayed and found out the truth instead of running off. She realized then she had always trusted him. She had seized the opportunity to leave when it was presented because ultimately, she had felt out of her depth and his comments the night before had deeply stung. Kate grimaced. To believe the worst had given her an easy out, and she willingly ran.

Kate's finger hovered over his name. She would call him. She wasn't sure what she would say, but she would figure it out when she heard his deep voice.

Before she could hit the call button, Meara's photo appeared on her phone. "Hey, Meara," she answered, looking around humorously paranoid. Did her sister have cameras following her now? Had Meara known how close she was to calling Marco?

"Kate, thank God you answered. Where are you?"

"I'm in front of the Pantheon, near the apartment."

"Get back to the apartment as soon as you can. I'm in the car, and I don't have time to send a driver for you."

Kate had never heard her sister so frantic. Her heart beat faster. "Meara, what is it?"

"Dad's had a heart attack. I've got the corporate jet fueling up. Get packed, and we will leave right away. Katie, it's bad," she added, almost with a sob.

Later, Kate had no idea how she navigated the narrow cobblestone streets, but she ran back in record time, packed, helped Meara pack and they were in the car within minutes. The jet was waiting, and they took off with no delay. Now that they were in the air, Kate tried to sleep, but she was anxious. She longed to hear Marco's voice, to have him reassure her that everything would be okay. She opened her phone and began reading his texts again. Would he even want to talk to her now? She had ignored him for so long.

Meara looked up from her computer, raising her eyebrows. "Who are you texting?"

"Uh, no one. Just thinking of texting Teresa." Kate flushed. "I'll see if she can go find out what's happening."

Teresa was a nurse at the hospital their father had been transported to. Kate hoped she might be able to go check on him.

Kate texted Teresa all the information they had. One of their father's employees had called Meara. They had been getting ready for the breakfast customers when their father had complained of chest pain. By the time paramedics arrived, he had collapsed on the floor and was unresponsive. Meara had called the hospital and bullied her way to speak to the doctor who was assigned his case. He confirmed their father was in the Intensive Care Unit after suffering a heart attack and they were running tests.

Knowing Teresa would answer her when she could, Kate shoved her phone in her pocket and closed her eyes. It seemed like a lifetime ago she was at the lemon grove. She wished with her whole heart she was there now.

twenty-nine

"I'm telling you girls, everyone is overreacting," blustered Finn Malone.

Both Meara and Kate looked at each other. They had arrived in the evening and had gone straight to the hospital. Their once big and loud Irish father looked frail in bed. His face was a disturbing gray, and he was on oxygen while a heart monitor silently recorded his rhythm.

Meara now interrupted their father's rant. "Daddy, of course we would come home. And it didn't cost a cent. We took the corporate jet."

"Ahhh, hear that, pumpkin? Your sister is big time with her own jet."

Kate tried not to grimace. "Yes, I know. I was on it."

Meara laughed. "Dad, it's not my jet. I'm just fortunate the company lets me use it."

To Kate's relief, the subject was dropped, and her father was busy asking about her trip. She gave him some highlights without drawing attention to Marco. Kate didn't want to go into the "Marco situation," as Meara referred to it on the way home.

"You're going to get your novel written now, Katie," Finn

assured her, covering her hand which was resting near his on the bed.

The doctor had been in to explain that Finn's heart attack had not done significant damage, but he needed double bypass surgery and they had scheduled it for the next day. Meara took the lead as always, drilling the doctor with rapid-fire questions. Kate watched her sister with a sense of awe—relieved that she asked the tough questions.

Finn's eyes closed and the girls quickly kissed him and left, promising to see him before surgery. Walking out of the hospital into the evening air, Kate took big gulps. The medical smells of hospitals always bothered her since her mother's illness—the fresh air felt great.

"I can't wait to take a shower," Meara said, as they got into the car where her driver was waiting for them. "We'll drop you off and then swing by in the morning." She yawned.

Kate nodded. Right now, all she wanted to do was see her apartment again and rest.

"IT'S WORSE THAN I THOUGHT." Teresa sighed as she dropped her bag in the chair near the front door.

Kate looked up guiltily from the couch, her spoon paused over a pint of ice cream. On the coffee table in front of her was another pint, a big bag of nacho cheese tortilla chips, and a box of red vines. Kate hadn't felt like ordering anything from a restaurant, and she had no food in the apartment. She remembered her last meal had been at the café in Rome—a lifetime ago to her stomach. Kate hadn't been able to touch the food on the plane, but Meara had eaten her meal just fine, admonishing Kate about needing her strength. Kate had just shaken her head in horror, finally popping one of the motion sickness pills Marco had given her.

When she got home, she suddenly felt starved and rummaged around. Wearing her sweats and Marco's NERD sweatshirt, she was now indulging in what she felt was a perfect meal.

Kate jumped up, plopping her ice cream down. She hugged her best friend fiercely. "Oh my God, I've missed you!"

Teresa smiled and gave her friend another quick hug before flopping into a chair opposite her. She still had her scrubs on, her short, dark curly hair flattened against her head, her curls sagging.

Kate sat down and grabbed her peanut-butter-and-chocolate ice cream, taking a big spoonful. "Hmmm, this tastes amazing."

Teresa laughed. "Didn't you just come from the Land of Gelato?"

"Well, yeah, but I needed some good ol' American junk food. Sorry I robbed your stash. I'll restock it when I can."

Teresa shrugged. "I don't care. I'm just so happy to see you. It feels like it's been forever."

Kate licked her spoon, eyeing her friend. "Long day?"

Teresa nodded. She was an obstetrics nurse, and Kate was so proud of her. She knew her friend was a skilled nurse who worked hard for the soon-to-be mothers. "Yeah, long day. I'll tell you later. Hey, sorry about your dad. I checked to see who his doctor is. He has the best cardiac surgeon in the hospital. And double bypasses are really common. I'm sure he'll be fine."

Kate thanked her friend, pushing aside her nervousness.

"So not to bring up a potentially bad subject, but is tonight's smorgasbord because of your dad or Mr. Hunky?" Teresa asked, eyeing her friend.

"I have so much to tell you," Kate said with a sigh.

Teresa grinned widely. "I have been waiting and waiting. Let me change and we'll talk." She got up and headed to her bedroom. "Save some ice cream for me," she called.

TWO HOURS LATER, Kate eyed her friend. Both cartons of ice cream gone and the chip bag empty, Kate put a hand to her stomach. "Now I feel sick."

"You're just out of junk food shape," said Teresa matter of flatly, opening the box of red vines. "You probably ate too much healthy stuff in Italy."

For a nurse, Teresa had a remarkable affection for junk food, always keeping a drawer devoted to it. She was great about working out, but not so good when it came to eating fruits and vegetables. Growing up as one of six kids and a working mother, Teresa had told Kate, though her mother tried, it was difficult to buy fresh produce and healthy food. She had grown up eating processed food and declared her junk food diet was part of her DNA.

"Thanks for listening to me." Kate stretched, acknowledging she had done most of the talking. "I honestly don't know what I would do without you."

Teresa chuckled. "Besties for as long as I can remember. I'm not about to leave you alone now! Besides, I keep telling you I'm living vicariously through you. I haven't had a date in ages. So now that you believe Mr. Hunky wasn't cheating on you, what are you going to do?"

Kate sighed tiredly. "I don't know. In the end, things are still weird. I didn't trust him, and he didn't trust me."

"Hmmm..." Teresa was deep in thought, before waving a red vine in the air to make a point. "If you want the truth, my guess is it's the Meara comment that really got you."

Kate nodded, looking down at her nails. She knew Teresa was right.

Teresa continued. "Sure, I get it. That was a low blow. But Katie, you've always been weird about your sister. I mean, at some point you have to get over that whole thing about Jacob the

Jerk. I honestly don't think that was her fault, and I know you don't either. You just can't get past feeling inferior to her. I don't get it. You're beautiful, and you work hard. You have amazing friends." She preened. "Let go of this competitive thing with her."

Kate stared at her friend. Only Teresa could talk to her like this. "You're right. I know. You and I have talked about it so many times."

"Here's what I think." Teresa sat up and stared at her seriously. "You're not happy with what you do, and that makes you not feel good about yourself. Look, I didn't either. I went from working night and day at the television station to going back to school to be a nurse. Thank God I did." She shuddered. "Even after days like today, I'm still grateful I found something that makes me feel better about myself. Once you figure out what makes you happy, you won't care at all about whatever Meara does. I mean, what exactly does she do? I know she wears expensive tight suits and flies on corporate jets, but that's all I can figure out."

Kate giggled, shaking her head. "When did you get so smart, Dr. Rossi?"

"I've *always* been smart," Teresa said smugly. "Oh, and by the way, *when* did you go to Stanford?"

thirty

Kate and Meara sat at a corner table in the cardiac waiting room. The sprawling hospital sported a cardiac wing, which apparently was thriving. Kate grimaced. There were many people waiting, trying to pass the time on their phones, playing puzzles, or games. Occasionally, a door opened, and everyone looked up to see which doctor it was, trying to see if there was news on their loved one.

"I wish they put treadmills in here," Kate told Meara, getting up again to pace. She was a ball of nervous energy. Meara looked up from the tablet and nodded, rubbing her neck. Kate glanced over at her sister, who was always dressed perfectly. Today was no exception, with Meara wearing black jeans paired with a silk blouse. Kate glanced down at her yoga pants and zip-up sweatshirt and shrugged. Better to be comfortable, especially when they didn't know how long they'd be waiting.

They had arrived right before their father was to be taken to surgery. He had been jovial as always, teasing the aide who came to wheel him to the Operating Room. They had stopped at what Teresa had told her the staff called the "kiss and cry corner" and told him they would be waiting. After they watched him slide away behind the double doors, they just looked at one another silently.

For Kate, being at the hospital resurfaced all the memories of waiting for her mom's surgeries and ongoing cancer treatments. Kate hadn't realized how much she had stuffed those feelings down and wiped away the tears from the corners of her eyes with her sleeve, hoping Meara didn't notice. She didn't want to explain it to her sister. They had never talked about their mom's death.

"Good afternoon."

Both Kate's and Meara's heads snapped up. Finn's doctor stood before them, dressed in his green scrubs, a mask hanging around his neck, a surgery cap on his head.

"Your father is out of surgery and in recovery. He's doing remarkably well. He's a strong one." The doctor smiled.

Meara and Kate grinned at each other, relieved.

The doctor sat in a chair near them and described the surgery, telling them Finn would remain in the Cardiac Recovery Unit for a few days before being transferred to a regular room. Once released, he would need to go to a rehab facility for extended care until he was strong enough to go home. After Meara's questions were exhausted, the doctor finally stood, telling them to wait a few hours, and then they could briefly see Finn.

"I better call the pub," Kate said. Most of their father's staff had worked there for several years and were like family to him. It was only at her insistence that they didn't come to the hospital to wait. She didn't have the strength to deal with their worry—she could barely manage her own. Meara nodded, looking away, blinking back tears.

Calls made, Meara suggested they go to the cafeteria for lunch. Picking up boxed salads and bottles of water, they found a table by the window.

"This reminds me of Mom," Meara commented softly.

Kate looked up, surprised.

"I know, Katie. I wasn't here very much. It's written all over your face. You can't hate me more than I hate myself," Meara said bitterly.

"I don't hate you."

Meara picked at her salad. "You and mom were always so close. I always felt like the third wheel. You looked like mom; you acted like mom. You loved to cook and Nonna adored you. I never wanted even to be in the kitchen, let alone cook anything."

Kate looked at her in surprise. "I never knew you felt that way."

Meara nodded, her face showing the pain she felt. "Here I was, towering over mom like an Amazon. Remember how when people saw us all together, they would joke and tell mom she got the wrong baby at the hospital? Even Dad didn't have red hair. I just didn't fit in. The only place I fit in was school."

Kate stared at her sister, wide-eyed. "You were always so good at everything."

Meara shrugged. "I loved to compete. And I knew Mom and Dad wouldn't be able to pay much for college, and I would need a scholarship. They always told me I was working too hard, remember?" Meara didn't wait for an answer. "They say things like, 'Meara, why do you always have to study? Meara, why don't you have more fun?'" she choked out. "What was I supposed to do? I knew to get where I wanted, it meant college and grad school. I couldn't saddle them with all that debt or tell them that's why I was working so hard. Mom made me feel guilty for not hanging out with you guys."

"You were so good at sports, though," Kate commented, trying to understand.

Meara rolled her eyes. "I only played because I read scholarships required extracurricular activities, so I signed up for everything. And you know me." She shrugged. "Once I got playing, I was so competitive I couldn't stop."

"Why didn't you come back when Mom was sick?"

"I tried. I really did. I'm not like you, Katie. You're so nurturing. You take care of everybody. Remember how the whole neighborhood used to fight over you to babysit? Not me. No one ever asked me. Well, thank God they didn't. You know me and kids." She shuddered. "But I wanted to be asked at least. And when mom got sick, I knew you would run around, caring for her, and it would be me standing here feeling like I couldn't do a thing. It was paralyzing. Then I saw the bills coming in."

Kate blinked in surprise. "Medical bills?"

Meara looked at her steadily. "Dad never wanted anyone to know. When I started taking accounting courses, he asked me if I would help him with the books. He said it was the worst part of the restaurant business. I love our father, but he is *not* a financial wizard." She rolled her eyes. "Dad's insurance wasn't great. In order to keep expanding the pub, he had cut costs where he could. His insurance was a really skimpy plan, which meant a lot of Mom's care was out of pocket."

Kate felt a sense of dread. "What did he do?"

"I paid it."

Kate stared at her sister, feeling a mixture of emotions. She had always thought she was the one who felt out of place, yet Meara had also felt that. Now she was hearing about her father's financial struggles—something she had never even known about.

"Meara, I had no idea. Why didn't you tell me?"

"Dad made me promise. He's so proud. I actually hid some bills from him, because he wanted to pay me back, so I let him give me a little money to make him feel better."

"I would have contributed," Kate interrupted. "But I guess that explains why Dad has always bragged about you and not me."

Meara rolled her eyes. "Are you kidding me? Every time he talks to me, he tells me how you brought him some lasagna or came over for breakfast and visited with him. I always feel guilty for being away!"

Meara shrugged, continuing, "I guess I should have been honest with you about the bills. But Katie, it's just a math problem. I make more than you—it's not a reflection on what kind of person you are or how successful we are. In fact, you're probably more successful than I am."

"Hardly." Kate snorted.

"It depends on how you define success. At least you have a life," Meara said dryly. "I'm not sure why Dad brags about me. You should ask him. I don't think he means to hurt you."

Kate nodded absently. She spoke slowly now, telling her sister how she had felt out of place, thinking Meara was the golden child. Meara's eyes widened before she shook her head. "I guess we should have talked about this sooner."

Kate agreed. "I think I need to apologize. There were times I have really envied you."

Meara shrugged again. "I own it too. I could have talked to you about all of this. But you know me. I don't let my guard down. I can't let anyone see emotion from me. If they do, they'll circle like sharks. I constantly have to prove myself. It's difficult for me to let anyone in—even family."

Listening to her sister's honesty, Kate finally felt free to admit her own feelings of restlessness and wanting to do something else with her life.

"I always thought it was a waste that you went into website stuff. You're way more creative than that."

Kate chuckled. Here was the Meara she knew! "Don't mince words!"

Meara laughed, too. "Well, it's true! You need to find something that makes you happy. What are you passionate about?"

"I don't know what I'm passionate about," Kate mumbled, playing with her discarded water bottle. "Even the novel I am trying to write isn't coming. Nothing seems to flow."

"You're passionate about Italy. I heard you talking to Dad. Write about that or do something online," Meara suggested, shrugging.

Kate looked at her cautiously. "Do you think I could?"

"Definitely. I can help you flesh it out. Even do a business plan once we get more ideas. I'd love to help," Meara offered softly. "But now we better go check on Dad."

They went to the Cardiac Recovery Unit and stood looking at Finn, who was sleeping quietly, hooked up to machines and tubes. Kate willed herself to breathe. The doctor had warned the next several days would be tough, but one by one, they could start disconnecting him and he would get stronger. She watched the heart monitor, showing the beats steadily. Kate glanced at Meara and saw tears in her eyes. She did something she had never done before—she simply held her sister's hand.

thirty-one

The sisters settled into a new routine for the next few days. They took turns visiting their father and then returned to the waiting room. Even though most of the time Finn was sleeping, they agreed they wanted to stay close.

When they set up the first morning in the waiting room, Meara had laughed when Kate had unloaded her backpack, placing a computer, tablet, paper tablet, and pens on the table. "No whiteboard in there?"

"Well, you said you'd help me," Kate grumbled.

Meara was already picking up a paper tablet. "I will. I will. Just giving you a hard time!"

It was amazing how much work could get done while waiting at the hospital. They turned a corner of the waiting room into their private war room. Meara had found post-its in Kate's backpack, and they now littered the nearby wall. Meara was bent over a spreadsheet and turned the computer so Kate could see it, showing her the numbers and timelines she had created.

"What do you think?"

"I think I've got Dad's genetics." Kate joked. "Meara, I'm terrible at this stuff. That's why you're helping me."

Kate suddenly sat back, looking down at her lap. She had a terrible déjà vu of her showing Marco the spreadsheet and discussing it like she knew what she was talking about. Of course, he had mocked her. She probably wasn't even reading them right.

"You're smarter than you think. Geez, you can write pages of code, and yet you think you can't read a budget or earnings statement? Give yourself some credit."

Kate stared intently at her sister. "Remember how you said you'd help me?"

"Uh yeah, that's what I've been doing here for the past three days, if you hadn't noticed."

Kate bit her lip. "I'm going to ask for more help, but I want you to hear me out."

Meara pushed away the laptop, her eyes narrowed. "Go for it."

IT TOOK A WHILE, but Kate finally concluded her story. She told Meara everything from the first moment she met Marco to the fight the night before Meara arrived. She didn't go into specifics about their argument. With their newfound friendship of sorts, Kate was embarrassed to tell her how much it had hurt that Marco had compared her to Meara.

When her sister opened her mouth to bring up Gianna, Kate stopped her and explained she trusted Marco, pure and simple. Meara surprised her—she still looked wary, but she didn't argue. Instead, she asked, "Are you angry with me?"

"Why would I be?"

"Because I came and ripped you away from him, showing you photos I thought were the truth, only now I trust your judgment if you tell me they weren't what they appeared to be."

"You thought you were doing the right thing."

"Only I wasn't. I should have let you stay and see what he had to say at the very least. He sounds like he really cared about you, Katie," she added softly.

Kate rubbed her neck. "Maybe he did. Maybe he still does. But these last few days have shown me I haven't been very happy with myself. I've spent too much time feeling like I'm not getting anywhere or I'm not worthy of something. I'm not going to be any good for him or anybody until I feel better about myself. And he has things to work through, too. I just want him to be happy," she said wistfully.

"This guy, Sal, sounds like a real piece of work. I trust your instinct. You've always had that ability to see through people."

"I know, right? It's my superpower!"

Meara chuckled, rolling her eyes, but Kate continued. "I know I'm right. I feel like he's sabotaging Marco. But I don't know how. Maybe I wasn't reading some of those files correctly. And that's where your help comes in," she said in a wheedling tone.

Meara raised her eyebrows. "Do you have the files?

Kate grinned smugly. "I thought you'd never ask."

"HE LOOKS A LOT BETTER," remarked Meara, staring at her father.

"I think so too. Look at his good coloring."

"I'm right here, you know," Finn said testily.

Kate and Meara laughed, looking at their father now settled in a private room, most of his tubes gone, the heart monitor silently still tracking him.

"I feel like a science experiment. Hospitals are not meant to get you well. Do you have any idea how many times a night they come in to poke at you? I can't get a lick of sleep here."

The sisters gave each other a smirk. Every time they visited

Finn in the last few days, he had been asleep. Kate nudged Meara a little. "Do you want to talk to him now?"

"What are you whispering about, Katie? Whatever it is, just tell me. Did they find something else wrong with me?" grumbled Finn. "They start cutting on you, and they won't stop."

"Dad, Katie and I went to the pub last night, you know, just to check on things." Meara didn't add that they had wanted to assess the situation. They had met with the accountant Meara had hired a few years before. She had showed them the waning sales, explaining Finn had slipped to operating in the red, refusing to reduce the menu and keeping a high inventory of food. Instead of implementing her suggestions, he had added breakfast, which was not breaking even.

They were dismayed walking around the pub. While the wide array of liquor bottles in front of the mirror behind the bar were impressive and the beautiful mahogany bar still shone, the tables and chairs were dated. The walls needed a fresh coat of paint, the floor was peeling, and things needed to be refreshed. Meara suggested attracting a younger clientele from the adjacent financial district. Perhaps liven the place up by adding a small area for bands.

Meara was taking the lead with their father, and for once, Kate was relieved. "Dad, remember Sean O'Connor from down the street? He was the oldest son." At Finn's nod, she continued: "Well, he's a contractor now. I asked him if he could meet with us tonight at the pub. He's going to look around and just do a few things to refresh the place while you're recovering."

Finn furrowed his brow. "I'm not sure Malone's can afford much, girls."

"Oh, we're not talking about a lot, Dad, maybe just some paint here and there," Meara answered casually. "We'll just close for a few days and get it done, and then it will be ready for you."

At her father's narrowed eyes, she continued persuasively. "Let us help. We want to. Just a few changes."

"You're not touching the bar," Finn told her fiercely.

The girls grinned and nodded.

~

THEY HAD PROMISED NOT to touch the bar, but it was a lot worse than they thought. Sean walked around, clipboard in hand, marking the needed improvements off. "It's lucky your dad's been able to pass some building inspections. The electricity, the plumbing—I don't even know what I'm going to find when we open things up."

Kate's eyes widened, but Meara wasn't going to be dissuaded. She grabbed Sean's contract and signed quickly. "Do what you have to do."

"The next thing we need to hire is a manager," Kate said, after they looked at their dad's office. Papers were strewn everywhere; it looked like a bomb had gone off.

"Dad loves being out in the bar, but he hates everything else," agreed Meara.

"I can't let you pay for everything," Kate told her sister.

Meara shook her head. "It means everything to me to be able to help. We'll call this a short-term investment. I will handle the remodeling and the initial salary for the manager, and then we'll evaluate how it's going. If we're still bleeding money in a few months, then we'll have to have some difficult conversations with Dad."

At Kate's pensive face, Meara continued. "I'm leaving you with all this. I have to get back to my job before the sharks start to take measurements of my office. You're going to have to be here for Sean, visit Dad and deal with his temper while he's recovering. That alone is way more than I can do."

Kate put her arm around Meara. "I guess we're doing this together."

thirty-two

M arco drove fast through the roads outside of Sorrento. He wound through the curves with ease, his powerful sports car making little of the miles. He felt at home driving in this region, his eyes obscured by his sunglasses, his favorite music blasting. For a few minutes, he felt free.

Marco told Sal that he was going to work from home for a few days in order to concentrate. Instead, he went to see two board members. The day before, he visited two others. He was uneasy that he hadn't said anything to Sal, but Marco had the idea to spend some time listening and cajoling the old men. It was possible he could win them over.

Marco found the visits to be pleasant and the shareholders to be less likely to attack him when they weren't in a pack. That said, they all explained to him they needed their investments to pay off as they were in their later years. They appreciated he was Angelo's nephew, but in the end, it boiled down to money. His job was to make them more.

Marco turned into the gates of his family's lemon grove and drove quickly to the house. He hadn't told his mother he was coming, but something drew him there. He had a lot of time recently to think about the things Kate said to him on their last night. It had angered him, but when he was honest with himself, he admitted he agreed. His brothers had told them they were unhappy but having her say it on top of her accusations about Sal had hurt. He prided himself that he was doing all of this because he loved his family. To have her spell out his family's feelings implied he not only didn't recognize their unhappiness but was contributing to it.

After parking, he walked up the front stairs and saw Max lounging nearby. Max got up slowly, coming up to lick his hand. "I know, I miss her too, pal," Marco said gently, petting him. Max had followed Kate around wherever she went.

"Mamma?" he called, dropping his briefcase and bag in the entry hall.

"Marco, I didn't expect you," said Margherita, emerging from the kitchen, drying her hands. "I was just about to make dinner for your brothers."

"Brothers? They are both here?"

"Yes, Stefano had meetings in Naples and came over for the night. Nico is here for several days, and then he's going to Sicily."

He followed his mother into the kitchen. "Sit, you can keep me company." She picked up flour, pouring it into a pile on the island.

Marco poured himself a glass of red wine and sat on a stool at the island, watching his mother crack eggs into the flour and mix the dough. "If you're making ravioli, my timing for once is golden."

"Yes, Stefano offered to make dinner, but he got involved with Nico doing something in that greenhouse of his. I thought I would whip up something. You know how making pasta always relaxes me. Something about all that kneading."

Marco grinned with her, but then grew serious. "Mamma, have you been working too hard?"

It surprised him that his mother didn't answer right away.

Kneading the dough, she eyed it before sprinkling more flour on it. She seemed to choose her words. "There are times where I get tired, Marco. And there are times I wished for a little more in my life," she finally answered wistfully.

"Such as?"

"Oh, I don't know. Maybe I would like to date."

"Date?" shouted Marco, almost spitting out the sip of wine he just took.

"Yes, date," Margherita said firmly. "I think I'm still an attractive woman. I spend all day with people, but there's a part of me that's lonely and I would like sometimes to have a companion."

Marco felt guilt wash over him. "Mamma, I'm sorry. Certainly, you should have some fun."

Margherita rolled the dough into a ball, putting it to the side to rest.

"You enjoyed having Katie around, didn't you?"

Margherita looked up at him for a minute, like she was again choosing her words carefully. She picked up a nearby bowl and mixed the cheese and spinach filling she had compiled earlier.

"I enjoyed getting to know Kate. It was nice to come home to somebody. Someday, I hope one of you will marry so I can have a daughter."

"Have you talked to her?"

"Well no, honey," Margherita answered, busy mixing. "She has been so busy after her father's heart attack and all."

Marco stared at Margherita, thunderstruck. Taking a deep breath, he asked more calmly than he felt: "When were you going to tell me about Kate's father?"

Margherita didn't look at him. "It wasn't up to me to tell you. Kate never asked me *not* to tell you," she clarified. "But I guess I just assumed you would reach out to her."

He put a hand through his hair. "I *have* reached out to her! I've texted her so many times, Mamma. I called her. She has never picked up. I don't think she wants anything to do with me."

"Of course she does. But she has some things to work out. And so do you," Margherita pointed out, finally looking at him. "Timing is everything, and once you both are in a better place, it will come together."

"I'm not sure about that," he answered sadly. "She left, and now I don't know if she wants me."

Margherita put down bowl and frowned at her son. "Kate is not Gianna. She left because you two had an argument, and you're as stubborn as your father. To think of the fights we used to have." She gave a small smile. "You're like him in so many ways."

"I'm not like him," he said bitterly. "I keep my word."

Margherita looked at him before drying off her hands on a nearby towel. She went over to where he sat now and put her arm around his shoulder. "Marco, when I say you are like him, I mean all the good parts. Giacomo was…" Her voice broke, and he reached his arm around her waist now. "He was a good man, despite what he did. He didn't believe in himself, and he felt Angelo was smarter than he was. Remember all the trouble you had in school? I often wonder if Giacomo also had vision issues or something that prevented him from learning. But we grew up in a time when people didn't know about that kind of thing. It made him feel less than he should have. He tried hard to be a good father, but he held himself back. He truly thought it would be better for all of us to be without him. He didn't leave us out of malice. He left because of fear."

She pulled away and looked at him intently. "I made my peace with him when he was dying. I can't say that there isn't a part of me who will always be resentful, but now I understand a little more. There were also things I could have done differently. Marriage takes hard work and understanding. I regret not talking about it with all of you as well. I should have, but every time I even brought him up, you would get angry, Stefano would withdraw even further, and Nico would cry. I finally decided it was easier to just not speak about him. I was wrong. I think its affected each of you differently."

"How could it not?" Marco sighed. "He was our *father*. And he left us!"

"He loved all of you so much." She shook her head, framing his face with her hands. "And when I say you are like him, I mean his brilliance. He was smart in so many ways and yet didn't know it. Giacomo was also generous, funny, and kind. Your uncle gets a lot of credit for helping people, but he was far more rigid than your father. Giacomo was all heart."

She wiped the corners of her eyes, and he reached out to hug her again.

"For God's sake, who died?" Stefano asked irritably as he walked into the kitchen, eyeing them.

"Marco and I were just talking." She laughed. "Where's Nico? I'm going to finish this ravioli and then we will be ready to eat soon."

Stefano looked at them, his eyes narrowing as if he was questioning their discussion. "He's coming behind me."

Nico soon arrived, covered in mud. While he ran up to take a shower, Stefano helped Margherita with the rest of the meal. The family sat down at the table on the terrace, chatting about nothing of importance.

"Do you guys really hate your jobs as much as I think you do?" Marco asked suddenly.

Stefano slowly put his utensils down, and Nico flushed, staring at his plate. "Marco," said Stefano stiffly, the muscle twitching in his cheek, "Nico and I both understand how hard you've been working, and we saw what you went through at the shareholders' meeting. It's not the right time to talk about our positions."

"But it is," Marco insisted. "If everyone is miserable, why are we working so hard? Zio Angelo worked to give us this legacy, but now I'm not sure any of us want it."

Margherita looked up sharply. "Do you think the corporation is his legacy?" she asked, her black eyes snapping. "His legacy was the three of you. Not some business that seems to swallow up all those devoted to it. I lost your father, I lost your uncle, and I refuse to lose all three of you to it!"

Marco reached over to stroke her hand. "I understand that, Mamma. But what is the answer?"

Nico shrugged. "Isn't this all a moot point? Can you fix things? You have a deadline coming up. Maybe that's when you walk away."

Marco sat back, his fingers twirling the stem of his wineglass. "I'm not sure I want to walk away. I have some thoughts," he finally told them. Looking over at Stefano, he added, "I'm going to need your help. You were always better at numbers than me."

Looking at his family now, Marco decided it was time for him to open up. Once he began, he found he couldn't stop talking. He told them about the last several months, his own angst at stepping into the CEO role. While he didn't go into his whole argument with Kate, he told them about the documents she had found. "I didn't want to look at them, but now I'm starting to second guess everything. I still don't want to believe what she said about Sal. He has been so good to me, and he was Papa and Zio Angelo's best friend."

"He wasn't your father's best friend!" snapped Margherita. "I told Giacomo several times that I wasn't sure Sal could be trusted. I could tell he was very jealous of Giacomo and Angelo's relationship. Sal seemed like he purposely tried to come between them. I believe all the stress in the end was what undermined their relationship and drove your father away. They had never fought before, but I think Sal was playing them against each other."

"Mamma, why didn't you tell me any of this?" Marco asked incredulously. "This could have helped me a long time ago."

She looked down at her hands. "You were so enthralled with the man and so heartbroken about Angelo's death. I pushed my feelings aside, hoping that Sal would do the right thing and show you what you needed to know. I thought maybe once he got your father out of the way, he had settled down and had our best interests at heart. I didn't think he would do anything to hurt the corporation. I'm still not sure he would." She shrugged.

Marco remembered how he had emptied his briefcase in his Milan apartment and thrown the thumb drive down on his desk in disgust. He had known deep down he should open the documents on the drive but had been blinded by loyalty.

"Stefano and I will get to the bottom of this. But when it's over, I want you all to know that we are going to do things differently going forward, no matter what happens."

Everyone nodded, looking at the more confident Marco that they hadn't seen for quite a while.

Margherita picked up her glass and raised it proudly. "*Mia famiglia.*"

thirty-three

K ate leaned back from her computer and looked at her phone. She had seen the alert that Marco texted, but her heart was beating so fast, she couldn't open it. Taking a deep breath, she swiped it. She glanced at her watch—it was very late in Italy.

Katie, I just heard about your dad. I am so sorry. Is there anything I can do for you? Whatever you need.

Kate's heart lurched. She had thought every day about texting Marco. She had stubbornly held back, still not sure what to say or how to even begin to mend their relationship. This text was so Marco—generous and thoughtful—the man she had known in Positano. Kate texted him back now, letting him know everything was going well. He immediately answered.

I'm glad he's going to be alright. Are you okay?

Kate's heart swelled.

Thank you for asking. I'm alright. A lot going on, but things are good.

You were right about my family. I talked with them tonight. Things are going to be different.

Kate's eyes widened. *I'm happy for you, Marco. I really am.*

Can we text again? Can I call you?

Kate stared at the screen. She answered him before she changed her mind.

Yes...in time. I think it's good for both of us to take a break right now. I have a lot to say to you—but let's wait for a bit until things get better for both of us.

I don't like that answer.

It's for the best. Just for a little while.

"Did Mr. H text you?" teased Teresa, walking into the apartment.

"Stop sneaking up on a person!"

"I walked through my front door!" Teresa protested.

Kate chuckled. "Sorry, the man makes me lose my mind." She got up and began gathering papers around the kitchen table that she had made into a makeshift office.

Teresa walked over and sat down; her eyebrows raised. Kate told her friend about the most recent texts.

"I think this is a good thing. I still feel like there's a chance for you two."

"I don't know if there is." Kate shook her head but smiled a little. She was afraid once Marco found out about what she had confided in Meara, he might be unhappy with her.

Kate's phone buzzed. Picking it up, she couldn't help the big grin that came to her face.

"What is it?"

Kate turned her phone so she could see the photo Marco had sent. It was their first selfie in Positano. Their heads were close together, they were smiling widely.

Teresa's eyes widened. "Oh my God, he takes my breath away. He's so handsome. And look how happy you guys are."

Kate nodded, busy staring at the photo. She saved it quickly and then put her phone in her pocket. She knew she would look at it a lot. That one photo held so many memories. Smiling at her friend, she changed the subject. "Want to order Chinese?"

KATE HAD NEVER WORKED HARDER in her life. Meara had helped her with her personal budget, urging her to give up the two contract jobs she had secured before Italy. "Live off your savings," advised Meara uncharacteristically. Kate realized her sister was right, knowing she had to concentrate fully on her new project.

In the mornings, Kate wrote as much as she could. Her book was almost finished, but it was not the romance she had started. Instead, she poured her heart out about Positano. She emailed Francesca and Allegra frequently. They gave her names of other people to interview, and she included insights and perspectives, how the region had changed and what it offered. It wasn't a guidebook but a love story about the town she had grown to love.

At noon, she visited her father, who was thriving at the care facility, navigating the hallways with a walker, sticking his head into every patient's room. She had found him organizing a poker game the last time she visited.

When Sean needed her at the pub, Kate went by to approve remodeling issues. The place was shaping up, and she was excited. Meara had found a new manager, Jimmy, who had moved from Boston, where he had run an Irish pub. "Dad has to love him"! Meara exclaimed.

Kate had brought Jimmy over to meet Finn. After the first tense-filled moments, Finn relaxed, and she left them enthusiastically talking.

In the afternoons and evenings, Kate worked on marketing. She began social media accounts devoted to Positano. She started slowly, posting a few photos, researching hashtags, making short videos. She followed accounts of influencers and travel companies. Late at night, she read books and listened to podcasts on how to grow a social media presence, often waking up with the light still on, her tablet in her lap.

Hitting send on the email with her book attached to her editor, Kate felt a little sick. She had poured her heart and soul into it. While she waited, she switched gears, putting effort into the online presence. Even Francesca and Allegra got into the spirit and began sending her more photos or quick videos. Alfonso became almost a daily contributor, which made her happy. She even nervously made a video of herself talking about Positano. Kate began slowly to hear from potential advertisers as her followers grew.

Marco was never far from her mind. She often pulled up the photos of them. The Blue Grotto seemed like a lifetime ago.

Kate scrolled through her phone to figure out what to post next. She stopped when she saw a photo she had taken of the lemon grove. The sun was setting, reflecting a golden hue throughout the trees. She selected that and found photos of some of the family's lemon products she had taken in the gift store.

She pulled up the Oro Industries' website. Their products were now featured prominently, and when she clicked on the image, it went immediately into an online story with "buy now" prominently featured. She smiled. Marco had taken her advice on that at least. She copied the link, added it to her post, and sent it off into the universe.

thirty-four

S tefano rubbed his eyes, sitting back on the couch, eyeing his brother with disgust. "What a mess."

Marco grimaced. "I should have shown you this when Kate left it for me."

They had been sequestered for a few days in Marco's Milan penthouse apartment, poring over the documents on the thumb drive. Marco had pulled up on his laptop everything Sal had shared with him. It was all so complex, they printed everything, with Stefano using colored highlighters to mark certain areas and then carefully making methodical piles.

Marco sniffed. "Whatever you're cooking smells amazing." Stefano had taken a break earlier, and now their lunch was bubbling on the stove.

Stefano nodded absentmindedly. "We better eat before it's ruined. Then we can come back to this."

Marco's phone buzzed with a text from his doorman asking him to approve a guest:

Meara Malone

Marco's eyes widened, but he quickly authorized her coming

up. He stood, glancing at his brother. "We have a visitor," he told him dryly.

The elevator doors opened directly into Marco's penthouse, and Meara entered. Marco had seen photos of her on the cover of multiple business magazines, touting the successful tech company darling. In person, her red hair was brighter and shiner, and fell in loose waves down her back. She wore a cream-colored suit, her jacket tied at the waist, the sheer edges of a green camisole peeking out. Her Italian leather high-heeled sandals added even more height to her impressive frame. She stood looking him in the eye now, her expression unreadable.

Sniffing appreciatively, she suddenly broke into a smile. "What's for lunch?"

IT WAS the strangest meal Marco had ever had. Over lunch, Meara had complimented Stefano on his cooking, attempted her Italian and spoke about her business. She was charming and gracious, giving no hint to why she was there. Marco glanced over at Stefano, who looked utterly transfixed. Meara was gently teasing him about something, her green eyes sparkling. Marco realized she knew exactly how to play it.

Now that lunch was over, Meara continued assessing Marco, her eyes narrowed, her chin up, almost defying him to ask why she was there. Everything he had read about her described her as ruthless, brilliant, and tenacious. He waited her out, daring her to make the first move.

Meara finally gave in. Leaning back in her chair, she eyed him for a minute. "Let's cut to the chase. Katie showed me the documents she left for you."

Marco opened his mouth, ready to tell her about their work on them, but she held out a hand. "Before you get your Italian up —I know it is your business. She showed me because she knew I could help. I spent almost the entire plane ride back to Italy on them and I have a lot to show you and even more questions."

Meara eyed Marco steadily. "Have you finally looked at them?"

The brothers nodded, not knowing if they were allowed to speak. Marco looked away, suddenly feeling a range of emotions. First, embarrassment—did Kate tell Meara how dismissive he had been? His heart gave a twinge—she had still sent her sister, even after what he had said. Did they have a future? He was suddenly hopeful.

For the first time since she walked in, Meara seemed uncertain, looking down and twisting a gold bracelet on her wrist. "Listen, Marco, I don't often make a mistake." At his raised eyebrows, she grinned. "I said not often. But I did with you and Katie. I should have trusted her. She has this innate ability to assess someone's character."

"It's her superpower," they both said and then laughed.

Meara continued, now smiling. "So I should have known everything I read about you probably was not altogether true. But Katie is special, and I've always wanted to protect her. I hired a private investigator, and when they got those photos of you and what's-her-name, I ran with it."

He hastened to set her straight. "That wasn't what it seemed. Gianna and I..."

Meara interrupted. "Save it for Katie. Just know that I was wrong." She raised her eyebrows. "Don't expect to hear that again. But I'm here to make it right. I have a team of tech people and forensic accountants. I know you're on a tight timeline, but I can help you find the answers."

Marco looked at his brother, who gave a subtle nod. "Very well. Thank you."

For the next few hours, the brothers showed Meara their work. She got out her own notes, firing off questions at them and asking for clarifications. She was like a human tornado and had an uncanny skill for zeroing in on a discrepancy immediately. Marco admired her, somewhat feared her, and was already grateful.

They turned then to strategizing how things should play out. Marco made copious notes and then made phone calls. Meara got out her laptop and was firing off emails. Marco hung up the phone, watching her chatting easily with Stefano. He felt compelled to tell her something. "You know part of the horrible argument I had with Katie concerned you," he told her, watching for her reaction. At Meara's frown, he admitted, "I compared her to you."

Meara threw back her head and laughed. "Oh man, that didn't work out well for you! My sister would not like that. We are very different people."

At Marco's nod, she continued, her eyes narrowing to slits. "She's a better person than me. And if you hurt her again, I'll find you."

TWO DAYS LATER, Marco's lawyers, plus Meara's forensics team, met in front of the main headquarters of Oro Industries. They entered the lobby, and Marco signaled for the company's security and Human Resources Director to join them. He called the HR Director the day before and asked her to draw up the separation papers. She still looked in shock, placing a shaking hand to her mouth.

Marco led the way to Sal's spacious office, which took up almost half of the executive floor. Sal was bent over his computer, and looked up, angrily surveying the crowd. "What's going on, Marco?"

"Hand him his separation papers," Marco ordered the HR manager.

"You can't fire me," blustered Sal.

"I can, and I will."

"Marco…"

Marco held up his hand. "Don't even try. This group of people behind me are here to seize computers from you and your staff. When we're done, you won't have to worry about me firing you. You'll have to worry about not going to prison."

The HR director scurried forward, placing the papers in front of Sal. He promptly swiped the papers angrily from his desk.

"Marco, I am a shareholder. I was your uncle's best friend."

Marco's eyes glinted, the muscle throbbed in his cheek, and his hands clenched at his side. "Don't ever talk about Zio Angelo," he said forcibly. "You have betrayed him. You betrayed us all. And you are no longer a shareholder. This morning's emergency meeting withdrew your shares and made them null based on the evidence we already have. I hope the next time I see you, we will be in a courtroom."

Gesturing to the security team, the two men hauled Sal away.

"You're just like your father," he yelled, red-faced.

"Thank you," Marco acknowledged with a nod. "Get him out of here," he barked. Security dragged Sal from the room as he continued to let off even more vitriol.

Stefano watched Meara's team immediately securing computers. He approached Marco, his face grim. "That was worse than I thought. Thank God it's almost over."

"Oh no." Marco grinned, happy for the first time in days. "This is just the beginning."

thirty-five

Kate looked at herself happily in the full-length mirror. Meara had sent her a dress from Italy. Kate had opened the box with trepidation, knowing she and her sister's styles were very different. She let out a whoop of joy when she saw the bright red floral dress. It was feminine and floated around her, making the most of her curves. She took time getting ready for tonight's grand re-opening of Malone's which also featured her book signing.

The initial box of books arrived a few days prior, but instead of opening it, she carried it to her father's. He had been allowed to go back home with a part-time nurse. She slit the box open and almost screamed with excitement, seeing the cover of her new book: *My Positano*. The cover featured a beautiful photo looking down the hill at the colored houses to the sea below. Slowly, she handed it to her father. He put his glasses on and looked at her over the top of them. "Katie girl, I never thought I'd see my name on a book."

She grinned. "Well, technically it's my name, but yours is there, too!" Kate came over and opened it for him, turning to the acknowledgements.

"There it is," Finn shouted, reading it out loud. He sat back in his chair, taking a breath.

"Dad, you okay?"

"Oh, I'm fine, just fine." He took off his glasses, his eyes misty. "I was just thinking about how proud your mother would be."

She looked at him for a minute, her eyes blurring. She finally couldn't resist. "Dad, are *you* proud of me?"

"Of course I am, pumpkin. Why would you even ask that?"

Kate gave a long exhale and looked away. She hadn't intended on having this conversation, but now the door was open. "It just seems like you talk about Meara a lot—about how successful she is and how much money she makes. You're always reminding me to take care of my money and asking if I'm doing okay."

Finn thought for a minute. "You know, when you were a kid, you and your mom were thick as thieves. I remember once I was driving you to high school, and you were just sitting there in the passenger seat, looking out the window. Do you remember what I asked you?"

When she shook her head, he continued. "I asked you why you didn't confide in me like you did your mom. You just looked at me like I had lost my mind, but I meant it. I knew we didn't have the same connection. I wasn't sure how to reach you."

He paused, lost in his thoughts. "I had more of a connection to Meara, especially when she started helping me with the books. And though she has done well financially, I never saw her as more successful than you. I just didn't do a good job of telling you that."

He looked down at his hands now. "I might have overdone it because Meara helped me out. I haven't been the best at business —I know your sister told you. It's difficult for a father to be bailed out by his daughter. If I was concerned about your finances, it was because I wanted to make sure you were independent, knowing that your old dad might not be able to help you out."

Finn looked at her steadily. "I want you to know that I intend on paying your sister back every cent of this remodel. I should have put away my pride and gotten a manager a long time ago. I think Jimmy can help me turn this around. But I am proud of you. There's never been a time I haven't been. And if I've never told you, I am very sorry."

Kate nodded, the lump in her throat swelling. "It's okay, Dad —I know I've also been too competitive with Meara. People always compared us, you know?"

"You and your sister are as different as night and day." Finn laughed. "Thank God, because I couldn't take two of either of you! But I'm glad I have one of each of you."

Katie got up and gave him a big kiss.

Finn looked at her, a glint in his eye. "You know, you've only told me a little about your trip. Do I have to wait to read your book or will you give me a preview?"

Kate smiled and began to talk, but this time, she included Marco.

"You found your star with your love of Italy," he said softly. "This Marco...is it serious?"

She shrugged. "There are a lot of issues. To be honest, I don't know anymore."

Finn nodded, patting her hand. "He'll find his way back to you, Katie."

~

"YOU LOOK GREAT," exclaimed Teresa, as she ran into the apartment, taking in Kate's dress in one glance. "I'm sorry I'm so late! I'll be ready in just a few minutes," she called.

Kate rolled her eyes, grinning, knowing Teresa could never

be ready quickly. It was still early, though, so she sat down and took out her phone. Nothing.

She had meant it when she had told her father that she did not know what the future held in regard to Marco. She was feeling more disheartened than she let on. He had been texting her over the last few weeks, sending photos, funny lines from movies, and snatches of memories from their time together. She knew he had been trying to stay connected. She was puzzled. The last few days there had been nothing. Rationally, Kate knew she could reach out to him, but now she was even more unsure where they stood.

Meara had called often to check on Finn and the pub. She also tracked Kate's efforts on social media, offering help with analytics, so Kate knew what was working, while also helping to negotiate with potential advertisers. It was Meara who had suggested Kate's first book signing be at the pub's re-opening. It was all coming together. For the first time in a long time, Kate was really proud of herself.

"I wish I could be there," Meara had said wistfully. "With being gone for Dad's surgery, I'm still catching up."

Several times, Kate wanted to ask her sister about the investigation involving Sal's activities. Other than reporting that she had connected with Marco and he agreed to let her help, Meara had not offered more. Kate debated asking her for details. She had to admit, there was just a small part of her that felt a twinge of jealousy, thinking of them working together. Shaking her head to snap out of it, Kate reminded herself she was no longer in that competitive space with her sister. Meara could have anyone and anything—just not Marco.

"KATE, it's so much nicer in here," exclaimed Teresa.

Kate smiled at her friend in her short bright pink mini dress and high heels—a look she pulled off so naturally. The dated and dingy pub was bright and lively, and customers were packing it. The menu had been updated, keeping the Irish classics, but adding some interesting appetizers and burgers and paninis (Kate's idea). Jimmy also convinced Finn to update the bar menu, adding some signature cocktails for the younger crowd. Finn, who thought anyone who didn't drink a whiskey neat or a pint of Guinness was being too fussy, finally agreed.

The girls ducked into the door under the "Grand Re-Opening Sign" to see the real surprise greet them: Meara threw her arms around Kate, laughing.

"I thought you couldn't make it," Kate accused.

"I've got a plane, might as well use it." Meara shrugged, smirking. "Besides, I couldn't miss this!"

Meara had directed the staff to set up a table on the side. It was covered with a white tablecloth, and sitting on top was a posterboard with the cover of Kate's book. The books were carefully arranged on the table with a pen for signing.

Glancing at the "Welcome back, Finn" banner over the shelves behind the bar, Kate said, "Meara, you thought of everything."

"I wanted tonight to be special for you and Dad."

Kate went over to the table, and as the night progressed, she had a steady line of people all queuing up to buy her book and have her sign it. Kate grinned, not even knowing what to write. She had never autographed anything in her life.

The bar was loud, with shouts of joy every so often, as long-time customers came in to hug Finn. The doctor had approved of him working part-time, as long as he didn't overdo it. So far, he was behaving, greeting customers and chatting with staff. Meara arranged for a small band to play, and they were getting ready to perform.

Kate signed a book for the last person in line and decided it was a good time to stop and enjoy the band. She was putting a few remaining books in the box hidden at her feet when a movement caught her eye. She lifted her head to see a pair of hands holding her book. Her heart hammered out of her chest. She knew those hands and watch anywhere. Slowly, she raised her eyes to meet Marco's uncertain black ones.

"*Buonasera,* Katie."

"Marco," she breathed. With wooden legs, she stood up and slowly walked around the table, her eyes searching his.

"I was wondering if you would sign this masterpiece for me. Especially right here by my name." He pointed to the acknowledgements page.

Kate never knew if she launched herself at Marco or if he pulled her against him, but suddenly they were locked in a long embrace. Marco put a hand on either side of her face, his eyes looking intently at her, wary and anxious. She leaned up and gave him a lingering kiss. He returned it, immediately deepening it. He pulled back abruptly.

"We have a lot to discuss, Katie."

She nodded, spellbound. "How, what...?"

Marco put a finger to her lips. "As much as I want to haul you out of here right now, let's wait to talk. This is you and your father's night. I debated on coming because of that. Meara told me I would be welcome. Am I?" he asked softly.

Kate grinned at him. "If those kisses didn't tell you I was happy, I don't know what else will."

Marco threw his head back and laughed, his black eyes sparkling with relief. He gave her one last kiss, his lips barely brushing hers and leaving her wanting more.

He straightened his shoulders. "Introduce me to your Papa."

She nodded, grabbing his hand shyly and going to detach Finn from a table with some of his friends. "Daddy, there's someone I want you to meet." Out of the corner of her eye, she saw Meara grab Marco in a big hug. It gave her pause for a second, but only a second.

Kate made the introductions, with Marco formally shaking Finn's hand. Marco towered over her father, who still looked a little frail.

Meara waved at Kate to come over to where she was standing near the bar. As Kate did so, she watched as Finn authoritatively placed a hand on Marco's back, directing him through the hallway that led to his office. Kate watched anxiously. "Meara, I can't leave Marco alone with Dad."

Meara grabbed her by the shoulders, dragging her toward the bar. "Yes, you can! Let them get to know one another. Come on, let's get behind the bar!"

When they were old enough, the sisters had each gotten their bartender's license to help at the pub. It had been the one time they actually got along. Meara had made Kate watch hours of videos online and they had practiced throwing bottles at one another, juggling them, perfecting flashy tricks and pouring cocktails. They eventually could put on quite a show. "Time to take a break, guys," Meara told the two bartenders, waving them out.

They got into position and laughed as it started coming back to them. Kate tossed a bottle at Meara, who caught it in one hand, pouring it out in one even motion. They twirled and tossed, with Kate finally getting up the nerve to do some of her more high-risk tricks of tossing bottles behind her back and up in the air. Their father had always yelled at them, saying if either of them broke the glass shelves, there would be hell to pay. They never had, though, they might have come close when they were practicing. Kate became a different person behind the bar—she felt a sense of confidence and it came easily to her.

She just finished shaking an espresso martini, dancing around with the shaker with clear abandon when she looked up to see Marco's amused eyes. Slowly, she blushed, but her heart-beat increased.

"Katie, head's up," Meara tossed a bottle of vodka her way,

and Kate picked up a nearby bottle to sling at Meara. The two went back and forth, the bottles staying upright, their pourers still attached. The crowd cheered as if they were watching a tennis volley. Finally, they did one last fling and bowed to an uproar. Kate met Marco's admiring eyes.

"Hey, Hunky. Finally showed up, eh?" Teresa eyed Marco, tipping her head from her petite frame. She put her hands on her hips and assessed him with narrow eyes. Looking quickly over her shoulder, she saw Kate approaching. Wiggling her finger for him to come closer so he could hear her with all the noise, she told him what she had to say. His eyes widened, and he nodded. Teresa beamed at him and walked away.

"Katie, a small pixie just came up to me and called me by some name. She threatened some pretty awful things." Marco shook with laughter. He whispered to her a few of the threats.

"Oh, Teresa must really like you. She usually says much worse."

Kate turned when she heard the band leader announce a special singer. Kate grinned, knowing what was about to happen. Sure enough, a customer was helping Finn up the couple of stairs to the elevated platform.

She watched her father sing an Irish ballad he used to sing to her at bedtime. It brought tears to her eyes, remembering how he would make sure to come home to kiss them goodnight before going back to the pub. She had forgotten about that. She rubbed her arms, as goosebumps tingled on them. Marco came up from behind her, wrapping his arms around her. Kate leaned into him and breathed. He had come back to her.

"I SMELL LIKE A DISTILLERY," Kate proclaimed, unlocking her apartment door. Now that she and Marco were alone, she was suddenly very nervous. She went about switching on lights and picking up things absentmindedly. Marco was watching her intently, and it was unnerving her. Teresa had stayed on at the pub with a friend. "I'll probably be really late," she had remarked, a glint in her eye.

Now that they were alone, Kate's anxiety was coming on strong. "Uh, I think I'm going to go change. I got pretty sticky. Meara's out of practice." She chuckled.

Marco nodded, his face unreadable. He walked over to the window, lost in thought.

Kate went into her bedroom and shut the door. Leaning against it, she tried to take several deep breaths. Peeling off her dress, she debated about what to put on. She might as well be comfortable. Pulling on a pair of jeans, she glanced around for a top. Smiling, she found what she wanted.

She emerged from the bedroom, closing her door with a small click. He was now standing in front of their fireplace, looking at the mantel. On it, sat the painting he had bought her in Positano.

As she approached, he said softly, "This seems like a lifetime ago." Turning around, his eyes widened, and then he burst out in laughter.

"You little thief," he accused.

"I have no idea what you are talking about," Kate giggled, walking by casually, dropping on to the couch.

He reached over to tug the sleeve of the sweatshirt.

"You were so angry with me, but you kept it," he said softly, his eyebrows raised.

Kate shrugged. "I love this sweatshirt."

"And it's owner?"

Kate flushed. "Oh, Marco. We have so much to talk about."

He sighed. "Let me go first, Katie, if I can. I wanted to call you so badly, but you put such restrictions on me." He smiled with mock sternness.

"Marco..."

"No, don't say anything," he stopped her. "You were right. We both had a lot to work through. I'm so proud of you and your success," he told her quietly. "There's so much I have to tell you."

"Marco, I don't care about the whole thing with Gianna. I should have waited for your explanation," she blurted out.

Marco frowned. "You understand there was nothing, right? I have to admit I was angry when I found out you left and didn't trust me. But after a time, I understood how it looked, and I should have told you about it all. When she first called me, I didn't know what she wanted, but agreed to meet. I thought it would give me..." he struggled to find the word.

"Closure?" guessed Kate.

Marco nodded. "I think I needed it. There was a part of me that was so anxious to move on with you, but I was not trusting any feelings because of what Gianna had done. We had a long talk. She made it clear I could have been anyone, but once she found James, there was no turning back. She tried because of the pressure her parents put on her, but in the end, she only loved James. There was a time when I wouldn't have understood her actions, but now I completely do," he added, not explaining further.

"She and James moved back from the States after he lost his job. She didn't ask, but I agreed to hire him back. Her parents have completely cut her off, and she is pregnant. I told her I would help. I reminded myself of my uncle." He smiled sadly. "He helped so many people out—even people who had wronged him. I guess I realized I had to forgive her. I even showed her a couple of photos of you—of us on my phone. She was happy for me."

"Marco..." Kate looked unsure, biting her lip.

"You can ask me anything," he said quietly.

"Why didn't you tell me you were in Rome?"

"It was the necklace—it was supposed to be a surprise. I picked it up from my private jeweler in Rome. I didn't know

Gianna was living there temporarily while James looked for a job."

She nodded absentmindedly. "You say you want me to trust you, but the night after the gala—I felt like you just pulled completely away from me."

He nodded sadly, reaching over to stroke her hand. "You're right, I did. There is a lot I haven't told you about why I was feeling so overwhelmed, and I probably should have."

"Such as?"

He took a deep breath and told her then about his learning issues, how it had always made him feel inferior. He explained how hard he had worked, but how those feelings had come rushing back recently.

"I didn't know," she said softly. "I would have gone easier or maybe not said anything.

"I'm glad you did say something," Marco told her. "All this time, I thought history was different." He gave her a quick account of what his mother had said about his father's departure and Sal.

"I never knew the whole story. I thought he left because of me and my brothers. It rocked me, and then it all came together like a puzzle."

"Oh, Marco, tell me what happened with Sal."

He raised his eyebrows. "Meara didn't tell you?"

She shook her head.

"Katie, you were right about everything. *Everything.*"

Frowning now, Marco told her the story from the beginning, from when he and Stefano started sifting through the contents of the thumb drive, to Meara's help and then confronting Sal. "The forensic accountants and tech wizards Meara brought in have been amazing," he said. "They discovered Sal had created a shell company and was altering the numbers to make some companies my uncle had bought look like they weren't profitable. Then he would get the board's authority to sell them, and his company would buy them. Looking back, he was working to undermine me at every turn—meeting with board members and keeping me out of the way for a reason. I believe he was the one paying the press to follow me, hoping for those sensational headlines to drive a wedge between me and the board. He might have thought then he could become CEO. We don't even know the full extent of the damage and the fraud he committed. We turned him over to the authorities. The investigation will take more time. We had an emergency board meeting, and the board approved me as CEO. There are no longer any deadlines."

"I should have trusted you, Katie." He put a hand through his hair. "That night I was so frustrated and stressed. And when you started telling me there were things I didn't know, it just lit a match to my already tattered ego. If I could take back what I said to you, I would," he finished softly. "I never should have brought up your sister."

She looked gently at him. "I was really hurt, I admit it. But so much has changed here, too. Meara and I have repaired a lot of hurt we should have taken care of years ago. I had to get over my own inferiority issues." She reached out this time and grabbed his hand. "I am so happy for you, if that's what you want." She saw something flicker across his face. "Though I believed I was right, I wanted there to be some other reason."

"I know. But you were right about my family, too. I can't take back the past, but I can make it better. Nico can go back to farming or doing whatever he wants. Stefano is deciding on whether he wants to go to culinary school, and Mamma...well, she says she may travel. *And* that's another thing you were right about. Turns out she has been spending time with Sergio." He gave her a small smile.

Kate grinned. "If nothing else, I can spot when romance is in the air."

Marco stared at her intently. "Really? What about ours?"

Kate was busy examining their hands, which were still

clasped. Her heart was beating so fast. Marco reached over and gently nudged her chin up with his other hand, so she was forced to meet his eyes.

"It's time for us to share more secrets. I'll go first. I have fallen utterly, deeply in love with you. Nothing really matters if you're not part of my life. I need you by my side. If it's here, then I'll move here. It doesn't matter as long as we are together. Please, Katie. Be with me, be my wife, my love forever."

Kate's eyes welled up, the tears ready to fall. She lunged forward, and he grabbed her, putting his arms around her, kissing her thoroughly.

"Oh, what you do to me, Katie. I had the biggest challenge of my life, and all I could think about was you. Being with you. Kissing you. Wanting more." Marco stopped to give her a long, deep kiss. "It has been torture being away from you all the days and all the nights," he said suggestively.

She rested her head on his shoulder, and they sat that way for a long time, soaking it all in. He suddenly pulled away, his eyes searching hers.

"Katie, I need to know how you feel," he whispered.

She gave him a brilliant smile. "I have loved you almost from the first. Certainly, when you were showing me Positano. I fell in love with you and Positano at the same time."

Marco put his head back on the couch, looking relieved. He sat up and smiled at her gently. "I'm glad I rank up there with Positano," he teased. "I was worried I no longer mattered at all. But your love for our town is paying off. Nico showed me your social media and website. You have worked so hard. I don't want you to doubt yourself again."

At her uncertain look, he frowned. "You really have no idea how big you're getting, do you? That one post you did on our products sent thousands to our website. Thank God I had taken your advice and hired a new IT manager. He has a whole team working on our website. We had just gotten the warehouse ready for retail sales. You made us a lot of money. And everywhere I go in town, everyone asks about you. Francesca and Allegra will no longer speak to me until I bring you back!" He laughed.

Marco got up to grab his briefcase that he had brought in. "I almost forgot; I have something to show you." Getting out his laptop, he powered it on, taking a minute to lean over and kiss her lingeringly. He then turned his laptop around for her to see.

"Marco, I'm your wallpaper!"

Marco smiled, looking at their first selfie together. "You once told me you put the people you care about the most on there. So I had to change it. It took me a few minutes and a couple searches online, but I did it!"

Kate grinned. "I have something to show you, too" She took out her phone and showed him her screen—there was the photo of them going through the Blue Grotto.

"Have I told you I love you?" he whispered, kissing her softly. Lifting his head, he asked, "Katie, where are we going to live?"

She looked at him steadily. "Can we live in Positano?"

epilogue

"**M**arco, hang on." Kate shrieked. He was holding on to the pole of the cable car with one hand like a typical tourist. He had wanted to spend a few days just being together in San Francisco, bringing back a carefree time of his Stanford days. They bought crabs and a loaf of bread and sat outside at Fisherman's Wharf. Marco thought cracking his crab was a sport, sending his pieces flying. They had listened to the sea lions barking, as they made their way through the Piers. They finally stopped and sat on a bench at the Presidio, overlooking the Golden Gate Bridge. Kate's head on his shoulder, he absently stroked her hand.

"Marco, you talked about making your family happy, but what about you?" she unexpectedly asked, sitting up to look at him. "Are you going to like running the corporation?"

He gently touched her face, happiness lighting his eyes. "You're the first person to ask me that." He paused for a moment, choosing his words. "You know, for the longest time I felt it was beyond me, but the last several weeks have changed me. I realize now how Sal played into that. I think he did the same thing to my father."

He continued, "I would like to try. But only if you're by my side. I was thinking we could spend a year and see how it works out. I don't mind handing the reins to someone else if we are not happy."

"Let's do it." She smiled. "I'll be right there with you."

KATE AND MARCO spent their last night dining with Finn. Marco insisted on talking to her father privately. "I am taking his daughter to live in Italy. I want his blessing," he said. They came out both grinning, Marco's hand on the older man's shoulder.

When it was time for Marco to leave, Kate had a hard time letting him go. Knowing it would only be a few weeks made it easier. Still, she clung to him as he gave her one last spectacular kiss.

Kate had agreed to move to Italy in six weeks and then decide on their wedding, but first she wanted to complete her book signings and focus on her business. Her book was selling well, and she continued to add additional events. She had appeared on two podcasts when she suddenly wondered, why couldn't she do her own? Marco had called that night, and she had told him about her new idea.

"Now that you're moving to Italy, you can expand to the entire country," he said. He had told her he would support whatever she wanted to do with her business. This new idea gave her pause. Could she really do that? There were so many places to focus on—she wanted to see all of Italy. Her mind had whirled at the thought.

Now Teresa was sitting on the bed, sorting through her pile of clothes. For Kate, it was all sinking in. Teresa had already found a new roommate, but they both knew it wouldn't be the same. Teresa tried to sound encouraging. "It's only a few months, and I'll be there right by your side to watch you marry that gorgeous man."

~

KATE LAY IN BED, smiling. Today was her wedding day! It had all been such a blur, but what an amazing few weeks. Smiling, she remembered how Marco had greeted her at the airport in Rome when his private jet landed. Sweeping her in the car with a bouquet of red roses, the drive was spent in his arms. They couldn't get enough of each other, and he had reluctantly brought his lips to hers for one last kiss before the car slid to the front of an exquisite hotel. When the door to the penthouse opened, Meara and Margherita had been waiting, laughing and hugging her.

"Time to go shopping," they had chorused. Her sister and her future mother-in-law had taken an instant liking to one another, and the two had already planned the following day's activities. The first stop was Rome's exclusive bridal store. Meara had called ahead, and they had pulled dresses for Kate to try on. All were a little extravagant for her taste. She had an image in her head and described it to the shop manager. The manager left, coming back into the dressing room to slowly show her a dress. "That's it," breathed Kate even before she tried it on. She knew it was the one when her sister's eyes widened and Margherita shouted, "*Perfetto!*"

The rest of the day they shopped for more clothes. Kate kept insisting it was more than one person needed. Margherita simply grinned, laying down Marco's black credit card.

Kate and Marco had talked about their wedding. He had two wishes: that it be soon and that they marry in the church in Positano. She had questioned if the church would remind him of his almost wedding. He had simply shaken his head. "This time I will be waiting for you, Katie."

The night they had gone to talk to the pastor, they strolled down to the church, hand in hand. When they got to a point overlooking Positano, they stopped to take in the scenery. Kate breathed in the fragrant air, so happy to be back. She turned to see Marco on one knee, holding a ring box.

After her shriek of "yes," he stood up, wrapping his arms around her. "I couldn't propose anywhere but Positano."

Admiring the emerald-cut diamond ring with its pave-set diamond band, he had slipped on her finger, Kate was speechless. It was exactly what she would have chosen. She did the only thing she could think of. She wound her arms around his neck and kissed him under the beautiful Positano sky.

THE LAST FEW DAYS, the lemon grove had been a flurry of activity for the couple's reception. Kate had loved seeing her family and friends enveloped warmly by Marco's family.

Meara appeared at her door, knocking softly. "Time to go get you married."

The women had spent the night at a nearby hotel. It featured a spa, where they now spent the day being pampered. Meara had brought in a makeup and hair stylist, and Kate had been shocked when they finally let her look in the mirror.

Her ivory dress was exactly what she pictured. It was exquisite in its simple design with delicate Italian lace hugging her shoulders with small cap sleeves, sweetheart neckline that cascaded into a satin full skirt. The veil was Margherita's—her something borrowed. Made of Italian lace, it cascaded down her back, over her hair, which she wore in gentle waves. Kate touched the diamond necklace at her throat. Marco had returned it to her almost immediately when she arrived. Her something blue had been easy—the bracelet Marco had given her.

Descending the stairs that evening toward the church on her

father's arm, she heard the bells pealing. She smiled at Meara, Teresa, and her two friends from home, Cathie and Debbi. Their bridesmaid dresses were all a different pastel color.

Kate glided up the aisle, focused only on Marco. He stood proudly at the altar's edge, reaching for her with one hand before she even arrived. *Ti amo,* he whispered, tears in his eyes. They recited their vows in loud, clear voices. When the priest asked for the rings, Kate eagerly turned to get the ring Meara was holding for her. Margherita had given her Marco's father's gold ring. Inside it was engraved with their wedding date, and Kate had added their date as well.

When she slipped it on Marco's finger, his eyes widened, recognizing it immediately. He glanced over at Margherita, who was beaming. She nodded her approval.

Those in the church laughed and applauded when Marco swept her into his arms to kiss her before the priest had told him to do so. It was surreal when the priest proclaimed them married.

Kate's gaze went to her father, who was busy dabbing her eyes. It was only then she noticed several friends and family from San Francisco sitting in the pews behind Finn. Turning to Marco, he smiled and shrugged. He had flown them in as a surprise.

The reception was everything Kate and Marco had wanted. Margherita had carried out their vision completely. Under the lemons, with candles and fairy lights as far as one could see, they dined together with the wedding party at one long table, the bride and groom at the end. Kate looked down at the table to see every person she loved. She turned to accept Marco's soft kiss.

Later, after they cut the cake, he swept her onto the dance floor. "I believe this is our dance."

Kate leaned into Marco, the music sweeping over her. She was drawn to another time, another place where they had danced. Pulling back slightly, Kate looked at Marco, and he smiled.

"Tell me a secret," he whispered, gathering her close, his lips traveling across her jaw.

"I think I fell in love with you the night we first danced."

Marco pulled away, his eyes glinting, the love shining through. Gently, he kissed her.

"For the first time, *cara,* we share the same secret."

upcoming books

Read more from the series "With Love from Italy"

Check out Lucca and Ellie's love story
COMING FALL 2023

To be the first to hear the details of upcoming books, get recipes and information about Italy!

Just for signing up, you'll get my nonna's marinara sauce recipe!

Sign up here:
Website: tessrini.com
Or follow me on social
Facebook @tessriniauthor
Instagram @tessrininauthor

authors note to the reader

Dear Reader:

Thank you so much for traveling through Positano for Kate and Marco's love story. Did my love of Positano—and all of Italy—and of course, the food shine through?

I'm half Italian—but feel like I'm 100 percent! Just writing this book brought me closer to my ancestors and the places I feel so at home.

If you want more...I can promise you there will be! Tour through Tuscany, Florence, Rome, Sicily, and more regions of Italy as this series grows. And always, we'll swing by the Amalfi Coast to say hi to our friends.

Go get yourself some delicious Italian food and enjoy my upcoming stories straight from Italia!

Cin Cin!
XO, Tess

about the author

Tess Rini has spent her professional life focused on non-fiction writing, from her journalism degree to her editing and writing magazine articles and content for local government. She has published one non-fiction book under a different name.

Tess was raised on a self-induced steady diet of Harlequin romances and so it was inevitable that she should try her hand at romance writing. The idea took off when she combined her love of Italy with her love for romance novels.

When not writing, she can be found relaxing in her Oregon home, traveling or cooking Italian cuisine (her specialty!) for her husband, four daughters and son-in-law. Keeping her company while writing or watching Hallmark movies is her adorable, but anxious, golden retriever puppy.

Sign up here:
Website: tessrini.com
Or follow me on social
Facebook @tessriniauthor
Instagram @tessrininauthor

Made in United States
Troutdale, OR
12/04/2023

15331056R00195